ALAN DUFF

Once Were Warriors

Alan Duff lives in Havelock North with his wife and four children. He is a weekly columnist for Wellington, New Zealand's *Evening Post* and several other newspapers. *Once Were Warriors* was the winner of the 1990 PEN Best First Book Award in New Zealand and was runner-up for the Goodman Fielder Wattie Award. He was awarded the Frank Sargeson Fellowship in 1991. Mr. Duff is also the author of the novel *One Night Out Stealing* and a work of nonfiction, *Maori: The Crisis and the Challenge*.

INTERNATIONAL

Books by Alan Duff

FICTION

Once Were Warriors
One Night Out Stealing

NONFICTION

Maori: The Crisis and the Challenge

Once Were Warriors

Once Were Warriors

ALAN DUFF

VINTAGE INTERNATIONAL

Vintage Books

A Division of Random House, Inc.

New York

First Vintage International Edition, March 1995

Grateful acknowledgment is made to the following for permission to
reprint previously published material: Dr. Margaret Orbell and
Richards Literary Agency, translations of Maori songs on pages 117,
120; Penguin Books, page 188, excerpt from *The Coming of the
Maori*, Sir Peter Buck, Whitcombe and Tombs, 1966: Victoria
University Press, pages 191–192, excerpt from *Maori Poetry*, ed.
Barry Mitcalf, Price Milburn for VUP, 1974.

Library of Congress Cataloging-in-Publication Data
Duff, Alan, 1950–
Once were warriors / Alan Duff. — 1st Vintage International ed.
p.   cm.
ISBN 0-679-76181-0
1. Maori (New Zealand people)–Fiction. I. Title.
[PR9639.3.D79205   1995]
823 — dc20   94-40298
CIP

Manufactured in the United States of America
10 9 8 7 6 5 4 3 2

Contents

Acknowledgments

Chris Else and Barbara Neale, my agents, of
Total Fiction Services, for their visionary advice.

My Publishers, Bob Ross and Helen Benton,
for their faith.

Richard King, who edited the book and
agreed to forgo the conventions.

1

A Woman in Pine Block

Bastard, she'd think, looking out her back kitchen window. Lucky white bastard, at that glimpse of two-storey house through its surround of big old trees and its oh so secure greater surround of rolling green pastureland, while she — Clicking her tongue, Oh to hell with him. Or good luck to him, if she wasn't in too bad a mood.

Good luck to you, white man, for being born into your sweet world, and bad luck to you, Beth Heke (who used to be a Ransfield but not that life was so much better then), for being married to an arsehole. And yet I love him. Just can't help myself, I love the black, fist-happy bastard. And she'd light another smoke, and always went ahh in her mind and sometimes aloud because she liked that first hit against the back of her throat, and she'd squint through the drifts. And wonder.

And sometimes she'd be upstairs, looking out her bedroom window at the view on the other side of the house, the front. If you could call it a view; just a mirror reflection across the street of her house and the half next door and the whole fuckin street of exact same state dwellings. A mile-long picture of the same thing; all the same, just two-storey, side-by-side misery boxes. Only thing different was the colour of the paint job, and even then you hardly noticed it. And your neighbour through a few inches of wall.

And Beth'd watch the kids; the scab-kneed, snot-nosed, ragamuffin-clothed kids of the area doing their various things out there. Beth wondering, all the time wondering. At them. The kids. The unkempt, ill-directioned, neglected kids. And her own kids. How were they going to fare? How were they faring now? If you could call living in this Pine Block state-housing area faring.

For hours at a time, sometimes, she'd watch the mirrors of her existence outside, down there below her and Jake's bedroom window. And feel like a spy. Spying on my own people. Them out there. Us. The going-nowhere nobodies who populate this state-owned, half of us state-fed, slum. The Maoris. Or most ofem are.

1

Feeling like a traitor in her own midst because her thoughts so often turned to disgust, disapproval, shame, and sometimes to anger, even hate. Of them, her own people. And how they carried on. At the restrictions they put on themselves (and so their choiceless children) of assuming life to be this daily struggle, this acceptance that they were a lesser people; and boozing away their lives and the booze making things all distorted and warped and violent.

And not having dreams. Like him out the back there, Trambert; of dreaming of one day owning a house like him, and a farm. Mr fuckin white Trambert with the big stately dwelling (Oh very funny, Beth) and endless green paddocks that backed onto the line of miserable state boxes erected on land he'd once owned but sold to them, the government, so they could house another lot of brown nobodies. To *dream*; of being like him, with acres and acres of land to feel under your feet, and hundreds and hundreds of sheep growing fat and woolly to add to your thousands and thousands in the fuckin bank. To dream. Of *peace* in the world; like Trambert must have peace in his nice white world. While here, down there on the street below, are kids practising to be the nothing nobody, but violent, adults of the future. Jesus, Beth, any wonder you feel you need a drink.

The footpath: it began life as a tarsealed walkway, then cracks started to appear, and then little sags. And a hole'd develop. And the kids, the mindless kids even in them days, they found you could pick away at a crack and soon you'd have a section of footpath, and they'd dash these biscuits of walkway to the ground, smashem to smithereens, playing like Samson because he was all the rage in those days. Wasn't long before there wasn't much footpath to walk on. A woman had to walk on the road. But she hardly noticed then. Not in them days, a newly married girl moved into a spanking new state house (her and Jake's half of it, that is) provided by a kind government who didn't charge much rental.

She had dreams then. But they got lost along the way. Sixteen years is a long time. For dreams to stay alive. And wasn't as if the dream was to be a Trambert, a Mrs Trambert, no. Just to have a whole house with her own bit of land under her feet that she and Jake and their kids could call their own. But nothing like a few hidings — from the man sposed to be part of the dream — to reduce life and its dreams to thoughts that grow to disbelief, how the mind went: Come on, Beth, don't kid yourself. You ain't going nowhere but Pine Block. Trying to fight it — at first — lying in

2

wait like some cunning animal for Jake to be in a good mood and then swooping in on him: Ah, Jake . . . I was thinking, you know, about us and, oh just, you know, life in general, and where it's taking us. But you think he'd listen?

Even in his better moments he just looked at a woman, gave her one of those smiles. Of dismissal. Telling her she was kidding herself. And he'd ask her why she wanted to be different from everyone else, wasn't she satisfied and who'd she think she was anyway? Ah, dreams.

Sixteen years is a long time. To live in hell. Well, maybe not hell, she wouldn't go that far. There's been good times, and not a few either. Wasn't as if the flames'd been licking at her feet all these years, now be fair, Beth. Hahaha, laughing at herself. Oh Beth, you're a one at times. But then again, it sure ain't heaven neither or what is Jake doing here? Hahaha, have to laugh, eh girl. Better'n cryin about it. (Though a woman did have her moments.)

Or she'd be watching the TV. An afternoon soapie. *Young and the Restless*. Time-killing, time-passing stuff if a woman was too broke to go join a card school somewhere or her face too beat up to go anywhere — (I ain't having em looking at me sniggering to emselves, whispering their told-you-so's to each other as if they got Husbands of the Year, laughing at a woman for marrying Jake when everyone knew what he was like, with his fists, how fist-happy he was. But so did she: I just thought I could see the, you know, potential in him. And anyrate, not as if he's his whole life punching me up. Only when he's drunk, and then not every time, not even half the time, what would they know, those sniggering whispering bitches out there? As if they can talk) — and she'd spot something; something right out of kilter, not related to the programme, not properly. Something, someone in the background.

A passing truck and she'd catch the flash of its sign on the door and might read something or other Seafoods, and she'd sit there thinking about what kind of seafood those Yanks ate, while the Yanks she was sposed to be watching were doing their usual drama stuff, beautiful people being nasty to each other, rich white bitches and bastards not satisfied with life being kind to em, they have to go and hurt each other. Or it might be a waiter in one of their flash restaurants the stars were always having dinner *and* lunch in, and Beth sitting there thinking how she'd feel having to wait on some flash bitch dripping with jewellery and silk all over and treating her like shit. I'd probably slap the bitch's face. But

3

I'd make sure I'd been paid up my wages first, laughing at that, at herself, her peculiar thoughts.

Other day it was a bookcase. Fulla books of course. Of course; what bookcases are for, aren't they? Oh come on, Beth, at herself for being stupid in her mind. Silly. Like a teenager. Like Grace. Her daughter. My thirteen-year going on fifty-year-old. Hardly like her. She smiled, her face'd crack. And it occurred to Beth that her own house — no, not just her own house but every house she'd ever been in — was bookless. The thought struck her like one of Jake's punches, dunno why. So much so she had to get up and walk around; paced up and down the downstairs passage, smoking, unable to ease her agitation. Bookless. Bookless. We're a bookless society. It kept hammering and hammering home. Soon it was like a sense of loss, almost grief. And she thinking, Jesus, what's wrong with me? So what if this house has no books, what's the big deal about books? But it kept nagging away at her.

She took her mind over dwelling after dwelling she'd been to, relations' homes, her own childhood home, friends. But no. It was bookless. She thought *why*? Almost in anguish. Why are Maoris not interested in books? Well, they didn't have a written language before the white man arrived, maybe that was it. But still it bothered her. And she began to think that it was because a bookless society didn't stand a show in this modern world, not a damn show. And I live in it, don't I? and my kids.

She went upstairs, went through the kids' rooms, trying to find a book and finding only comics and magazines, karate mags, boxing and rugby mags under the two older boys' beds, and — (Oh, what's this? A *Penthouse* snucked right away underneath Nig's bed. The eldest. Her favourite. My Nig. Flicking through the pages — good God. What's this? Recoiling in horror at the sight of a woman in full-colour naked glory with her — her fanny exposed for the whole wide world to see. Slamming it shut. Staring at the ceiling, at the door, she didn't know where to look; at the poster-covered walls deceptively adorned with pictures of males in fighting poses, boxers, karate jokers, thinking: well, well, well. My boy's growing up. Not having seen a *Penthouse* before. Thirty-four years old and I haven't seen or even known of a magazine like this. Finding herself opening the mag again, discovering several sections of glossy photographs of women stark naked and looking pretty, you know, sexy for it despite their brazenness. Beth's heart thumping just a little more than normal. And a tingle, just a little one, down there, of sex. Of wanting sex. Oh wow. Far out, girl.

4

You're thirty-four and you're getting turned on by a few photos of naked women. Are you around the twist? But it wasn't a latent lesbian desire suddenly brought out of her, she knew that. Just sex. She quite liked sex. With my husband. When he feels like it, and I don't mean feels like doing it for himself.) — and after she was recovered she searched on, in the girls' room, Grace and Polly's. Mags and comics. No books. Teenage girl mags with pages and pages of pictures of prissy white girls dolled up, or in skimpy swimming outfits, why would a Maori girl with dark skin even for a Maori want to read look at stuff like this when she had no chance of looking like them? No chance. Then Beth realised she was thinking like Jake about her thirteen-year-old daughter's prospects, her future. Oh, let her read this kind of stuff if that's what turns her on. But no books. And Polly, she was ten and her school reports had her getting poor grades for reading so she wouldn't likely have books under her bed, though Beth did check just in case Polly surprised her. So she went downstairs and it wasn't necessary to go into the sitting room cause sure weren't no books in there, up to the kitchen where she sat down feeling quite drained. Thinking over and over again: bookless. We're bloody bookless, all of us.

Then the council came along with men and machines and they laid a concrete footpath in place of the ruined old. Fixed the vandalising little kids right up. So they, the kids, painted things on it, with old paint from backyard sheds, or stolen from somewhere; obscenities, hearts with arrows through them and initials inside of who loved who, and hearts with who hated who and the heart dripping with blood; they marked out hopscotch squares, noughts and crosses grids, with paint and lipstick and from spraycans (till they discovered, this new generation, the high to be got from sniffing the fumes from a can of spray paint) for years the kids put their marks on the footpath. So it looked no different to the area, the tone of Pine Block: neglected, run-down, abused. And, you know (a woman'd have to think hard to find the right word), prideless.

Made her want to weep sometimes. And not so much for her as for her kids. Their future. If you could call it that.

Walking along the street, not just Rimu Street but any of the nine or ten that crisscrossed each other in this perfect pattern, the car wrecks. More and more the car wrecks appeared on front lawns, down the side of a place (and out back) and stayed there. Sat out on front lawns, up on wooden blocks or bald tyres,

5

promising to be fixed, done up (Tomorrow, man. Gonna start on it tomorrow.), rusting away, making the place look more and more like a wrecker's yard, stead of a place you were meant to raise your kids, send em out as decent citizens. Rusting monuments to these people, their apathy, their couldn't give a fuck bout nuthin or no one attitude.

Ooo, made a woman wild sometimes. Had her wanting to march up to some ofem ask em, didn't they have any fuckin pride, doesn't it occur to you to *do* something? But of course she couldn't. Not in Pine Block. Not as a Maori to another. They'd lynch her. And anyway, who'm I to talk? Way I carry on myself at times, specially when I've had a few. Not as if I'm some angel living amongst the heathens. These are my people. I love em. Or so she forced upon herself.

The kids played in the car wrecks. Used em as playhouses. You could see them at any time of day wriggling and crawling and wrestling away in there, or just sprawled out amongst the cobwebs and the spiders and exposed seat springs and the rusty jagged metal edges that added to their infected, half the time pus-oozing wounds, and the steering wheels sucked on by every mouth that ever sat in a wreck, because they must be suckable you only have to watch the kids. As Beth might find herself doing without even knowing she was half the time.

And there was one house had an old wringer washing machine stuck right outside the front door, bold as you will, it'd been there for years, ever since Beth could remember. And the grass — sposed to be the bitch's front lawn — grown halfway up its fat, chipped girth, weeds sticking out its belly, and a slimy moss formed all over the rubber wringer rollers like a disease. God. Even some of the people looked upon that Barton woman's pridelessness as a standard to which they'd never fall. Not that far.

A woman'd come home from town — in a taxi, feeling like Lady Muck, for a change, steada Lady Blues who ain't got no money — her supermarket shopping filling the taxi boot and she, Lady Muck, in the back not wanting the ride to end, as if she was a princess. And she'd be looking out the window and she'd notice the Pakeha houses, how most of em had well-kept lawns and nice gardens with flowers and shrub arrangements and some with established trees and others with the foresight to have young ones planted, and Lady Muck'd start feeling depressed. Then the vacant lot of land separating Two Lakes from Pine Block that no one, not in sixteen years, had ever built on, it'd fill a woman's vision with its ugly overgrown look, remind her of what was to come. Pine fuckin Block. And she'd feel like whatshername, Cinderella, in her taxi, waiting for it to turn into a pumpkin at the sight of her residential reality, and the rotten little kids everywhere, and the mean-faced teenagers, and the gang members sauntering around like they owned the place. No gardens here. Not trees, nor plant arrangement, not nothing.

And she'd pay the driver, and she'd be stood there, on the soiled concrete footpath, with her eight or nine plastic shopping bags at her feet, thinking of the six mouths she had to feed as well as his, Jake's, the animal, and his fuckin boozing mates coming around drinking all night and then wanting to be fed, and she'd trudge up her footpath feeling old.

An old woman at thirty-four.

And she'd come back for the other bags, careful not to take each load inside or there wouldn't be anything to come back to. And she'd turn and there'd be her through-the-wall neighbour, Jill, just happened to have come outside to sit on her front doorstep the way they do, wanting to know everything, to see some action, something they could wag their tongues over. But Beth having to smile through her teeth, Hi Jill, to the woman because she and her husband were good to borrow from, especially beer. And smokes. Fixem up on payday, Thursdays, out of what Jake gave her from his unemployment, which was half. The other half was his. And you forgot to add an extra bottle or two as a thanks, they didn't talk to you for a month.

Inside, in the kitchen, slumping in a chair, it was usually the kitchen for what use a sitting room with hardly any furniture to speak of and what there is you wouldn't get two bob from the second-hand shop for, only the TV down there, oh, and my good old record player, but I wish I could afford one of these flash stereos they have these days even the kids've got em I do love my music, and the TV hardly worth watching, those soaps didn't fool a woman, inspire her to wanting to be like them, the nasty vicious unhappy beautiful creatures, Jesus Christ, if they're real then who wants to be a Yank whitey?

And her mood'd feel like this heavy weight pressing down on her, a kind of blackness with it. But I'm a fighter, I ain't the type to lie down and let people, life, roll over me. Even him, the fuckin animal, I don't exactly crack up shaking to death or screaming when I know it's coming, a hiding. To hell withim, there's been times when a woman laughed in his face, with her blood pouring from it, and toldim: You go right on, mister. You're still an arse-hole. O life, but sometimes I wonder about you, what I did to deserve what you threw at me.

When it rained, the rubbish in the gutters'd block up the drains, have the street awash with its own gunge, its own discarded filth — oo, we Pine Blockers are our own worst enemies — and it might rain for days and so it'd rise up, the flooding, and creep up over the front lawns — if you could call some ofem lawns — form little lakes, ponds, puddles, and the kids — always the kids in Pine Block, the place is teeming withem, we're shit breeding more shit faster than the sewers can handle — the kids'd turn up.

They'd turn the lawns to sludge pits, quagmires, traipse mud and dirt around withem. Even to bed. Even beds with no sheets. Bloody animals — not the kids, it ain't their fault — the parents. Catch one of mine going to bed without at least a wash and there'd be trouble. As for no sheets.

Parents too drunk or half the time missing, boozing up somewhere, at the pub, in another blimmin *town* some ofem, where they'd ended up in their drunken state and with a whole tribe of kids left at home with not a brass razoo to feed emselves on. Jesus Christ, but a woman'd never done that, as drunk as she'd been. I make sure my kids come first. Their food, anyrate. What can a woman do about their future, their education? It ain't in my hands. Not on my own. Not living here, in Pine Block, Two Lake's dumping ground for its human rubbish. It's all of us; we need to get together — talk and try and sort ourselves out. Before it's too late. If we haven't already missed the bus.

And when the rain'd stopped and the lawns'd dried out and the council'd come (late, as usual) and unblocked the drains, the mud patches became deserts; little deserts and dustbowls that the horrible untamed kids could come back to and sit by, twiddle, and scratching with their mindless, hardened little toes that'd hardly known a shoe between em, using implements, a stick, a nail, anything, scraping scratching digging gouging at the earth till dust filled the air and clogged up their flared, wild little nostrils. Then, satisfied they'd done some damage, they moved elsewhere to wreck ruin something else.

And when the rain came back and filled the craters they'd made, the kids came back and sailed blocks of wood with a nail hammered centre and scissored (if a pair could be found) sails made from plastic shopping bag or pierced cardboard or newspaper, down there on their hardened little knees blowing like crazy, urging their vessels on, swearing and cursing at the things as they practised being rough and tough. You could hear em from upstairs, the little buggers. Then, bored, they'd move off to another place.

Might be a car wreck; in there amongst the cobwebs and rusty, dangerous protrusions and springs shot out like broken Jack-in-the-boxes, and oases patches of upholstery, and soil marks, and dried food scraps, and the smell of piss, and sperm stains — (once Beth'd watched a kid — oh, the poor little bugger — one rainy afternoon out her bedroom window, a wreck across the street, and knew from the jerking movements the poor little fucker was masturbating. Made her weep. Turn her eyes away and weep. Love, she thought. That's all the kid is wanting, love. And having to take it from himself because there ain't no other source, Beth instincted out. Made her feel like rushing down there and bringing the youth back to her bed and giving him, you know, a real good rooting. Just to make him feel good.) — And for some, the car wrecks were home.

You could go past of an evening and see em huddled up in there with some old blanket or nothing at all, just this pathetic shape cringed in the frozen outline of a broken-down car. And the strains of music coming from inside the house it was sat outside of. May as well've been a gravestone. And those arseholes in there drinking up large, having a ball thank you very much and fuck the kid out there huddled up and dying, his heart anyway, he got sent out there because he was bad, he done something we didn't like, or he exists and we can't stand his existence, he's such a, oh, we don't know, we just don't like him. Even though he's of their loins. Jesus. Any wonder some ofem grew up wanting to join the gang that'd won the struggle in Pine Block, the Brown Fists. Though there were kids who'd joined with their archrivals, the Black Hawks, across town, and so got to do battle, often fatal, with their Pine Blocks brothers and cousins and childhood friends. Maori against Maori. And thousands ofem each side across the country. And hardly a one working; the government, the good old government, paying em to do crimes against each other and society.

Beth'd heard a whisper from her children that her eldest, Nig (my Nig), was looking to joining up. Had a woman confronting her seventeen-year-old, asking him outright, and he saying, None of your business, how they do these kids they don't remember nothing of what you did forem. And she warning him, you better

9

not be joining up with no Brown Fists, mista, or you and me are through. She didn't mean it. Only wanted to scare him; Beth assuming that the intensity of her love for her son was matched by an equal reciprocating love. Nig just looking at her that way he did (oo, he knows how to hurt me), saying nothing, just looking with those glistening brown eyes looking hurt, those handsome features so much like his father, but Nig's more refined, more handsome. Just looking. So Beth conceding, giving a little: Well, alright, I didn't actually mean we are finished, kaput. But, son, you got to think of the future.

Nig saying, what future? No future for a Maori. And walking off. Rocked a woman to the core.

And her other children, they were coming up to the same troublesome age as Nig. Abe, fifteen. Is he next? Boogie, fourteen, and already getting into more and trouble at school. Grace — well, I don't know about her. I never could get through to her. Something about her, I dunno. But she's growing up all the time, she's even got hairs on her whatsit. And her period. Polly, only ten and she still sleeps with her doll, and Huata, he's only seven, so a mother's got those two at least for a few more years. Though the years they do go by. And all too soon. Why, I can remember like yesterday being a teenager myself. Now I'm double the age. And about five times the misery! hahaha! A woman has to laugh or she'd cry. And Beth née Ransfield, she was no weepy weakling. Just confounded, that's all.

Funny place, this Pine Block: you could predict it, the moods of the people, tell what day it was by the signs. Thursday to Sunday — the clink of beer bottles in their crates, the wafts of takeaway food aromas from Kentucky Fried to Chinese to burgers and, staple diet of Pine Block kids, fishnchips.

Mondays, starting to go on the cadge some ofem.

Tuesdays, hide your surplus you got any or someone'll break your heart and your cupboards while they're at it with a sad story.

Wednesdays, broke. The lot of us. Or nearly the lot. Even those with jobs, they're only workers on a worker's wage. So Wednesdays, they dreamed . . .

Tomorrow, man, gonna get my dole money and buy me some Chinese. Gonna buy me *lotsa* Chinese. And fuck the power bill. Spare ribs, man, oh far out. And a loafa bread. And butter *thick*, man, gonna dip it in that sauce they do and gonna *stuff* myself.

10

I am, man. Yeow, brother, you dream away. Ain't dreaming, man. Tomorrow, gonna do. And after I've had the ribs I'm gonna buy me a cooked chicken from the Hindu's. The Hindu's? Man, they ain't chickens, they're *chooks*. Y'c'd string a tennis racket withem, man. Aw, c'mon man, they ain't that bad. They fuckin are. Well, I like em. You like anything. So what, man? So you got to have the *bread*, brother. The bread to pay for the stuff. Well like I said, man, tomorrow I'll *have* the bread. Ah, man, you call what they give you on the dole bread? Well it ain't fuckin porridge, man. And it ain't bread, neither. Less'n a hundred bucks a week if you're single, you call that bread? Well it beats having to *work* for it, man. I mean, work . . . just the thought of it makes me tired. I'd rather have a job that earns decent bread, man, steada this hanging out all fuckin week for a lousy less'n hundred bucks. How long does it last? Brother, it ain't gonna last me one day by the time I'm finished tomorrow. Buyin pork bones too. I'll be waiting for his truck to come, the Pork Bone Man. Gonna be waiting with that look, you know, real cool, casual, eh, like I just won something. The horses, like I just won a big trifecta or sumpthin. Or this Lotto. Man, what I wouldn't do to win that. Million bucks first prize. But hey, what would I be doing standing in the middle of Pine Block waiting for some cunt to arrive with overpriced pork bones? Eh brother? You wouldn't see me for dust. So where would you be then, man? I'd. I'd — a frown creasing the brow, having to think about that one, really think about it — Well, not Pine Block thaz for sure. Maybe, brother, but you'd be back. Back what? Back here, where you started. Come on . . . When the bread ran out you'd be back. Ran out? Man, how's a fuckin cool million gonna run out? Same way as it ran in, bro — luck. When it's in, it's in. But it always goes. And half the time don't come back. What we all count on in this shit joint, Pine Block — luck. No wonder a man's gettin himself drunk all the time: it's the — the — the. No word for it. Not even so simple a word as frustration. It's being what we are, man, that's what'll bring you back. That's what keeps us drunk. Luck.

Luck. Beth! Beth! The hell is she? Jake that day had come striding out to Beth hanging out yet another load of washing. I got lucky, Beth! Carrying an armful of something, looking like he'd just won this new craze, Lotto. But not first prize. Despite Jake's tone, despite that armful of parcels. That'd be wishing for the impossible.

11

So Beth turning her back, back to the washing and that ever-reminding view of lucky Trambert's acreage, his big old house half hidden in the trees over there. And Jake standing there saying, Beth, Beth, listen to me. Look what I got for us. And for you.

All six foot three inches of hard-muscled towering man of him, and Beth playing it cool, and just a little bit coy because you never knew his being lucky might run into her being lucky (he hasn't touched me in ages) and smiling at him making an appearance between a shirt of his and a pair of Grace's underpants. I got lucky. Smiling all over. But Beth sighing, what kind of luck? The kind that you can bank? And him grinning, Maybe. Her heart doing a little leap at that: What, you mean no worries about where the next meal is coming from? Surely not.

So she stopped her doings. Looked up at him, his head poking over the washing line wire. No fooling around, Jake. I ain't in the mood. What luck? And him doing a sway, with a sexy grin, or maybe he was just being stupid, and drawling, Guess what I got for you? And her thinking, it can be anything. Don't care what. Because it'll be the first time in years. Playing along with his game, thinking he'd finally had a win on the horses that he spent half his dough on. Come over here.

Beckoning her to step away from the washing, he doing so first, going down on his haunches on the long grass of back lawn it took him all his time to borrow next-door's mower, cut the damn thing, having to spread with his big mits an area flat where he laid out his newspaper-wrapped parcels. Couldn't be much of anything flash, not in newspaper. But Beth feeling sort of excited about it. So tell me, she sat herself down beside the parcels, counting em, four, five, six. Six surprises. Must be something good.

Jake opening the first, taking his sweet time, doing it page by page and Beth being able to read last year's local news about the mayor presenting someone before the contents finally revealed itself. A crayfish. Crayfish? Jake, you haven't been up to nothing bad, have you? Nah, don't be stupid. Grinning. Alright? Beth brushing her forehead, Wow. Course it's alright. She hadn't had crayfish in that long it wasn't worth trying to remember. And the bees buzzing away in the background (and fat blowflies too, don't forget them, Beth) and someone with a motor mower going, and a plane humming around up there somewhere in the nice summer blue, oh but this is a nice change. Crayfish.

For us? And Jake unwrapping another of the lovely red beasts,

I don't even have to cook em. Jake stroking — *stroking* — the things, and oh, it must be big for his mit not to dwarf it. Jake laughing. Her starting to believe it, that he'd been lucky.

Another parcel, this time a whole snapper. Big. Two more in another parcel. Oh, but this is a food-lover's dream. This is what a Pine Blocker has a Wednesday wet dream over. What next?

Mussels. Dozens of the sweet little creatures. Greenlips, the farmed jobs. They'd be fat as anything. Fill the shell from edge to edge those farmed mussels. And what's he got in those plastic pottles, not what I'm thinking, surely? He *must*'ve won big at something. Jake, what'd you win? Come on, stop teasing now. (And wondering what was in the sixth and last parcel. For me. For Beth Heke, who's had to put up with this man for sixteen years and don't remember getting anything for me like this, let alone with a feast to boot.) Can I do the last parcel? — but Jake was already doing it. Grinning.

Jake . . . ? in that voice, girlish, come-onish, a you-can-have-me-if-you-like tone. Remembering the pottles: What you got in these? Oh them? Jake making out he was so cool. Oh, juss some oysters. A pause then erupting in laughter. Making a woman warm all over for her man. (Why, I can't help loving him.) Oh, just ten dozen little ole oysters, dear. And laughing again. Oh, why can't life always be like this? Beth thinking. Why can't we have a few more *wins*? a bit more of this *luck*, whatever it is.

Last parcel. (Oh, don't tell me, I can't look. I can't look.) Beth closing her eyes, wanting to near squeal with excitement — no, not so much excitement as happiness. At just being happy because he, her man, is happy. At how it must be near all the time for some (like him over there, Trambert) because life keeps throwing you winners, a bit of luck for a change.

Sea-eggs. Your favourite, Beth. She looking at him with grateful eyes but thinking he must have her present hidden on him. But of course you don't ask, you wait till he's ready. May as well enjoy the feast beforehand, Beth told herself. And sea-eggs were a favourite of hers, she loved em. (Funny thing, Jake, being a Maori, and near a full-blood at that, unlike Beth, being about half with white blood on both sides of her parentage, Jake didn't like sea-eggs, kina the Maori called em. Look like little hedgehogs, Jake described em. Did too, but the roe inside was sweet, even if it was a black purply gooey mess to get at the tasty part.) She had one right there, cracking it open against the steel pole of the clothes-line, delicately removing the inner slivers of yellow roe, letting em slide down her throat just barely broken by her teeth to release the taste. Mmm-uh! Let life stay like this. And Jake he started on one of the crayfish.

Ah, the two ofem out there, eating like a king and queen; chuckling at each other, shooing away the flies that came rushing, feeling greedy, selfish about it: the delicious food, the shared moment. Of just me and him. Me and my man pigging out on a fine summer's day.

Jake winking at her. Beth hoping it meant what she thought it did. Careful not to wink back because he didn't like the woman to be the instigator of that particular activity, nosiree he didn't. Sex was a man's choice first and foremost; in fact, a woman was careful she didn't show she enjoyed it too much or it made Jake wild, he'd start asking questions, or sulk, not touch her for another month. But she had her ways of reaching her objective without Jake knowing she'd reached such a height.

Then she asked about the luck, what it was, how much. And he laughed and laughed. Rolled about on the grass, a crayfish front horn in his hand cracked with his teeth and ready for eating. I got the sack! Laughing. The sack? From your job? And he was laughing? Aw, come on, Jake, you're joking. Not joking, woman. Laughing again, telling her it was last week, his firing from his job as a labourer at a quarry where he'd been for fourteen of the sixteen years he was married to her. Sacked? Last week? So why tell me now? And why all this food? You mad, Jake Heke? Feeling angry with him. About to give him a piece of her mind — and to hell with the consequences and to hell with this food and to hell with whatever else he's got for me, personally — but Jake explained: I got granted the benefit. What benefit? The unemployment. The unem-*ployment*! Beth wanted to slap his face. You got it, lady. I'm on the dole as from now. Got the letter today. And they sent a cheque with it. And you've eaten some of it! Laughing.

Telling her it worked out at only seventeen bucks less than what he was paid at the quarry, and to think, all them years of working it was for nothing. (Beth quickly calculating her half of Jake's income to meaning half of seventeen bucks less a week. Not the end of the world. And Jake'd find something soon.)

That was over two years ago. Jake just another of the long-term unemployed of Two Lakes. The country suffering its worst-ever unemployment figures. Why, half of Pine Block was out of work. Though a person had to be blind and deaf not to see the figures published in the papers, on the TV, about Maori unemployment being much higher than their white counterparts. It was because they were less skilled. And now, Beth knew, a damn sight less motivated if Jake and a good many of his cronies were examples. And to think, he was so *proud* of himself, as if he'd had it over not only his former boss who'd sacked him (for absenteeism) but the rest of the world for thinking they were better than Jake Heke. Luck. A woman wasn't so sure about this luck business that it was really luck and not just plain hard work, self-motivation. Luck.

As for the present Jake had for Beth, he'd meant the sea-eggs. Sea-eggs for chrisake. Call that luck?

2

Two Kids on a Bench

Boogie looking up at the wall clock for the umpteenth time —
Fuck. Fuckin thing hasn't moved since I last looked at it, telling
his sister: Grace, that clock must be broken. His own voice broken,
close to tears. No it's not. Just stop looking at it all the time, Boog.
Can't help it. Know you can't, but it ain't broken. So 9.30 a.m.,
crawling, finally, past, the time Boogie'd set his mind on, because
ten o'clock, man, that was just *too* long. Now he could do the next
half-hour endless crawl.

Just sat here, a boy and his (good) sister in the foyer of Two
Lakes Courthouse, on a Friday morning when his mates (what
few he had) were at school, probably laughing about me, I bet.

Grace? You think they'll be, you know, laughing at me? Who?
The kids. At school. My mates 'n that. Dunno. Grace shrugging.
And if they are then they can't be very good mates. But you think
they are? Shush, Boogie. You got more to worry about than mates
laughing at you, and no, they won't be. You sure, Grace? Course
I'm sure. Oh Boog, you're such a sook at times. You really are. No
wonder the old man picks on you. Can't help it. I know that.
Well? Well what? So why're you calling me a — Because you are.
Sometimes.

Grace touching her less-than-a-year-older brother reassuringly
on the arm. Only sometimes, Boog. Forcing a smile his way
because she was lying. Sensitive kid that he was, a girl felt older
not younger. And him being a boy. And the son of Jake Heke.
Still, that didn't stop a sister loving him, maybe she loved him
more for being a sort of freak, a standout from the rest of the Pine
Block roughies, let alone a son of Jake. Boys: they make such a big
deal of being *tough*. It's *the* most important thing in the world to
em. Specially Maoris. Not that the Pakeha boys at school are that
much better. They're all stupid. Even that cop standing over there
with his sleeves rolled up, arms folded, face set in concrete trying
to act tough. It's males. Grace was sure of it.

Boogie asking the cop — for about the third time — when his

16

turn was gonna be on the list, the cop telling Boog to wait his patience, boy. Something in the tone of boy that wasn't right. Like hatred was lurking just beneath his uniformed surface. Hatred of people like Boog, and her by sisterly association, Grace.

Maybe a hate for Maoris, hard to know. Though God knows there were plenty at school didn't like Maoris. Not that a girl blamed em half the time; they're a rough tough mean lot, those (us) Maoris. Even the kids. Learn young.

But it hurt knowing a segment of your school peers didn't like you on account of your race. What about the good ones like me? Not saying I'm an angel, but I ain't bad. I *ain't*. Then Boogie muttering in her ear, Givim patience if the old man was here. He'd fuckin *waste* the white cunt. Hissing the word out. Grace telling him don't talk like that or I'm off. And thinking that their father'd do no such thing, not whacking someone on Boog's behalf. He didn't like Boog. Hated him in fact.

Grace could hear father's voice echoing in her mind: Ain't no kid of mine they can't look after emselves. His own kid. And being disowned because he couldn't fight. What about Boogie's other qualities? Always near the top of the class, very kind, and *very* sensitive to the kids that everyone else forgets about, or scorns. Nope, you got to be able to fight first. And even then you weren't exactly guaranteed Jake Heke's love. Jake the Muss, that's what his mates — his *crawwww*ling mates call him. Muss for muscles. They love him for it. Never mind that last — or it was early this morning — he beat up my mother. That doesn't bother them, he's still their hero.

People starting to arrive: making their appearance head first as the rest of them followed up the wide stone steps. High heels clicking, shoes scuffing, heavy leather work-boots clumping, near every one ofem with a Maori inside. Grace recognising so many of the faces as Pine Blockers; the kids and some of the mothers come withem. Only one father so far. Hardly surprising.

The odd one saying hello to Grace, no one acknowledging poor Boogie. Making Grace feel more protective toward him, yet a part of her mind confused at feeling an opposite hatred, a contempt for his physically inadequate condition. And wasn't as if he didn't have the physique: he was tall, like his father (we all are) and muscles were developing, she'd seen him in the bath, running around the place. Yet he hated fighting. Violence. Anything to do with it — for himself. Oh but he didn't mind telling kids his old man was who he was, and he was always boasting about his big

17

brother Nig gonna waste the whole flippin world once he got into the Brown Fists. Yet say boo to him and he'd freak out.

A big man appearing in a suit. Bennett. Mr Bennett, the child welfare officer. Grace knew him, he'd been around regarding Boogie, his behaviour at school and outside of it, his stealing from shops and being caught, playing truant. And now here, an appearance at the Children's Court in front of a magistrate.

Morning, everyone! the big welfare officer greeting all and sundry, anyone'd think this was a Sunday picnic. But Boogie and Grace both giving him shy smiles of greeting, instincting what they did of his likely good fatherliness, the qualities he seemed to give off. Then he disappeared into the courtroom, Grace presumed, behind those big wooden double doors.

Others in suits or nice dresses, court officials no doubt, hurrying by and disappearing the same way. Most ofem Pakeha, white. Funny that, how one side of the double doors are one race, and the other this race: Maori. Made Grace want to crawl into a hole with shame. Or had her wanting to disassociate herself from them, jump up and explain she was only here to give her brother moral support because she knew her parents wouldn't be here to do same, and she'd even got permission from the headmaster at school to be here, just as long as she didn't take the whole day off should her presence be no longer required, as the head put it. She was a good girl. Maybe a little different from many or most of her peers, and certainly different from her Pine Block peers, but she was a good girl. I mean I have good thoughts. So she supposed that made her good.

Last night there'd been a big fight. They'd wrecked the place, or what there was to wreck of it, which wasn't much. More broken glass and spilled beer and plenty of blood. First it was Jake roaring his head off at some man — it must've been a man because Dad was calling him cunt — that he was a tougharse and the cunt was a wimp and why didn't they prove it (*prove* it?! Prove what? Grace awake upstairs in her bed'd wondered), and the other fulla yelling that Jake didn't fuckin worry him, rep or no rep, telling Dad he wasn't backing down to no man, Jake the Muss Heke be damned. So Dad hitim. It must've been Dad because he was the one yelling immediately after the familiar, yet still sickening, sound of fist crunching into flesh and bone, *Stand up!*

Then a woman started on Dad, accusing him of being the biggest arsehole cunt under the sun and why didn't he pick on someone his own size and Jake's voice just hearable as telling the

18

woman, Aw, shut ya mouth, woman. As if she hardly existed. But the woman building to a screaming pitch and being joined by others — Grace figuring that it must be a kind of madness comes over em when they're boozed up; and maybe it's also fear, so they yell and scream, just like kids do when they've been unexpectedly frightened. They yell. Close their eyes and yell like hell. And it was Jake they were afraid of. Dad. My father. The man who did that to my mother and created me. Oh God, I hope it's not inheritable. Whatever it is that Dad's suffering from.

Then men's voices joined the din and soon there was thumping and bumping and crashing going, and glass smashing and wood, beer crates, splintering; women yelling, some ofem bawling, and there was even one laughing. Grace heard her — in snatches — this woman her mocking laughter at the mayhem happening around her, sort of like a TV documentary describing a scene, the sequence of mad events taking place before and around her: Yah! and now Moose is sticking his big nose in! Go to it, Moosie! Hahaha — And then she'd be cut off, then come clear again: G'won, Mary, cry ya little eyes out, as if that's gonna make these bastards and bitches stop. G'won, Mary, weep! Hahaha! Yer mad! The fuckin lot of yas, yer ma — Cut off again.

The struggle, this humungous struggle resuming dominance over a girl's ears and no doubt those of her other five siblings. What must they be thinking? Specially the younger ones.

Calling to Polly, You wanna hop in with me, Poll? But Poll saying no, she was alright. Her and Sweetie, her doll, they were looking after each other. So Grace calling to Huata the same invitation and getting sobbing in reply. God, she'd heard it so many times before, and she knew it went on all over this place, the kids, always the kids, suffering most. Poor Huata.

She got up and climbed in beside her seven-year-old brother, cuddling up to him, feeling the damp of his tears on his pyjama top, the wet and then familiar stench of his piss. Oo, it's alright, Hu. It's alright. And Hu heaving with sobbing. And the fight still going on down below. And snatches of commentary from the laughing woman. And such a nice starlit night outside too.

Sorry, darling. Yeah, me too, dear. And I'm sorry for hitting you. No, no, *I'm* sorry for hitting *you*. Here, comein givus a kiss. A hug. A handshake. Yet another handshake. Put it here, brother. Take my hat off to you, man, you pack a punch. You too, bro. Here, put it here, man. I fuckin love ya. You're my cuzin, you know that, eh? You and I are related. Here, put it here, brother.

19

On my mother's side, eh, that's the connection. And here we are fighting each other. Here, shake, cuzin. And don't let us — blood-related — be fighting each other again. Sorry, sorry, sorry, here shake, put it here, gimme a hug, a kiss (a fuck), we won't do this again we were juss drunk, eh, cuzin? Have I shaken your hand? Here, put it here, cuz, just in case. My fault — No, *my* fault. No, it was my fault, I shouldn't said what I did — Man, it wasn't what *you* said got me wild it was . . .

On and on and on into this lovely night, this lovely night and lovely children corrupted, ruined, *raped*, and all you can say is shake? Put it here, brother? And next week, next month, next year, for all the years of your terrible existence you lot'll be doing the same, Grace in her brother's bed thinking, as his small body seized every regular so often with a sob ascending from his troubled sleep.

Hearing the sounds of their shift from the sitting room to the kitchen. And someone starting up the guitar, telling everyone, Be happy now. Like that song: Don't worry. Be happy. As if it is all so easy. As if the events just passed have not taken place. As if it hasn't tramped across another lot of kids' minds, crunched under-foot more of whatever it is that, left untouched, has a kid growing up normal, kind of pure.

Then voices in song, harmonised song, floated up to the bed-room. So you would not believe — you would *not* —that from the same source had sprung, just minutes before, such chaos, such encrazed chaos.

And maybe an hour later, a girl didn't know, drifting as she was in and out of dreams and waking dreamscape, the two jumbled, mixing in, she hearing the same voices just shot. Gone. Just bursts of notes lasting a line, a verse, a word.

Someone telling the guitarist, Hey! Hurry up and tune that fuckin thing. I wanna sing a song for you fullas. Someone telling that person, it was a woman, to shud her fuggin mouth, she couldn't sing to save her black self, that she'd heard a fuggin *cat* screechin better'n her, and telling the guitarist, Tell her to go fug herself, Sonny. Bitch can't sing to save her black self. And the insulted woman replying, The hell you think you are talking about me like that? I c'n sing better'n you. Oh yeah? Yeah. Oh yeah? Yeah. Shit, woman, may's well bring the fuggin cat in here than listen to you singing. So juss fug up. *You* fuck up. Don't play her song, Sonny. Play Strangers in the Night, Sonny. Play My Cat Sings in the Alley, Sonny. Come on, Sonny, let me show this bitch. Ah, go catch some mouses, woman. Catch you in a fuckin minute.

Come on then. And the men whooping, Yeow! Go to it, ladies!

So the ladies going to it, you could hear their struggle, and it wasn't hard for an experienced girl to picture em hanging onto each other's hair, clawing at each other, taking big raking gouges out of one another's facial skin, spit flying, froth bubbling out of frantic mouths, eyes bulged blood red with the effort, the booze, and that certain madness that afflicts a girl her own race and only them, she knows it — oh but does she know it. And the men yelling and laughing, and saying, *Whooaa* at probably the combatants falling over them, pushing em away, laughing, Go fight over there, spill your blood on Bully's shirt, I had my share. Laughing.

It's a joke. It must be a joke. A lifetime joke, the same one said over and over, like their aftermath handshakes, on and on and fuckin on.

No wonder a girl felt she was going half mad, or didn't want to live no more, not here, in this house, in this street.

And eventually the women's fight over and their tears shed and sorries gushed, and the guitarist going danta-danka-dunka-dinka-dang-ding down his strings, a chord, a tuning chord, forever tuning when he's not playing or drinking. Then Dad. Tennessee Waltz, Beth. Do Tennessee Waltz. Grace waking both ears to that. And Huata fast asleep and gone of his seizures, but wet as anything. A girl could hardly bear to move her leg lest she register it too fully, her brother's piss against her form. Thinking, Go on, Mum. Sing. She sings so beautifully. And her mother saying, You sing it with me, Jake. And Dad saying, I might. I might. Then someone, one of those stupid women, sticking her nose in: I'll sing it with you, Beth. I'll harmonise you, eh? And her original antagonist telling her, Beth don't want a fuggin *cat* miaowing along with her song. So fug up, woman. Ah, fuck the singing, one of the men drawling, what's to eat? And, funny thing, at the same time the smell of cooking reaching Grace's nostrils: now, Thursday, so it'll be pork bones and watercress with spuds and doughboys. Soon as they've fed they'll be falling asleep where they are. Grace falling away back into dreams.

She thought it was a dream: someone asking for eggs. Then someone, her mother, saying, What, eggs with a boiled feed? You must be joking, mista. Grace fearing for the mother in her dream till she realised it wasn't a dream.

Awake, listening. Too damn quiet down there. Just mumblings. Huata soaked to the skin beside her. Her own pyjamas wet from contact with him. Creeping out of his bed, stripping her soiled nightclothes, getting into bed naked, ahhh, the nice feel of sheets against her skin. Now what's happening? as arguing started up.

I ain't cookin fried eggs with no boiled feed. Damned if I am. What I serve up is what you get. You're not satisfied then take a walk, Jim. This ain't a fuckin restaurant and I ain't no one's slave. Not even his. Grace presuming her mother'd be pointing at her father. And Grace fearing for her. Her mother's physical well-being, and wondering *why* does she bring it on herself half the time? She knows what he's like. Someone saying something, Grace couldn't quite make out, but her mother clear enough: The hell you mean, Maori way? You call yourselves Maoris? Then Jake telling her to shuddup, woman. And she telling him to go to hell. She's got her opinions and she's got a right to say em. Back she went: Maoris, eh? Can any of us in this room speak the language? No reply. What do we know of our culture? Her voice emotional, the way it gets when she'd had too much to drink, or is like anyway when she gets a bee in her bonnet. Men's voices, a chorus ofem, telling her to shuddup and siddown and that she had a damn cheek talking to them like that. But Beth went right on at them. She told them the Maori of old had a culture, and he had pride, and he had warriorhood, not this bullying, man-hitting-woman shet, you call that manhood? It's not manhood, and it sure as hell ain't Maori warriorhood. So ask yourselves what you are.

But the men weren't listening: Grace heard a voice go, That's it. I ain't sitting here while no woman talks like that to men. The sound of chairs scraping then Jake: Say sorry, Beth. Silence. *The hell I will! What've I got to be sorry for? Tell* HIM *to say sorry!*

Next instant the noise ofem all leaving. The door finally slamming. Silence again. Grace squeezing shut her eyes, pulling the blanket over her head waiting for the inevitable to follow. And it did.

And Grace laying there, moving her jaw rapidly but regularly from side to side and making a low ahhhhhh under the blankets as she did. It blocked the sound out completely. Didn't even allow thoughts of it to enter her head. They didn't come till later.

Up in the morning, dizzy with lack of sleep. A note on the kitchen table addressed to Nig to get the kids to clean up and don't wake me, love from Mum.

A pool of her blood on the floor at the table where she must've sat after he'd finished with her. Poor *poor* Mum.

Nig not up so Grace sending Huata to wake him, Grace

starting on the sitting room, Polly following faithfully after her lugging that doll of hers, a thing with blonde shiny hair she thought of it as her baby/sister/other mother all in one.

Sitting room a mess. Broken glass, smashed beer bottles, wood splinters of beer crates, the overpowering stench of beer. And fags. Settee tipped over on its back, the armchair one more fight older with more blood splatters, beer stains; a circle of beer crates on their ends where they must've sat around in a circle continued drinking or saying their sorries and thrusting put-it-here hands at each other. The whole scene bathed in sunlight pouring in through the black cloth blinds on permanent B for broken, in different stages of up or down, overlooking the back lawn, which hadn't been mowed in ages, with bits of junk sticking up out of the high grass, a beer crate, a cardboard carton, a big tyre; and beyond, out there in the vast green expanse, but you wouldn't believe two such different worlds could be so close, Trambert's sheep grazing on his acreage, and the stand of pines you could see from Grace's window (and used to be filled by a frightened girl's imagination with witches and terrifying creatures of her haunted mind, but she was tougher now, so they were just the pines the area was apparently named after) and aptly ugly macrocarpa.

The floorboards sticky with partly dried beer, and cigarette butts everywhere. Abe walking in, heading straight for the over-turned settee and plunging his arm at the seat junction, no good morning, kiss my arse, nothing, just wanting to be the one to find any coins even a note or two that'd slipped down there.

Nope, nothing. Fuckem. On to the cigarette packets, rushing about like a flipping vacuum-cleaner whipping up the packets flicking the lids, saying nope, nope, nope till he let out a whoop that he'd struck gold. Choice! Three, man! Stuffing them into his school shirt pocket. Grace going, Abe! But Abe not even glancing at her. Then Nig — shadow of his father — standing at the door. And Abe stiffening, touching his breast pocket. Gimme, gimme, Abe, Nig chuckling but menacing.

Not that he was a bully. Not to Grace he wasn't. He loved her and she him. But Boogie, poor Boogie out there in the toilet having to clean the worst part, the spew, the runny shit spots up around the toilet bowl rim; and no one liked Boog except the girls. And Huata was too young yet to know Boog'd failed the test of pending manhood, but he'd learn. He'd be one of the judges one day against one of his own peers. All boys are judges against their own. And now, waiting for a real judge to pass judgment on poor

23

Boogie, given that name out of contempt because he was scared of the Boogie Ghost as a kid, more scared than normal, terrified in fact. The rot'd set in early.

Now look at him, sitting here with his face on permanent S for scared, he's been running scared all his life. And then Bennett came out.

They here yet? Who? Your mother and father. Or one ofem'd do. Boogie shaking his head, looking at Grace for support. But Grace no picture of self-confidence herself, not to a man in a *suit*, so looking down, reddening. What, they still asleep? Uh, yeah. Both ofem? Uh, they had a late night. And Grace glancing up to see the big welfare officer take a step backwards, cry, Aee. Maoris, eh. Always the late nights. Always the excuses from their lawful responsibilities. But Boogie shrugging his lack of understanding, and Grace just grasping what the Maori welfare was saying. Sighing, Well alright then, you're first to be called, young Heke. Then taking his huge frame over to the main cluster of people opposite the Heke siblings.

Grace following Bennett with her eyes, a phrase flashing in her mind as she looked across at the people: The Lost Tribe. The Lost Tribe, The Lost . . . it kept repeating. Mystifying her. Eyes riveted to the human scene, and that Lost Tribe phrase going on and on in her head.

The mothers with fags in their mouths, in hands that had a tattoo, an arm with one, two of them that Grace could see. Most ofem — there'd be eight or nine mums — fat things. And most wild-looking. The Lost Tribe . . .

Leaned against the wall, scowling, two gang prospects, Grace knew em from Pine Block; just a couple of kids maybe fourteen, fifteen, mad keen to become Brown Fists; already covered in home-made tats, their hands and exposed arms purple with tats. A glance at Boog to confirm that he was trying to catch their eye, eager to greet them, givem the old lifted eyebrows greeting, anything, just to be in sweet withem. But they'd not return his greeting, didn't he know that? No one in Pine Block, let alone gang prospects, is gonna be seen acknowledging the existence of a wimp.

Teenagers of all shapes and sizes lounging around, slouched, pacing, fooling with each other, talking loud or not at all, Maori every one ofem but two. And look how *they* were trying to crawl their way in with the Maori toughs.

Lost Tribe . . . Oh look, that mother's breastfeeding. Oh, isn't

24

that sweet. When I have babies I'm gonna breastfeed em for as long as I can, because I read it makes em grow up healthier, and anyway it's good forem in creating a bond between baby and mother. And I sure want that with mine. *If* I ever get married, that is . . . if I find a boy who'll have me; ugly thing like me — (Oh, but inside I'm not ugly. In fact, I feel, you know, somehow beautiful inside, though spose ya can't exactly cut me open to find this out.)

A couple of toddlers runnin around. (Oh, aren't they cute.) I love kids. One ofem started to make a hell of a racket: banging the metal ashtray up and down on the floor, Grace givin the kid a little smile, thinking so what, he's only a kid. But next minute the kid was scooped up by — Grace supposed — its mother. Up in the air she had him . . . and Grace having those words, The Lost Tribe . . . going through her mind as she watched the incident like it was in slow motion.

Fat bitch's arm went back. And Mr Bennett just turning his head. Arm coming in (oh hell!) and the kid's body jolting like a train'd hit it. (You bitch! You fuckin bitch!) Bennett saying, What the — when the woman came back with another swing. *Mrs Renata!* Bennett scolded, obviously knowing the woman. And Mrs Renata giving the welfare officer glistening eyes of hatred whilst Bennett's tongue went tch-tch-tch. She lit a smoke. She sucked hard on it. Several times. Her fat chest went up and down with drawing in angry breath. Then her face was half hidden in a cloud of smoke. Then Grace heard her say to Bennett, And don't you be stickin your nose in my affairs. Bennett saying nothing, just telling Boogie as he came past back to the courtroom, I'll be calling you next.

Grace's mind going over and over with, The Lost Tribe . . .

25

3
They Who Have History

Oh far out! Grace at all the wood everywhere, the quiet, the paintings on the wall. The whole atmosphere of the place. Like a church.

Sitting down where Bennett indicated. Oh wow, at the ceiling with its fancy plasterwork, scrolls and things. Oh, but you wouldn't think it exists just through those big doors. And them on the other side, what a girl has grown up with, she knows them (though does not understand nor empathise with them) and here, a kind of palace, a church, a place to respect and fear all in one on the other side. Who'd believe such a place exists here in little ole Two Lakes? Grace thinking this must be how the Trambert big house looks; or sort of.

Oo, so *quiet*: the court officials talking in whispers. Maybe they don't want us to know. Maybe it's like a secret club where the members jealously guard their secrets and special codes and exclusive membership.

Grace looking at Boogie to see his reaction, and not surprised to see him with hands wringing, eyes to the floor. Oh poor Boog, can't blame him. Mr Bennett said he might get sent away to a Boys' Home. I'll come and visit you as much as I can, Boog, Grace promising herself. I'll get a job in the supermarket in town after school, they hire Maoris there even if you're from Pine Block, probably because most of Pine Block does their main shopping there. There and the pub.

Those pictures: great big things in fancy frames and every one ofem a grey-haired white man. Hah, imagine a Maori in one ofem. Some chance. Only Maoris in here get to sit where we are, I bet. Unless they got a high-up job like Mr Bennett here. But how many Maoris like him around?

Grace staring at each portrait in turn, counting them. Each man with headmaster-type gown up around his shoulders, and each with the same headmaster-type solemn look. Smile and their faces'd crack, as Mum says about me. Nine of them. Nine portraits of men who must've done something good to be up on the wall here. Might be some ofem are dead. In Pine Block you die, you die. Grace'd known many a person, usually young, in their teens, early adulthood, one minute alive next dead. And the kids in the street talking about it, describing the gory detail of the accident or murder or manslaughter that killed the person. One day a living, breathing entity, next, a nothing. A lifeless shell and no fancy portraits hung up of them.

Man, what a place. Reminds me of the Queen, Grace registering the familiarity of the coat of arms above the magistrate's bench. The Queen and her loyal, faithful servants, that's it. So where do we fit in this picture? Me and more especially my poor brother here? Then startled by a voice booming out: ALL RISE!

And in he swept.

Silver hair. Suit. Bet he's gonna appear on the wall one day. Where's his robes then? Maybe his missus forgot to iron them (hahaha!) Grace couldn't help herself, it was nervous inner laughter more than anything. She got like that when she was nervous, scared. Giggly, too. Oh please don't let me break out in the giggles.

Five of them, the court officials. Three women, two men. In nice outfits and suits. One of the women good-looking (oh *real* good-looking.) It's not fair. Bitch knows it too. Grace studying their faces, clues niggling away at her, instincting something about them — prefects. That's it. They look just like school prefects: prim and proper and better than you; they'd pimp on you soon as look at you. Specially you, Maori kid. Yes, and distant like school prefects, of knowing them when they were ordinary like you, and day after their appointment you were looking at a stranger.

Then magistrate (God) spoke from his on high position of slightly higher elevation.

Made Grace's heart jump. An inner panic that for some extraordinary reason he was speaking to her. (Oh I'd just *die* if he spoke to *me*.) The parents, Mr Bennett? I don't see any sign . . . and Mr Bennett getting to his feet, Uh, no, your honour. They haven't appeared at this stage. At this stage, Mr Bennett? You mean this is going to be in several stages? Uh, no, sir. I meant — Simply, Mr Bennett, they are not here. No, obviously not, sir. And are they likely to be here? Bennett glancing left of him and Boogie waiting with a shrug, Grace managing to squeak that she didn't think so. *Hoping* he wouldn't ask why. No, your honour. I'm afraid Mark

27

Heke's parents won't be here in all probability. Magistrate sighing at that, shuffling through papers, the rest of the wood-panelled portraited room silent.

Now, let me run through this with you, Mark (Boog's real name) Heke, the history leading to your appearance here in this court . . .

And all through it Boogie not lifting his head once, and Grace willing her brother to do so, just once, don't let this man make you feel worse than you already do.

Grace inspired, angry enough to push her normal shyness aside, looked at the man ranting waffling on about her brother as if he was some kind of — kind of — She didn't know, but it sure didn't feel nice even being the sister of the subject under scrutiny.

She built up a picture of the magistrate, his background, how he must come from a nice home, he'd never seen his father beat up his mother for not cooking one of his friends fried eggs with boiled meat and potatoes.

He'd never been woken from sleep or been unable to sleep for the din of brawling going on beneath you. He'd not experienced any of what the people before him like Boogie have had to endure. Yet here he is telling poor Boogie what a bad boy he is.

Telling Boogie, We *all* didn't like school as youngsters, young man, but most of us went because we had to.

Oh it's not fair. Boogie plays the wag from school because half the time he's scared of being picked on, or he's being led by other kids and he's too afraid to say no. He doesn't go to school because he can't see what good school is going to do him anyway. Lots of us don't.

Alright for him up there, I bet he went to some posh school and oh of course university; and just like the Pakeha kids in my class, I bet he got read to when he was young, encouraged with his homework, even taken to special tutoring if he had difficulties with some of the subjects. They do that for their kids, do the Pakehas. Not the rough Pakehas, but then most Pakehas aren't from rough families. And they do a lot more besides.

Like taking their kids to different places, different things to do. And they *don't* spend half their life in the pub drinking like our fathers and lots of the mothers do. Man, if I had a head start like they do I could be a magistrate too. Well, maybe not that, but something high up.

Silence. Magistrate had imposed his desire for silence on all. Only his breathing, the odd rustle of clothing, someone shifting position. A cough. A sigh. And Boogie won't stop scuffing his feet! A long sigh from the bench, then: Mark Heke, I have no choice but to declare you a ward of the state. The state? Grace thinking. Like in a state house? Where you shall be under the control of the child welfare authorities . . . Grace not able to figure it, what it meant in terms of Boogie's future and yet knowing it *was* his future that'd just been decided by a stranger.

A complete stranger, who Boog'd never set eyes on before in his life, and he was making Boog a ward of the state handing him over to the welfare — Oh poor Boogie, Grace letting out a tiny groan before catching it at mention of a Boys' Home, where, the magistrate was promising or assuring or threatening, Mark Heke would find discipline and — through discipline — direction.

Grace's mind reeling, and what'd Boog's mind be doing? Looking at him, oh you poor kid, even though she was younger she felt older, and his eyes fixed to the floor, head shaking, hands clutched tightly together. She saying, I'll come and visit you as much as I can, Boog.

Wanting to put an arm around him but afraid to, not in here, the magistrate might say something, he was sure not to like gestures like that: love for your brother. Not showing it. Not here in this precious damn room with all his mates up around the walls supporting him, giving him not only the law on his side but them, the ones up on the walls in their big fancy frames, the education they must've had, the head starts. History. (He's got history, Grace and Boogie Heke, and you ain't.)

Then the magistrate was wishing Mark luck — *luck*. Asking for the next case. Just like that.

4

. . . And Those with Another

Through the big doors, out into the other world waiting their turns to be judged; you could smell the feet, the socks that hadn't been washed, and armpits, and that smell of fat people in a tight confine or airless space.

Grace could smell the violence too, she could almost see it, it was like shimmers from a sunbeaten road.

Bennett holding Boogie firmly by the arm, steering him in the direction of the main cluster. Everyone looking. (Oh God. No way to hide.) Grace fast on the heels of the big welfare officer, but seeing the looks poor Boogie was getting and no doubt because he was crying.

Someone, it turned out to be one of the Brown Fist prospects, asking, Whassa madda, bubs? The beak hit you with his powder puff? Laughter.

Then another, this one a woman: Oh, we got our little sister to hold our hand have we? Though that woman was immediately told to shut her mouth by another female adult voice.

Come on, come on, out of the way, Bennett going to some ofem. Cigarette smoke and armpits and obesity and the shimmers of violence and the echoes of taunting laughter, and the *looks* they were giving a girl after they'd finished with her sobbing brother. Except for that lone supporter catching Grace's eye and telling her, Don't you mind these buggers, girl. Good on you for sticking with your brother. Grace too shy to smile her appreciation, just wanting out of here.

The walk taking *ages*.

Bennett stopping at a door and fiddling with a key, taking an eternity, and comments being made from a girl's teenage fellows from mostly Pine Block, smartarse, mocking. A voice behind calling out: TURANGA! William James. And a collective ooooo! going up, watch he don't hit you with his powder puff, Billy. Grace hearing quite distinctly — because it was a very common utterance of her father's: Fuckim (Fuckim, fuckim, fuckim, echoing on and on in her head like that Lost Tribe had) as Bennett finally got the door unlocked.

Sweat broken out all over Grace's face; sticky, clammy, feeling smelly herself. Bennett's voice from seemingly far away telling Grace she had ten minutes with her brother then, he was sorry, she'd have to go. The door closing, cutting short the last of the teasing, and laughter, and powd — of powder puff.

Oh so much quieter in here. The world changed again. But not Boogie, he hadn't changed, sobbing away there.

Poor Boog. Poor, soft, failed Mark Heke. A sister wondering who'd done this to him, this giving a kid a flaw in his makeup and borning him in Pine Block. A wimp thrown into a den of warriors. And she put her arms around him. But she could not cry.

5

Tennessee Waltz

Beth woke — and stayed awake, not losing the struggle this time of sleep pulling her back into its merciful embrace. Oh, but I don't want to be awake. Wanna die. Closed her eyes, felt immediate pain in one of them. And her heart ached just as bad.

She lay there, staring at the ceiling, gathering her thoughts, the events of this early morning rapidly reshaping. But she tried not to let self-pity creep in — Fuckit. I'm made of stronger stuff than that. She moved her hip ever so slightly, felt his presence beside her; never ceased to be amazed how they slept in the same bed even after he'd beaten her. She touched her face — gingerly. Ooo, that bastard. One day I'll kill you. It hurt all over.

She got quietly out of bed, went to the bathroom.

Oo, look at me — *look* at me, at her reflection in the medicine cupboard mirror with the silver starting to break up behind the glass and mould formed in the lower two corners. And this face — if you could call it a face — framed there, beaten to a barely recognisable pulp. And him, the doer of this to me, laying back there in bed — *my* bed — as if nothing happened. I'll *killim*. I'll kill the black bastard.

The right eye puffed shut, nose broken — again — lower lip swollen with a deep cut about midway and leaking blood. Bruises all over. Beth sighed, shook her head in a kind of astonishment. You mad mad crazy bastard, Jake Heke.

The house was quiet. Kids must've gone to school. Wonder what ti — Oh God. Boogie. He's in court today. Ten o'clock. She hurried downstairs, to the kitchen where the clock was — so clean, oh, you good good kids. Clock. Where the hell is it? On the windowsill above the sink — *What?* Five to *one?* In the afternoon! Oh poor Boogie, I should've been there. Rushing back up to the bathroom, the mirror . . . Look at me, son. Look at the state of me: I couldn't've come looking like this. I couldn't've. The guilt, or something, bringing tears to her eyes — and oh, *stinging* the bad one. Grinding her teeth together in frustration and rage. Standing there for several minutes willing herself not to lose control.

She found herself in the younger ones' bedroom; again, tidy. I trained em well, no one can take that away from me. Over to Huata's bunk, her youngest; could remember like last week him suckling on her, that special feel of feeding your own with your own body, its produce. The love imparting through it. The tears sprang anew, she wiped at them forgetting the damn eye, jerking her hand away in pain. *You black cunt!* I hate his guts. She ruffled Hu's pillow. Felt the emotion rushing up again. The hell's up with you, woman? You've had hidings before. So what's new?

Above to Polly's bed, and Sweetie tucked in under the pillow. Kid'd had that doll since her first birthday, little thing with its shiny blonde hair. You'd think you could buy Maori dolls too.

Oo, Beth got a sudden new perspective of Polly's doll, it looks like a damn corpse with its eyelids closed and blonde locks spread out beneath her. Beth touched the face, There there, Sweetie, I didn't mean you were dead, only you look like it. She touched her own face to reassure herself that she couldn't possibly have appeared in court in this mess. I couldn't, Boog.

Over to Boogie's top bunk above Grace's, for some reason being reminded of Grace's request for her own room and Beth asking her daughter where the extra was going to come from, as it was a three-bedroom house and was gonna stay that way like it or not, Grace telling Beth that she could apply to the Housing Corporation for a bigger house, she knew other kids' parents had done that, and Beth telling Grace she'd think about it.

But nothing done. Nothing done, story of my life: too much the thinking not enough the doing. Right, soon as my face is healed up I'm applying for a four-bedroom. (Can't blame the girl, she's nearly a woman now even though she's only twelve, close to thirteen.) Startling, and cocking her ear when she thought she heard a noise, hoping it wasn't him getting up. Not ready to face him. Need time. To gather my strength so I can tell him where to go — oh *why*'d I fall for the man? Stepping over to the window, taking in the same old sight of the Trambert farm, calming herself inside. Then, better, she moved out to the next-door bedroom, Nig's and Abe's.

Stood in the doorway looking at the walls covered in posters of boxers and karate men, and Abe with a few pop stars amongst his similar fighting posters. And this thought welling up in her

33

mind of: My Nig. I just love him so much. My first-born, and I
wanted a son for my first and so did Jake. Remembering how they
used to make such a fuss of him, spoiling him rotten, sitting up
together with him whenever he was ill. Ah, those were the times
when your father and I were close, and when I never even thought
that he wouldn't want to share my dream of, you know, our own
house, not a state rental, and family togetherness. My Nig.
Managing a little twitch of a smile despite the pain.

Stepping inside, noticing that all the boxers were Negro. Fancy
that, never noticed that before. Now they're what you call real
niggers. Not like a Maori nigger. They're often called that, some
Maoris, it's a common nickname and given out of affection not
contempt.

One of the black boxers took her eye. Yuk. Bald. And his pate
shiny with sweat, or something shiny, and muscles rippling all
over. Reminds me of him, Jake. Oh fuckim. I hateim. But still
looking at the Negro boxer and comparing to her husband, the
build, the meanness of face, the eyes . . . the eyes, searching for
something she could see but not put her finger on; as if the fighter's
eyes were giving away something of the exact same look in her
husband's eyes, almost a hurt. Yes, a wounded hurt. As if he's
saying, I'm gonna punish you, not because I'm bad but because
you hurt me. Then the thought went away as Beth remembered
immediately her beating and what she'd done to deserve it. You
made a fool of me in front of all my mates! he'd yelled at her
before he started on her with his fists.

A headache came on. Must be getting my mate. Hah, some
mate, dunno why we call our period a mate. Not as if it's something to look forward to. Jake, he hates it; only have to tell him
I'm close to getting it and he won't touch me. Good way of
keeping him off when a woman don't want him, like when I came
to bed and him saying sorry and wanting to make up, and his way
of making up is sticking himself inside me — thrusting at me, like
I'm some damn dog bitch down the street. Think he gets a buzz,
a you know, a kick from doing it so soon after he's beat a woman
up. Still, a woman'd had her moments of that being the very thing
she wanted: to fuck. For relief, I spose.

A smoke. Need a smoke. Off downstairs, careful-careful on the
threadbare carpet not as if you walking on six-inch-thick shagpile
over at the Tramberts', lady. Magine her, Mrs Trambert, tiptoeing around her own house afraid of waking her husband in case
he felt like starting on her again. Or woke wanting to fuck her —

not make love. Fuck. Jesus. Then realising she was in her nightie, but that's alright, I'm a clever girl, I got spare changes of clothing everywhere.

And she went to the linen cupboard where the hot-water cylinder also was and she pulled out from under it a plastic bag containing a dress, a change of underpants, and casual shoes. Out in the backyard shed (unused, naturally) Beth had another change of clothing, and underneath the house yet another. Bastard'll never throw me out on the street naked again with a woman's privacy exposed for the whole — waiting — world to see.

Changed. Just like that. Pleased with herself, her forethought. The kitchen. Fridge. Oo, my face hurts. Hope there's some beer left, and licking her lips with immediate regret. The pain. Bastard. Lifting — one good and one swollen shut — eyes to the ceiling. I hate your guts. Peering into the noisy old refrigerator for the familiar headrise of quart beer bottle. Ah, yes. Counting them: one, two, three, oh good, four ofem. Four of the lovely sweet things.

Over at the table, pouring the first glass and the sun streaming through the windows behind her so warm. Ah. So very nice and warm. Oh, now look at that. Smiling — and to hell with the pain — at the sight of foamy white head atop her beer. Smokes. Must have a smoke to go with it, not the same having a beer without a smoke. Horse and carriage, love and marriage, smoke and beer. (Beer and fists. Beer and personality change. Beer and . . .) she went over in her mind as she went out to the wash-house to fetch a packet of cigarettes from her hiding place in the cardboard box where the potatoes were kept. Cunning, cunning, clever clever, Beth. (Beer and happiness — ?? happiness? For me it is. Beer and culture. Culture? Beer and Maori culture. It's our lifeblood. We live for our beer. My parents did, and as for Jake's, the stories he's told me about how they drank. Any wonder he's half mad.)

Back to the table, having the first mouthful, just a taste. Lighting a cigarette. Ahhh. Nother taste. Just a sip. Tease myself. A deep pull at her fag. The hit at the back of her throat. Another swig, but this time a decent one. Ah, now that is *nice*.

Sun warm — *warm* — on her knees. Pulling her dress up — Oh, that is so good. The sun's heat like an intimate caress, reminding her. Up your black arse, mista, thrusting two fingers at the ceiling, pushing aside a wisp of hair fallen over her forehead. I used to be beautiful. Well, maybe not beautiful, but everyone used to tell me I was spunky. Or I'd hearem: See Beth over there,

35

she's a spunk. That's what the boys used to say. Made a girl come over all funny, except she didn't know what it was that felt funny, but now knew it as sex. Sex-u-ality, Beth. Get it right. Hahaha, gotta laugh, eh. And the first quart bottle going just like that.

Nother one, madam? Aloud to herself with a giggle restricting itself to her throat so as not to aggravate the cut lip. Don't mind if I do, thank you. Getting another bottle. Looking at the beads of condensation running slowly down its brown glass sides, and the sun rays, how they let you see right through the liquid, see the label in reverse. But her face pounding with a gradual rise in pain, a regular thumping, throbbing ache. Must be the first effects of the beer. Have another glass. Mmm-uh. Thank you. Downing it greedily, like medicine. Or love. Or maybe they're both. She wondered about that thought. And up your arse, Jake Heke, she every now and then gave the two-finger insult to the ceiling.

Boogie, pictures of him, of his face and the look of having been let down by her dancing into her mind and being shoved away as soon as they appeared. (I couldn't *help* it.) The third bottle. Easy, easy, Beth, not as if you got your own brewery. But knowing she could borrow from next door, nor having to worry about no one being home because someone was always home next door. If one went out, the other made sure he/she'd stay. You'd think they had a treasure in there to look after stead of a usual Pine Blocker's miserable possessions. To hell withem. Though Beth needed them. And they both knew it.

Music. I need some music. That'll keep my thoughts off Boogie, my blues, him still asleep up there because that's what happens to half these Pine Blockers when they're out of work, they sleep. And when they wake up they drink. And money doesn't come into it because they *find* it, or they have it from keeping back a good part of their benefit meant to feed a whole family on. It's beer first with a Pine Blocker. He'd run a mile for a sniff of the stuff. Beth's swigs getting healthier as the throbbing pain subsided. Beer.

Music. Sitting room. Look at it. Oh you good kids. Must buy you all something next payday. Or soon as I get a good win on the cards. Though it'd been some weeks since Beth'd won at poker. Boogie. No! She touched her face for reassurance that she *could not* have appeared on his behalf today. Knowing that Grace'd got the morning off from school to go give her brother some support because he was like that, he needed it, and so was she, Grace, she had it to give. Good kid, even if a woman had no idea where her

36

daughter was at, coming from; such a mysterious, quiet thing that she was. Good kid, though. Specially with her brothers and sister. She'll make a good mother one day. She's a good one now: whenever a woman's too drunk or too beat up to do the household chores, Grace'll step in. Good old young in years Grace.

Beth sorted through the variously owned and collected records; single and long-players, spanning several decades, from the forties, inherited from her parents' generations and retained because those times they had melody, and harmony, and romance in the songs, the fifties and sixties, and not this modern stuff the kids liked, soul and reggae and rap. Not that a woman didn't hear the music in the new, just that it lacked romance and sentimentality for her. We're a musical people, us Maoris. Comes natural to most of us; plays a bigger part in our lives, I think. Though Beth couldn't be entirely sure on that, since she hardly knew a European, not to talk to go to their house see how they lived.

They're like strangers — they are strangers, to most Maori I know. May as well be from another country the contact the two races have. Oh but I can't blame em half the time when you see all the crime, or too damn much of it, is committed by us. Hell, I dunno, must be something in the Maori make-up makes us wilder, more inclined to breaking the law. Yet we're a good people. Basically, we're good. We share things. We'd give our shirt off our back to another. (Till you'd lived in Pine Block a while, that is, and then you'd grow hard along the way, most of you.) And we have this . . . Beth thinking hard, trying to match up instinctive understanding with a suitable word — passion. We got passion, us Maoris. Or maybe it's style. But not like that Negro style you see on the TV of being swank, hip, cool, moving with their black rhythmic groovin, not that kind, but a cross between that and the less showy whites. Oh, and humour, we got humour. Chuckling to herself. But things, we ain't got *things*. Meaning possessions. Material possessions. And who needs em? No Maori I ever knew ever lusted after having *things*. It's here — Beth patted her heart area — it's here where we want for ourselves. Patted her belly, And here. Laughing. Food. We love our food. Even when we know it's bad for us, killing us early even. We say what the hell, it don't matter, it was sweet while it lasted. What they call it? Laid back, that's the term. We're a laid-back race. Cept when we're drunk. Then we lay out. Other people that is. Lay em out as soon as look atem. Half our trouble: beer and fists and having passion. They don't mix.

37

Aee, my Maori people, for you this woman sometimes despairs. But have another drink in the meantime, Beth.

Oh, and we're shy. Musical, good dancers, natural born entertainers, yet we're shy. Like him up there, Jake the arsehole: can sing the pants off anyone — when he's drunk. Sober, he won't sing a note. Drunk, and every Maori's a star. Go to any party you can see em with heads back, eyes closed, singing to their hearts' content. And so *good*. But when the party's over, so are they. Such a shame.

Dancing. Jake when he dances it's like he's got air under his feet. Such a tall man too. He flows — *flowwwwws*. And when he twirls you he does it so gently and with perfect timing and his white teeth flashing on his dark handsome face, and . . . Beth remembering better days. (Of when he'd pull me close to him and I could feel his manly strength, the muscles, the security it gave me. And soon that other feeling'd come on . . . of wanting him . . . of wanting him inside me — Oh, but I could never tell him that. Never.)

The fourth bottle going down fast. And no music yet because she was afraid of waking him. So back up to the kitchen to check the time and glad to see school'd soon be out. She could send one of the kids next door to borrow more beer, or pay for it if they went that way, which they occasionally did just when they knew a woman needed em most the bastards, that bitch.

Number four finished. I'll smoke while I'm waiting. Good time-filler, smoking. Good full stop. Don't wake up, Jake Heke, not yet, not yet . . . The pain not so bad now. Feeling a little sleepy, or like sleeping. They're different. Lighting another smoke. Ahh . . .

Kids home. Ooh, Mum, look at your face, it's — Yeah, yeah, I know what it looks like. Think I can't look in a mirror? So how was school? And where's Grace? Her two youngers' horror at her facial injuries not lasting long, as she knew it wouldn't. They were very experienced kids, and hungry kids. What's to eat? Fresh air, you can't even give your mother a hug. Hugging em. Oh, it's such a good feeling this love. And telling em: Love, it's the only thing counts on this earth. A tear in her good eye. Yeow, Mum, love and food. So what's to eat? I'm starving.

Feeding em something, shooing em off, go play, be happy, grow strong, know love. Yeah, yeah, Mum: love.

No Grace. No Boogie. Means the worst. Shit.

Abe home: Abe, go next door and ask to borrow some beer.

38

Four bottles. DB if they got it. I'll pay em now if they get shirty about it. Abe going next door, not asking about her injuries, returning with the four bottles, Where'll I put em, Mum? His attitude changed: Pine Block surliness growing on him. Like moss. Like that green slime on the Barton woman's old washing-machine wringers. Or a disease. He's caught the Pine Block teenage boy disease: he's starting to scowl at the world, just look at his lips the way they're shaping. (Can't you give a mother some medicine, doctor, for her ailing children?)

They cold? Nope. Warm as. Not like you, eh son? Huh? Warm as. Huh? You're not warm as. So? So? Beth went in imitation of her sullen son. So? she repeated to make her half-drunk point. G'won, get yourself something to eat and go do whatever it is you young fullas do that you never used to dream of doing when you were young (and hope was still with you). Kids. What's the use?

Sticking the bottles in the freezer section of the fridge. The sounds of Jake finally risen. Oh, we're up, are we? The night-shift drinking starting soon, eh? Giving him the fingers. Up your black arse, mista. More out of bravado than anything, and tensed for him to come downstairs and start on her again. Gritting her teeth in anticipation. Fuckim. I ain't backin down. Wishing the beer would hurry up and get cold. Can't stand warm beer.

Grace. How'd — Oh, what's the use in asking? I can tell by her face. They send him away, Grace? And Grace standing there and Beth thinking her daughter had no feeling for her, then suddenly Grace bursting into tears. *It's not fair!* And a mother finding herself holding her daughter, and being held in turn, and though sad and upset for Boogie, Beth aware that she and Grace had not done this kind of thing often. Not holding each other. So feeling uncomfortable. As though in the arms of a stranger. A stranger. It's always strangers. We humans are all strangers to each other; not just them over the fence and over dale yonder in the big house, but even a mother to her own children. Look at Abe: I may as well've been his teacher, his worst most hated teacher at school. And there's my Nig, who's itching to get into the Brown Fists. And now it's Boogie, my own son taken from me and likely to have become a stranger to me on the spot because I didn't appear as a good mother should and say good things about him so he might have a chance, and then there's this girl in my arms who I don't even know. Thirteen years and I don't know her from Eve.

We'll visit him. Alright, Grace? I'll save up and we'll go visit him. In a rental. How about that, Grace? Oh Mum, but you *can't*

39

save up. We never save anything. No one in this place does. Grace crying. And for more reason than just Boogie, Beth realising. But what could a woman do?

Look at me, Grace. Look at me. Stepping back from Grace to show her her face. Oh Mum, why can't we leave here? We will, Beth patting her girl's back. We will one day, I promise. Just like a scene from a TV movie. Now off you go, honey. Here, go buy you and the kids a treat, giving Grace a ten-dollar note, but Grace refusing. Save it, Mummy. Save it what for? Beth quite forgetting the promise of only a minute ago, just something she'd said. For the rental to go visit Boogie. Oh, that. Well, you take it anyway. No. Save it. Grace leaving. Save it, save it, save it . . . She's right you know. I should save it. I should make this my very first ten towards that trip. So hiding the money in her empty plastic bag in the linen cupboard. The beer'd be cold by now.

Back in the sitting room, stepping into the room — Well, would you look at that. At her radiogram bathed in gold from a beam of sunlight centred on nothing else but the radiogram. Music. It's telling me to play some music and to hell with him upstairs. Putting on an old Sam Cooke: I'm in a Sad Mood Tonight.

A smoke. A coldish beer. And music. Wanting no more, for the moment, than that.

Jake poking his head in, a ready scowl on his dial. (I know you, mista.) Beth ready for him with a defiant look of her own. Him appraising her through those wild brown eyes, that flashing look in em. Coming into the room a few steps. You wan' somemore, woman? Drawled out. (Fuckim) Go ahead, mista. If it makes you feel good, go ahead. Standing up from her seated position on the floor — a little shaky on the ole legs. (Ooops. Must be drunker than I thought.) But I ain't backin down to him. Offering her jaw to the several paces distant Jake. Here, if you can find a spot untouched. He narrowing those eyes, and she knowing he was trying to work himself into that hurt state, where he felt anything he did was justified. But reasonably confident in herself that he'd see the damage done already was enough.

She was right. He marched out. Slammed the door when he left. The front one. I know it was the front because I heard the sound of breaking glass. And she checked: sure enough, the bottom pane of glass was in pieces from the force of Jake slamming the door. Breaking glass. Seemed like she'd heard that most of her life.

Drowning herself in the sweet release of beer, colder and colder beer.

What time is it? Must be getting on, it's dark outside. Dark? So what's new? It's dark outside this house even when it's daylight. Beth close to the stumbling stage. Yet her mind lucid. Or feeling it was. Certainly something of clarity'd been released or triggered by the intake of beer. Yeah, even when the sun's shining it's still dark in Pine Block. *Oh, have another beer, Beth Heke who used to be a Ransfield!* shouting to the ceiling, which she was seeing in her mind as the sky and then it wasn't the sky, it was really a theatre, a huge theatre of people who were watching and listening to her. They're my audience. I tellem what's wrong with this world, with *my* world, with the MAORI world — Yep, the MAORI world, in big capital letters like that. I tellem like that because it's a big problem being a Maori in this world. We used to be a race of warriors, O audience out there. You know that? And our men used to have full tattoos all over their ferocious faces, and it was *chiselled* in and they were not to utter a sound. Not one sound. The women, too, they had tats on their chins and their lips were black with tattooing. But I think they let us cry out when it was being done; I spose they thought us women are weak anyway, though we aren't.

Now where was I and what was I saying? Oh who cares? *Who gives a fuck?*

And we used to war all the time, us Maoris. Against each other. True. It's true, honest to God, audience. Hated each other. Tribe against tribe. Savages. We were savages. But warriors, eh. It's very important to remember that. Warriors. Because, you see, it was what we lost when you, the white audience out there, defeated us. Conquered us. Took our land, our *mana*, left us with nothing. But the warriors thing got handed down, see. Well, sort of handed down; in a mixed-up sense it did. It was more toughness that got handed down from generation to generation. Toughness, eh. Us Maoris might be every bad thing in this world but you can't take away from us our toughness. But this toughness, Pakeha audience of mine, it started to mean less and less as the world got older, learned more, and new technology all this fandangled computer stuff, oh, but even before computers, it all made toughness redundant. Now thassa good word for a Maori, eh, redundant?

But we — or our men, anyway — are clinging onto this toughness thing, like it's all we got, while the rest of the world's leaving us behind. It's not toughness we need anymore, it's — it's — Shaking her head. So what is it we need, O solver of the world's problems? Beer! hahaha! laughing. Rocking back and forth with it. And downing another glass in one long, sweet and increasingly mindless pull.

Aee, Beth, nemine the crying for your own race. I were you I'd be crying for you, girl. Just you.

All these message-like wordings appearing in Beth's brain, her half-enlightened, half-befuddled mind. And the comings and noisy goings of her children — what remained of them, with Boogie gone (and no official notification a mother her child, not yet anyway), and Nig, he was mostly not at home, spent all his time hanging out with other Brown Fist prospects, fighting, building up his reputation, his credentials for entry to that terrible gang. Hearing the street coming to life: cars revving, or gunning past, exhausts backfiring, exhausts roaring, exhausts rumbling; and she'd imagined the lights blinking on all over Pine Block, so to light up the sordid activities she knew so well. Drinking drinking, but Lord what it did to the people when it was finished withem; she even picked up, between records, the rattling clink of bottles being toted in wooden crates — I know it so well that sound — and laughter, Maori laughter: explosive, spontaneous, it made you want to laugh without having to know the joke, it's like a mirror, an emotional mirror of yourself.

Grace feeding the kids in the kitchen, such a *good* kid, Grace; Grace talking in her quiet way to them; even when she growled at the younger ones it wasn't like growling, more like mild scolding, oh but that's a word you'd never hear in Pine Block: scold. What's that other tame word you hear the Pakehas use on the TV? Cross. That's it: *cross*. Cross. If you do that again I'll be *cross* with you, child. Hahaha.

She saw his — *his* — HIS — lights flick on across the way there, most of it obscured by trees; tried to imagine what he and they might be doing this Friday autumn evening. Bet it was nice, whatever the Tramberts were doing.

Drinking. Sending Grace next door (with the secreted ten dollars) to buy the next lot of beer. Heedless then. To near everything but the emotions. And music. Love my music.

I was dancing — (oh yes) — *with my darling* — (mmmm) — *to the Tennessee Waltz!* Beth adding her voice to that of Patti Page, the song echoey in the sparsely furnished room, sliding — *sliiiiding* her bare feet over the varnished floorboards, *I remember the night*, arms out holding her imaginary partner, who happened to have a face like Jake's. Setting her mouth possessively at the part about the woman's darling being taken from her by another, Beth thinking no bitch'd take her man without a fight. Feeling proud, vain about her possessiveness. And loving the deep rich voice of Patti, because Patti's distinctive, deeper than normal tone somehow made a woman's possessiveness stronger, more real. Such a lovely melody too. Not like this modern stuff, it goes bang-bangbang, thumpthumpthump all the time. It should float, it should be like the sea, it should make a person feel romantic. Twirling — oops, nearly tripping over herself.

And outside a pair of eyes staring at the apparitions of her mother going back and forth across the line of sitting-room windows; hurting for her, hating her for succumbing even her terrible miseries to the booze — it's always the booze in this place — and the strains of a singer with an unusually deep (and sort of hauntingly lovely) voice about losing her darling at a Tennessee Waltz. Oh Mum. Mum, Mum, Mum, at that apparition flitting across the screen of windows lost to herself (yet she's not bad at dancing if it wasn't for the tripping). The girl giggling, but that was the only time because Grace Heke she was a more serious girl than most, she couldn't help it, we're all born different.

This grotesque face with its wounds fresh and swollen sliding — *sliiiding* — across a girl's vision like out of a dream sequence on that backdrop of yellow/white squares illuminating a woman, a mother, a beaten wife, a member of a troubled race, her condition for this side of the world to see.

The arms outstretched holding this imaginary partner; it must be Dad because she's holding him at about his tall level where he'd be. Shit, why does she love him? Yet Grace wondering why she herself felt this aching in her heart whenever she thought about her father, which aching felt like love. And such a lovely night of stars above.

Love. Tennessee Waltz and love being taken. A girl hurt at that, thinking that love should belong to the first to claim it, assuming it is reciprocal. Oh, I'm just a girl, what would I know?

And that figure flitting back and forth over another Pine Block sitting-room screen.

43

6

Jake and the Broken of Hearts and Spirits

Jake Heke looked like he was chewing on gum the way his jaw muscles were always twitching. But Jake was no gum chewer, just that his teeth ground. It was worse when Jake was asleep; his wife Beth'd have to tell him, Hey, roll over. Like sleeping beside an all-night rubbish chomper. Though she had to be careful waking him like that, he might be having one of his bad dreams. And she'd cop one then.

Jake knew he was a grinder, but so what, wasn't any big deal. Didn't bother him as, say, a sure giveaway of his inner turmoil. Didn't give a fuck. He ground his teeth, that's all. Just as he woke from any length of sleep, head running strong with violent dream. How a man is. So he'd always ask Beth, Whassa big fuckin deal about teeth and dreams?

Just as he woke, almost invariably, with a desire to punch someone, which grew quickly to vivid imaginings of wrongs done him, slights, looks, and so he feeling hurt and then — naturally enough, as he saw it — wanting to right things by the only way he knew how: with his fists.

Man, I juss wake up wanting to *punch* somefuckin one.

Jake's world was physical; and he was aware it was physical. He assumed damn near the whole world was seeing it the same. It was there when he woke each day (or night) in the canvas of his mind as physical. He saw people all over — but mostly men — and they were engaged in physical combat, the subjects of combative consideration, their fighting potential, how fast they'd likely be, how good a hit they carried and was it in both hands or just a normal one, right or left (in that order too) could the dude be from this more modern style of scrapping of using the headbutt, the knee, or just anything that came to hand. His mind covered the field of physical confrontation. He saw others in terms of their fighting potential first, before he saw anything. Even on the TV,

44

when he watched the damn thing, he always looked at some dude and wondered if the dude could fight or not. Specially these smooth ones with fuckin hair that didn't have one hair out of place; they made his teeth rasp together, he wanted to hop inside the TV and smash the cunt's pretty-boy face to a pulp. And so strong was this hatred, he assumed — never even gave it a thought — it to be perfectly justified. And equally, the odd times he got to smash some pretty-boy's face in his real world (for simply having what Jake deemed to be pretty-boy looks) it never occurred to Jake that there might be something wrong with his outlook, perhaps his mind. It couldn't: damn near every man he mixed (drank) with thought the same. He was sure they did. Besides, wasn't as if a man was *only* about fighting — course he weren't. He thought about other things. You know, sport — he liked sport, especially rugby league. And rugby (except there weren't as many fights in rugby union and they mostly tackled cleanly, whereas league they tried to put the big hits on the other fulla, they had a whole list of foul methods like stiff-arms, coat-hangers, elbow in the throat, eye-gouge, ball-scrag — man, anyone scragged *my* balls in a game I'd rip his right out — you name it.) and he just *loved* the boxing, the bigtime stuff they showed on the TV, Sugar Ray Leonard — oh man! — guys like him and the greatest, Ali, when he was around (man, that cat moved sweeter and quicker than even me); a man'd be inspired for weeks after watching one of them black master boxers fighting: he'd practise in his bedroom (preferably when Beth wasn't around, because she teased a man, made him feel real stink for his love of scrapping, didn't understand it was an art), he'd throw shots in front of the mirror, a pane of glass, anywhere he could see himself, the beauty therein. And anyway, he thought about other things too . . . other sports . . . ah, even political things — not all this shit about who's teaming up with who, but the main players, they sort of interested a man, though he couldn't name specifics. Oh, and life. Sure, why not? Don't everyone think about life, you know, how it fuckin works, why things happen (specially these unreal things, what they call it? Coincidence. Specially that.) Even love. Why not love? Every man needs love: a woman's love (her twat, more like it), his mates (very important), his kids (in a man's own way, mind. Don't wanna be a fuckin sook about it. Gotta get their respect or they'll walk all over you.) But it was violence that Jake Heke was most tuned to.

Jake'd woken late, damn near five o'clock at night. Man must've been tired from all them late drinking nights (and giving his wife a hiding, hahaha!) and age catching up onim. Be thirty-six in a few months. Though he didn't really feel age had affected him adversely in any way.

Man'd had another funny dream too: dreamt he was on this boat and someone'd thrown this fuckin big octopus at him and the thing'd attached itself to him, spread all over him. Jesus fuckin Chrise, he could still feel its every little sucker sucking onto him, sucking the blood from him. And trying to get it off him: every time he ripped a tentacle from one spot, another'd suck onto a new spot. And the *slime*, man. Man coulda been having a real experience. He'd finally got rid of the monster and then it was time to get the cunts who'd done this to him: he'd punched and broken and torn limbs from their sockets and *pulverised* a face till it was flat (and yet talking in this squeaky voice that was sad — I mean *sad*, brother — and asking why he'd done what he did. So a man having to take this little flat face up in his hands, cradle it like a baby and hear himself singing a sortof, whattheycallit, a lullaby. To a face. It was more like a fuckin pikelet with eyes.) Then he remembered how Beth'd more than deserved her hiding because she'd insulted one of their guests. Though when Jake left and slammed the door after him he hadn't meant to break the damn glass, it just broke. He was only wanting to let Beth know it wasn't *him* in the wrong it was her.

A bus'd pulled alongside him as he headed up his street and Jake'd waved it to fuck off, he wasn't no fuckin bus-catcher. A bus? Man, he'd rather crawl to where he was going on his hands and knees than be seen dead on a bus. Buses? Man, they're for losers and housewives and kids and old people with no bread. Dooly'd give a man a lift to town, the pub. A fuckin bus . . . Maybe Dooly'll wanna join a man at McClutchy's, and if he ain't home I'll try Bub. But I ain't fuckin walkin, no way; not on a Friday night, everyone going to town for late shopping and going past a man saying, Hasn't he got his own car yet? Fuckem. I had the bread I wouldn't be buying no fuckin car anyrate; I'd get something else nice. A stereo. Or one a them big colour TVs with the screens like a fuckin pitcha theatre. Magine watching the big fights on one a them. Don't need no car though. Or maybe a man'd buy her, Beth, a car if he had the bread. Save her catching the bus or getting a fuckin rip-off taxi, having to lug a hundred shopping bags with her and half our tribe. (See, Beth? Man thinks of you when you don't even know it.) Man didn't like his missus being seen walking, catching the fuckin bus, running around in cabs: people'd think her husband didn't, you know, take care of her. Or that he was a broken arse. No job. Not looking for one neither. But why should a man when the guvm'nt was paying him as much to stay at home? Man'd be a fool to himself to go work for the fuckin stuff when all he had to do was walk down the footpath to the letterbox on a Thursday morning and it'd be there. Three hundred and sixty smackaroos. For sittin at home. Fuckem. They stupid enough to pay, a man ain't so stupid not to collect. And I give her half. Clean down the middle. Even stevens. I don't try and cheat her out of her share. She's got the house to run. Bills to pay. Our kids eat like fuckin horses. And my mates like a feed once they had their fill of piss. Me too. Straight down the middle. Not like some ofem, they hardly give their missus's anything, then they still expect to come home to a feed. Cunts're dreaming: ya can't fill a pot on fresh air. As for a man's own half, he can get by; long as he stays away from the fuckin geegees, they're his one big downfall. Can't pick my nose when it comes to the horses. And not as if a man don't study em for long enough, that's all he does half the time is get the racing guides, the papers, and study the geegees, their form, their every little history. Come to think of it, a man ain't no star when it comes to cards neither. Soon as someone ups the ante a man gets scared — nah, not scared, ain't scared a nuthin or no one. But nervous. Spoils his game, even when he's got a good hand. Nah, rumbling's my game; man shoulda been one of them olden-day prizefighters, he woulda made a fortune. A fortune. Hell, but who cares if a man can't gamble, he c'n still walk into McClutchy's at opening with not a brass razoo and come out at closing pissed out of his brain and maybe even a few bucks to go buy him some ribs from the Chinese. That's cos people they respect a man in McClutchy's where he always drinks. What happens when a man can really handle himself: people wanna buy a man a beer. Damn near line up to buy him one sometimes. Shit, been times when a man had his whole table covered in jugs from the people. Covered. And a man knows, they're buying his favours, his promise that he'll leave em alone, or look after em if they get picked. They're buying Jake Heke the man — and so they should. Not as if God or sumpthin handed a man his rep on a plate, said, Here, take it. It's for free. Might be free beers sometimes in this world, but there ain't free scrapping reps, not with Maoris. You got to earn it. And you got

47

young ones coming up all the time wanting to take it. Us Maoris, man, we used to be warriors. And that mighta been a long time ago, but you walk into any public bar in the land where there's Maoris and tell Jake Heke that warriors are a thing of the past. And you only have to look at the league and the rugby teams to see there's still warriors left in our race.

Eh Dooly? Jake to his friend driving him to McClutchy's, They wanna buy us a beer because they're scared of us, who're we to argue, eh brother? Yeow, Jake the Muss. Dooly laughing along with his drinking mate. If that's what turns em on, eh Jake? Lettem. Yeah, lettem.

Cruising slowly down Jake's street, no hurry, no hurry. We got all night. And Dooly telling Jake, I hope they there in good numbers tonight, bro, cause I ain't got any bread. Jake sitting up at that. Wha'? How come, man? You only got your dole yesterday. Frowning at Dooly. Wondering aloud if Dooly'd lost his unemployment, or his share of it, which Jake assumed to be around the half mark, on the horses, maybe a card game. But no, Dooly shaking his head and telling a man he gave it all to his missus this week because they had bills. Up to fuckin here, man. Slicing with his hand at chin level. *All* of it? Jake couldn't believe his ears. Bills, brother. Got to pay the bills. Who says so? The fullas who send the bills, man. Dooly's laugh unsure because he'd picked up Jake's loaded tone in the Fuckem. That's what I say, but the missus she says pay. Jake twisted hard in his seat to Dooly: What, she just comes up to you and says gimmee? She sure does, brother. And you leter? Man, I ain't got no choice. Not 'nless we wanna run around the house with no power on having to cook over — Aw, c'mon, Dool. Come on what, man? You know what. Jake — Dooly slowing right down and looking at his mate — we don't pay the bills we don't fuckin eat. You the one told me that yourself! But Jake shaking his head, No way, Dool. Half. Half what, man? Ta give the bitch half, and she can't run a house on half, kick the bitch out. Aw c'mon, Jake. No fuckin c'mons, man. But I *like* my missus. Jake's eyes flashing briefly wide as the sentence tried to cognite in his mind. Then his face relaxing when he rejected the pronouncement as his friend meaning he liked his missus for what she had on live-in tap for his choice of taking — her sex. So he chuckled and said, Yeah, sure, bro. Sure.

It was Jake told Dool no rush, because he liked to drive (be driven) slowly through his own streets, sort of like a king going over his kingdom making sure people still knew who he was;

suited Dooly Jacobs too, he had a souped-up old Valiant he'd done up himself, liked to catch the looks it and he got from the young fullas around the Pine Block streets. Car might be fifteen years old but it still turned the fuckin heads. Was Dool's pride and joy, he spent half his unemployed life working on it: doing the engine up, cleaning it, inspecting, there was always something to do. Big motherfucka hemi V8 in it, man, just its fuckin growl'd scare most ofem off the road. So they cruised down Jake's street, Rimu Street (and Jake kept his eyes frontwards when they went past his house, thinking, fuck the bitch. She shouldn't've made a fool of a man in front of his mates.)

Turned right down Manuka Street, going slowly slowly, easy easy. With arms out the windows, and Dooly tapping a beat on the roof, and Jake's bent elbow on the outer door with sleeve rolled high to remind any might-bes and likelies what they were up against in terms of sheer muscle. (Just let any punk try and he'll wish he hadn't.) And Jake kept glancing to see if veins were sticking out on his arm. And a face'd go by and Dooly'd raise his fingers from their complicated beat, Hey man! Howzit! Grinning away, then back to his incredible finger beat that Jake was thinking just flowed out of him, a little envious, thinking he'd have himself a practice at home tomorrow see if he could produce something similar.

When Jake greeted it was just a lift of his big left hand, a flick of casual greeting, the hand flopping back on the sill, and Jake mostly seeing only the size of his mit, how it never ceased to amaze him he'd been blessed with such big hands, almost as if God'd known Jake Heke was gonna need big mits. And he liked how the veins bulged up on his mit, the one on the door sill not the one rested deliberately hanging off the edge of the seat so the blood flowed down and swelled those veins.

Not a lot to see out there, just the same old two-storey houses shared by two families, fuckin mirrors of each other, and heaps and heaps of kids of all ages runnin wild and mongrel dogs roaming all over. The car wrecks on the front lawns Jake and Dool'd long stopped seeing, they were just part of the scenery. Cruisin.

Hoi! Jake yelling out the window in jocular but aggressive tone to a group of kids fooling around and not much older than five or six. Haven't ya got mothers? The question just jumping from Jake's mouth without forethought nor afterthought. And grinning all over. And Dooly going, Huh?

49

Out of Pine Block, the vacant land that no one wanted; who wants to live next door to a slum full of mad Maoris having all-night weekend parties? The pair laughing at Dool remarking this, they understood. Can't blame em, eh Dool? Even Jake understood. And Dool responding: Man, I was a Pakeha, *I* wouldn't come within ten fuckin miles of this joint. Laughing again in that unspoken understanding of men with no means of articulation.

And then the rest of the world, the other side of Two Lakes, with privately owned dwellings, and neither man bothering to remark on how good it must be to own your own home and not have a neighbour through a few inches of wall listening to your every fart and fuck and fight; a home with a garden, a carport, a garage. Shit. Whassa use? Ain't gonna change a fuckin thing.

But the farther they drove from Pine Block and the more the houses changed, got better, slightly larger, slightly more appealing than the last, it had Jake Heke imagining em, the home-owners, safe and snug in their privately owned boxes with the cars they all seemed to be lovingly cleaning and polishing like it was some fuckin pet or favourite person, Jake was getting to fume more and more over the car-loving successful-appearing white maggot shits. Fuckem. Cunts worship the things, their cars. They do. Man felt like yelling sumpthin out of the window at one ofem, except he didn't know what he wanted to yell; instinct telling him there was something amiss about anybody who gave a lousy car so much attention.

Couple of miles, four kays in the new language a man'd never been able to think in even after all these years, it must be ten or more, and over the railway line and they were in town.

Two Lakes, wow, Jake drawling as if it bored him, did nothing for him, when truth was town made him feel uncomfortable. In fact, from the moment they hit the other residential side of Two Lakes, Jake Heke was ill at ease. Only when he was (safe and snug) at his drinking hole, McClutchy's, did Jake feel at home again. Though he wasn't aware of that discomfit. Just a funny feeling in his gut that was there one minute and next it wasn't. He never connected things.

Main street. So what, big deal, who gives a fuck, town's not even a city, and ya call this a main street? More like a hick-town street. So where do we hitch our fuckin horses, man? Having a chuckle inside at his thoughts. A long main street though: must run damn near a mile to the lake sitting at the other end. Taniwha Street it was called, after the water monster from Maori myth,

50

though Jake knew plenty who thought taniwhas really existed, though he didn't. So what does a taniwha look like? he'd challenge a believer. And so far he'd never had a satisfactory reply.

Damn place lit up like a Christmas tree. Jake hated this end of town, it was the flash end. Maoris tended to the other end. Like that chemist over there. Bastards. Jake'd never forgotten his one and only time going in there with a prescription for one of the kids sick and the place so fuckin clean and with a funny smell, like a school dentist or a real clean toilet or like at a doctor's. And this woman in a white coat coming up and running her eyes up and down a man, thinking he was blind. He knew she was telling him she didn't like his dirty work clothes, but she could go fuck herself, he just couldn't wait to get out of there. And lookit that clothes shop, the menswear: damn dummy things they got in the front window all dressed to the fuckin nines, I'd give a cunt a bunch a fuckin fives he walked into my pub dressed like that. And how come the dummy things've got white-man features? What, they think they the only race on this earth? Fuckem.

Dooly slowed for a pedestrian crossing; Jake looked sullenly at the crisscrossing of people, thinking of most ofem: The fuck you think you are? Mostly because he perceived their generally tidy dress as being flash, dressed up.

Again at the lights, Dooly halted; sitting there waiting for the fuckin thing to change and half of Two Lakes deciding they just *had* to cross the street, and Jake feeling more and more like a sardine in a — no, a monkey at a zoo. People looking at me . . .

Jake sitting there fuming, hating the people, the fuckin lights for not changing. I'll spit at anyone they look at *me* too hard, like *I'm* a fuckin monkey. Givem monkey. Then he let out a sigh to cover for his changing position as he pulled his arm back inside and quietly wound up the window. Ah, that felt better. And he sat there, eyes dead ahead. To hell withem; even someone I know comes past wanting to say hello, why should I? Man didn't come down here to say hi to every Tom, Dick and Harry.

Hey, why'd you come this way anyway? in an accusing tone to Dool. To look, brother. Look at what? At the *people*, man. Fuckem. But they're your fellow *cunt*reemen and women, Jake. Dool laughing. Fuckem. Oh c'mon, Maori boy, thassa wrong att-ti-tude. And Jake shooting Dool a look in case Dool was having him on. Better not be. (Friend or no friend, man, I don't take shit from no one.) We all New Zealanders underneath, brother, Dool continuing in his breezy vein. I said, fuckem. And still the lights stayed red. Then, no sooner did they get the green, it was another pedestrian crossing. Jesus Chrise. Jake clicking his tongue in frustration.

Jake's patience ran out — Drive through, man. Wha'? Can't do that, this is a zebra crossing. Don't see no zebra out there, man, only a packa wankers. Next one to look in here and I'm gettin out cloutin the cunt. Hey, eeeasy, brotherrr, Dooly tried to lighten it up. You not that thirsty are y'? Drive through, man. Aw, c'mon — Drive. Dooly revved the engine as warning, which brought some dude to a halt, stood there staring in outrage at the deep-rumbling Valiant. And Jake was winding his window down as fast as he could, enraged, and out shot his huge clenched left fist: *You get the fuck outta our way, mutha or* — through clenched teeth. Jake, Jake, easy easy, pal. Ain't no big deal. And Jake swinging on Dool, but with his fist still out the door, You shoulda gone the other way, Manner Street. Why'd you come this way? Then quickly back to the fulla outside, except he'd gone. Lucky for him too. Aw, Jake, where you living, man? This is 1990 not 1890. We're all one and the same underneath, Jake boy. Neath what? Jake glowering at his friend as they moved forward. Our skin, brother. Gimme that shet. What, you think a Maori's different underneath to them out there? Dool sweeping his hand across him. But Jake satisfied his sullenness gave explanation enough. More than enough.

Through the second set of lights, getting a green straight away, all of a sudden Jake came out of his sullen sulk with Dool for taking em the wrong way, leaning back and sweeping an expansive arm and smiling. Man, now this is what I call the real people, at the prevalence of Maoris out there doing their late-night shopping. *Brown* faces, brother, Jake saying with unnecessary force to a similarly brown-skinned friend. Brown and black and fat and rolly polly, hahaha! Jake laughing and pointing at all and sundry, their more casual, even untidy, style of dress, the way they walked, and talked; or stood around in groups sharing from a newspaper-wrapped parcel of fishnchips, or standing there cracking freshly bought mussels in the shell against each other and slurping — I mean, *slurping* — out the contents, a man could identify with that, these people. (And their laughter, man: *rocking* with it, the way (we) they do, and nemine the self-conscious I'm-in-public shit, it's let it all hang out. Juss look atem the way they walk: that ain't walking it's *styling*. It's rhythm. It's going to that beat every (physical) man or woman and even the kids've got in your head. Your soul. Pakehas, they don't under-

52

stand it. That's because they got no rhythm. And no, you know, passion. Or passion and violence.)

Slow, man, slow, Jake instructing and his arm going out the window and pressing it hard against the door to start with just to get the veins up. Givin em a glance, his arm, the veins, the size of his fuckin great mit. And to them out there, even though he felt he kind of loved em, a hard-eyed look. Just in case.

Outside Tam's Chinese takeaways another group ofem and all pigging out on sumpthin Chinese. Hoi! Jake yelling grinningly out at em, Save some for me! They returning his laugh, and one even tossing Jake something or other from his plastic container but Jake missing the catch. Next time, brother! yelling to the fulla and grinning all ovah. All ov-ah.

Till they hit the next Chink takeaways and it was a group of Brown Fists all bunched up trying to look the heavies with their filthy gang regalia and tattooed faces and bare arms covered in em too. Jake giving em his most menacing glare, and holding it till his eyes stung with not blinking. And asking Dool: Who they meant to scare, man? with all the contempt of a man utterly confident in his fighting skills, his fistic power.

Jake waving to a woman he knew from a party way back, and Dool teasing him, Hey, who's that, your bit on the side? But Jake shaking his head, Not me, man. Aw c'mon, Jake, big handsome fulla like you? No way, bro. Yeah, sure, man. Dool's tone disbelieving. And Jake muttering shuddup to Dool, drop it. I ain't no womaniser. Ah, so you like your mi — Man, I didn't say that. Turning the corner into the street where their drinking haunt was, and immediately Dool giving a little whoop and Jake echoing with a chuckle.

McCLUTCHY'S read the sign in red neon, no blinking on and off, no other colours used, no need to. Not when the regulars'd never change for love nor money.

Past the taxi rank, and people already lined up and not even dark yet, near every one ofem history. Crates or brown paper bags of beer at their feet, their swaying gaits a giveaway. And not yet dark. And every one a brown man. Dooly reminding Jake to look straight ahead in case they saw someone they were bound to know and thus be obliged to give the person a lift home. Hell, only just got here.

Parked way up the street from the bar because of cars everywhere, walking along briskly, a mild urgency in their stride, and laughing, then Dooly pushing Jake playfully and Jake using the slight imbalance as an excuse for a (very good) imitation of an Ali shuffle. *Hahahaha!* their twinned laughter echoing down the narrow canyon of two-storey buildings, though only one building mattered to the pair.

McClutchy's. Man, oh man. McClutchy's.

Cross the street, ignoring the drunken calls from the taxi rank of How're'y's? or Here, put it here, brother: shake. Fuck the shakes, silly old codgers can't take their piss. G'won, off to bed ya old buggers, Jake mildly at the line-up of mostly elderly male waitees. And a chorus ofem — but right out of synch — jabbering, Ooo Jake! The toughest cunt in Two Lakes! that sorta thing. Making Jake feel good.

Up the three concrete steps to the big double doors and the bouncers in their bow-ties giving Jake, in particular, deferential greeting: the way men of violence defer to those they know or perceive as their physical betters. And Dooly, buoyed by the rub-off of kudos of association with the big man with the big rep and the even bigger mits, pushing the door open with a hard bottom-of-the-shoe kick like in a western movie, sumpthin tough like that. Then they entered another world. Just a set of double doors away.

It hit em like a blast — it was a blast — of, firstly, sound. SOUND. Sound upon sound within sound. A bizzare humming. A swollen jibberjabberjumble. A great big cacophony of drunken SOUND. And it struck, immediately, as not quite right — even accepting the induced state — as grossly out of balance with something, at odds, terrible odds with the normal world. Even to a Jake, a Dooly, it hit em like that. But only for an instant. Then, unless you were a stranger, the discordant turned to music; sweet jabbering humming music. So they grinned at each other. Made their way to the bar.

Shrieking explosions of laughter, exclamation, SOUND. Oh man! Dool having to shout to Jake beside and then behind him, It's *packt*! with joy in his voice. Layers and layers ofem, of babbling jabbering moaning cursing swearing beer-pouring humanity — cursed by something, a stranger'd think and a regular'd know, except it didn't matter. What the hell, this whole joint is one big mirror of each other so it's alright, man, it's alright.

The tinkle of breaking glass. The *pop* of a fist exploding in someone's face, the immediate yelling and screaming of someone — a woman, some bitch, Jake registering — then a roaring male:

I'LLFUCKIN*KILL*YA!!! — Laughter. Humming dying, heads turning to the incident.

Point your ear anywhere and the sound'd be different, clashing with one another and yet it all felt the same. Or it'd stereo, then hurtle off of each other a violent collision.

Gats going everywhere, there must be four or five ofem: strumdedum, jingjikajingjing, in clashing accompaniment to each cluster of singers, and they weren't so much singing as *transporting*, away somewhere, on stage probably, or in some state of emotional rescue, thinking they were saving some long lost event happened to em, heads back eyes closed mouths agape and sounds and emotions escaping from the gaping holes like poison from an ever-infected wound, ya can't kid me, even Jake Heke, even I c'n see why half ofem get carried away when they sing it ain't singing it's . . . ? But Jake unable to escape his word limits, his boundaries, to nail the perception down. Onward.

Hey Jake! Put it here, brother. And here. And here. And there, and over here, Jake, everywhere. Man. And the jukebox going feebly in the background but only because the barman had volume control and you didn't know the barman and he didn't like your music then fuck your five bucks of fifty cents this ain't a democracy it's a dictatorship!

More glass breaking, and someone toppling over . . . sloooowwwly, slow-motion stuff, onto a table of full bottles and jugs and glasses. Hey! *Pop*, the fulla's nose being punched, bone snapped just like that. Spill our fuckin beer.

The press of bodies, heat, human heat and stink and sickly sweet wafts of (cheap) scents meant to enhance a person, usually some cheaparse woman, or maybe Old Spice on a man if you could callim that wearing that sorta shit in here. Crowd closing, even against him, Jake. Someone shoved by Jake, the someone twisting and asking, The fuck you shoving, mate? before he'd seen who it was. Oh Jake. It's you, brother. Here, put it here, I thought you was someone else. A nervous chuckle in case the Man of Muscle'd taken offence regardless. Smiling all ovah at Jake putting an arm around him, those broad hard shoulders showing their seventy-one inch spread, or the right-hand half of it anyrate. No worries, man. Jake smiling at the fulla. Gotta move. And Dool following alongside when it suited, behind when it didn't, in front if Jake gave him the lead, got stopped by someone wanting to shake his hand.

And the air swirling with smoke, damn near every one ofem

smoking, or just put out or about to light up or cadging one. Need it, man, and right now. No skylights. No windows to speak of. The lighting bad. Only the bar lit up like Taniwha Street you'd think it was fuckin Christmas. Another woman upset at sumpthin and dropping to Jake's left. He expressing a mild interest till he saw who it was: fucker. Bitch is always askin for it. His interest really taken when a fulla jumped in and poleaxed the woman's assailant, dropped the cunt like a stone. Good punch. (Hmm, good punch.) Jake taking note of the dude. (I'll get him after.) Just in case the fulla thought that king-hit made him king. Not here it didn't. Onward.

Then instantly another fight. Man, looking over his shoulder at Dooly Jacobs, Gonna be one a them nights. Pleased at the prospect. He had a big left hook just sat there waiting in him — he could feel it, even see its trajectory, the very *shape* the punch'd take, whoever was unlucky enough to be wearing it.

The bouncers, the ones stationed inside, bulling their way to the last scene, pushing and shoving and even punching people aside in their greedy haste to get to the action and give it some of their own. But Jake didn't give it another thought, only the dude's face who threw the big hit frozen in his mind for later.

People greeted at every step, near. Laughin their crawlin laughs, patting him, shaking his mit, even the left one'd do in their eagerness to be in withim; asking him who he was gonna sort out tonight. Shet. Lodging their greetings with him so he'd not forget, falling at his feet damn near; brushing, touching, squeezing a man's rock-hard muscularity just like I'm a fuckin god. Shet.

Then the pretend mums and dads and uncles and aunties laying bullshet claim to their relation, kissing and hugging and slobbering all ovah a man, made him feel stink, just wanted to get away from em. But shaking a hand, accepting an embrace, wearing a sloppy kiss because, well, they were his people, he was one ofem. (I think.) Jake never completely sure who he was one of. The popularity sometimes adding to his unsureness, hard that it was in knowing people's motives. Yet accepting, on the surface of his thoughts, that he was one ofem alright. If not the one.

Some were already succumbed to the booze: slumped out on tables, barely able to stand, being propped up by friends, a wife, a relation; some curled up under tables just like little babes or kids not wanting to go home. These the bouncers didn't mind so much just so long as they were tucked away out of sight of Mr M for McClutchy himself. If it was Jake he could be anywhere in any

56

state of drunkenness and that was alright. Any bouncer tries me on and I'd take the cunt apart. So.

So people going, all over the joint they were going. Out of their minds, that is. Heads rolling, eyes too, things coming out jumbled, rubbishy, and aggression growing; spit-drops on every spat out word, sentence, a gibberish, a mixed up, fucked-up gibberish from a person sposed to be a human. Man. Did a fulla get as bad as that? Jake always found it hard to believe of himself whenever he did happen to come in sober.

The ones going you could see the different signs, a punch — feeble, mostly — flopping out at some invisible or real opponent, followed by fush and fugg meant to be fucks, or hurling insults at the ghost every drunk carries in his mind and probably in his heart too. And the gats going. But not, like, out of it. Just going as gats do: jingjika strumdestrum . . . jukebox going up an down in competition depending on what was played; and over at the jukie, look atem, a middle-aged couple dancing out their dumb fantasies and the coloured lights from the jukebox thrown on their oblivious features sort of telling a man sumpthin about em but what, Jake did not know. Except it was to do with love, and love being mixed up, confused. (Then later the same fulla'd be punching his lover dance partner for giving someone the (imagined) eye or because he thought she'd gone off him. Man, don't tell Jake Heke, he knows these things: punching, the hurt that causes the punches, Jake understands.)

And you could only just hear Mavis Tatana the Voice Magnificent singing alone to her guitarist strumming for her, an old number from the days when music had melody (and romance) and the words you could, you know, sort of dig them, what they were saying, even if you didn't always feel like listenin.

Mavis. Shet, people said she coulda been a opera star, any kinda singing star she wanted, if she wasn't struck with the ole Maori shyness, oh, but that's the Maori for you, too shy, too scared to throw him and herself forward in case people are looking, listening, maybe laughing and certainly talking; it's better to stay put and shut up. Till you're drunk that is. Poor Mavis. Not like whatshername, the famous Maori opera singer, the *real* famous one, Kiri, that's it. Kiri Te Kanawa. Even Jake Heke's heard of her; why, she even sang at that wedding, you know, the royal one with the pretty thing built like a fuckin racehorse married the fulla with the big nose, Charlie, that's it. Well, them: Kiri sang at their wedding. A Maori, can ya believe it? On the TV too, all over the fuckin world! The world, man. None a this Two Lakes stuff for her. The world. Aee, Jake'd heard em say of Kiri over the years, I cried that day to see a Maori — a *Maori* — singing for royalty in front of the whole world. Cried. Only thing, I didn't like that damn dress she wore, made her look like she'd bought it from the Sally Op Shop, eh. And people laughing at that and saying it was the Maori coming out in their Kiri, her lack of taste in a Pakeha world with all their headstart years of so-fist-i-cay-shun. Laughing at that too, their own ability to laugh at emselves. And everyone always remembered or was inspired to comparing their Mavis Tatana to our Kiri Te Kanawa because when Mavis sang she gave you no choice she bowled you with her talent, almost frightened you with the scope of herself, the tones and shades and hues and sheer range of her notes. Except you didn't understand what was happening to you, especially not if you were Jake Heke, yet you could hear — *hear* — and so you had this thing inside happening to you but you did not know what. For the life of you, you didn't.

So there she was, as usual, Mavis Tatana, the lone star amongst the burnt-out bodies and yet representing something of you, everyone knew this. As if she was representing them, the people, at some championship. The championship of life — LIFE. It must be, or why else did she move you so?

Oh, kia ora! Jake being greeted in Maori, the language of his physical appearance, his actual ethnic existence, and yet they could be speaking Chink-language for what it mattered. Course a man understood kia ora, who doesn't even the honkies do, but as for the rest. Made him uncomfortable if they spoke it to him, so Jake always replied in emphatic English, and sometimes a speaker might exclaim, Aee, the Pakeha took away our language and soon it'll be gone. But that was before this kohanga reo stuff they introduced, of getting the language spoken in classes, on the TV. But a man still didn't feel comfortable in its presence. They were older, these speakers of the stolen language, and they ruffled his hair (oh man, but I love my hair being done like that) felt his bicep muscles in that Maori way like they're sizing up a steak, a good feed, or like a man's a racehorse; and the men they gave him the google eyes and did their imitations of his imitation Ali shuffle, some ofem pretty damn good for old fullas, gave him looks of mock fear and touched his face, *stroked* a man (like his daddy never did) made him feel humble. And warm all over. Sentimental. I need a beer. Gotta go, Pop. Catch ya later. Off into the crowd again. Teeth grinding up like an engine restarted.

58

Giving a wave to the table everyone called the Alkies' Corner. One small corner of a vast bar in a vast world (or that's how Two Lakes the greater felt). Jake never forgot that corner, and he didn't mind telling people it was because he never knew, might be him one day over at that table. And people saying, Aw, come on, Jake. Not you. So a man not really believing he might either. Yet his eyes lingered for a fraction longer on that quartet of daily drunks, and he did feel at some sort of empathy withem, but quickly the main bar claimed him as one a them, a member of this great big happy family of booze lovers, beer guzzlin darkies, that's what we are, and — oh, a man can't put his thoughts into words. Just pictures. And funny feelings. Like meeting someone you knew in your childhood and it's like he or she's never left you.

Two hundred — nah, there'd be easy three hundred ofem. And Jake and Dooly's progress could be seen as a swath cut through an obliging but seething, beer-bloated, mindless humanity; three hundred broken dolls, three hundred flopped-out puppets dangling in the hands of some god-cunt making em do things you wouldn't credit animals with. Then — Huh? (Boogie.) Boogie? It just popped up in his mind. O *shit*, a man forgot Boog had to go to court and I was sposed to be there. Jake stopping in his tracks a moment even though a path'd been widened for him to take a few more steps. (Sorry, Boog.) Ah, fuckit. Wasn't me got him in trouble with the courts. A kid is his own master of this world. He's a wimp anyway. Ya wouldn't think he was a son of mine. And anyway, too many people calling out hello to a man, touching him, to waste his thoughts on a stupid kid who can't fight to save himself and maybe if they sent him away it'll do him some good, he might *have* to toughen up. Fuckim.

Six, eight minutes it must've taken to get to the bar. Jake telling Dooly, My shout. Dooly grinning, I know that. I'm flat broke, bro. Jake saying, I know that. And the two looking at each other wondering if it was funny or what and laughing anyway. Two. Jake lifting two fingers to indicate the number of litre jugs he wanted. DB for the brand. Giving the Rheineck lager tap a look of pure contempt as if to drink that pisswater was worse'n bein a woman. And he stood there, waiting while the jugs were filled, aware of people's awareness of him; he felt like a chief, a Maori warrior chief — no, not a Maori chief, I can't speak the language and people'll know I can't, and it'll spoil it — an Indian chief, a real Injun, not one a them black thievin bastards own half the fuckin shops round town, a *real* Indian from comics and TV and America . . . Jake pouted his lips ever so slightly and pulled the corners of his mouth down by use of the cheek or jaw muscles, or maybe it was both it don't fuckin matter; he flared his nostrils, like a, you know, a bull — I know! Like Sitting Bull. Chief Sitting Bull. And he part lidded his eyes. And he'd done this enough times in the mirror to know what he looked like, so he stood there swelled with pride and vanity and this sense of feeling kingly and inside a voice was going: Look at me. *Look* at me, ya fuckers. I'm Jake Heke. Jake the Muss Heke. LOOK AT ME (and feel humble, you dogs).

The jugs came over. On the house, Jake. Thanks, man. Much appreciated. Jake pleased with his manners, pleased with the respect he commanded, handing Dooly a jug. Here ya go, boy. Get that freebie down ya. And Dooly, being broke, going along with Jake's magnaminous act, Ah, thanks, man. Thanks. Thinking: I'm here for the free piss not my stupid fuckin pride. They moved off.

Over at the table, the elbow-height table, Jake Heke always drank at; even if it was taken when he arrived, it was vacant by the time he got to it. Or it'd better be. Hello to his regular school of drinking mates, tougharses the lot ofem. How I like my mates: tough. And if they ain't tough then they better have sumpthin about em. Mitch Daniels talking about a hell of a scrap'd happened just before Jake and Dool's arrival, Jake all ears. That right? His eyes just that little bit wider, and disappointment already strong in him for missing it. Tell me, man. But having to make out he was cool about it.

So Mitch telling Jake and Dool about it, how this dude — never seenim before, but I think he's a shearer from outta town working this way on contract, sumpthin like that (and Jake trying to build up a mental picture of this dude so to get everything quite clear in his mind) — packed a punch like a fuckin elephant, how he took on three and dropped the three ofem: Pow! King-hit on the first one — What was it, Jake butting in, a left, a right? what? Straight right. A left and a right on the second fulla, and oh man! spun him one way then the next, eh. All in the space of — how long you reckon, Rangi? Oh, bout less'n a second — There you are, under a second and two *big* hits, eh. Everyone's eyes lit up with excitement, of reliving it or hearing it for the first time. The third fulla, he didn't wanna know, eh. Cunt was trying to back out of it, started walkin backwards with his hands up when *pow!* this tough dude smacked a left into his face. Y'c'd hear it all over the fuckin bar. Eh, Rangi, you could eh? I'm telling ya, man. Even your punches, Jake, good as you are, I think this fulla hit hard — no, not harder, but nearly as hard as you. He did, eh, Rangi? Yeah, man. And Jake getting just a little worried; it was the kind of story people told about him, not some other dude. And a stranger at that. (In my fuckin pub.) What, he still here this fulla? Jake wanting to know. And quite prepared to allocate his ready-made left hook to the stranger. Nah, he left. Juss up and walked out. Jake then wanting to know what the bouncers did and being told, Nuthin, man. Packa wankers, all they good for is smashing up old fullas and little guys. They stood there and did nuthin. What was he, a Maori or what? Well that's the funny thing, Jake, he wasn't a Maori, eh. And Jake surprised himself: this wasn't a bar for non-Maoris; you had to be related to one, be an idiot, or be as tough as this dude evidently was to have white skin and come in here a stranger. Pointim out to me you ever seeim again, Jake told all to look out for.

And his heart rate'd picked up, the talk of fighting doing that. And the first lot of freebies went real quick, as did the next lot bought by someone at Jake's table. And they talked about the king-hit Jake'd witnessed himself when first they came in, who was the dude? Jake hadn't seen him before either (and wondering, really wondering about all this king-hitting going on when it was sposed to be his thing. I mean, what if someone up and put one on me? Man wouldn't be able to show his face in here again.) though they knew he was a relation of so-and-so, which is why it wasn't so bad him getting involved, not with being related to a regular and anyway, that bitch who got smacked first she'd been looking for it for ages but he wasn't to know, the stranger related to so-and-so, that Ronty the Shonty (no one knew her real Christian name) Pohatu was a bitch. But the fulla can hit. That's him over there, Jake. I know who he is. Jake picking the fulla out in the crowd and the semi-gloom and the smoke, assessing the dude, working out to stay left of that right — if the fulla got to throw it, that is — to lessen the distance it travelled. And quite sure he was gonna get the fulla even though no reason.

Eyes going elsewhere, at the sea of people and how out of it most ofem were, and downing his own drink as fast he could to catch up withem. Someone plonking a jug in front of him just as he emptied his second, and winking at Dool and indicating it was theirs, the jug. Ours, brother. Together we stand, together we fall. But laughing, mind.

So it wasn't too long before Jake Heke was adjusted. Feeling just nice, thank you. And darkness fell outside.

Mavis Tatana, the big fat bitch, was up singing again. Oh, she c'n sing alright. She coulda been a opera singer that one, people saying to each other, over and ov-ah again but still they said it. Another Kiri Te Kanawa it wasn't for the ole Maori shyness. So how come Kiri isn't shy? Well, that's because she — I don't think she had a Maori upbringing. Nah, that's what I heard too that she was bought up posh, eh. Oo, have to be, eh, to sing that blimmin opra stuff. Shet, I call it. Me too. But some people like it, eh? And she is a Maori after all. Still shet. *You* the only fuckin shet round here. Laughing. Going back to listening to the woman who woulda been . . . *say that you're my sweetheart*. Oh, I *love* that song. Whatsit called again? El Morata, thatsit. Shhh. . . . *my one and only sweetheart*, the behemoth's voice ringing out even over the din and they, the people, going ahh and aye in exclamation their appreciation. Seeing so much too: of what this huge woman meant to them, the hope. Yet not understanding. Never understanding. Not the profound. Even though they had a part in it.

Then Bim — that fuckin bitch — the Baby Killer getting so carried away by Mavis's singing she forgot her unpopularity and came staggering out of the crowd into the half-circle of space cleared for Mavis so people could see her, give her more focus, sorta like a spotlight but without the light hahaha! Bim. Bim with the two cot deaths that everyone said can't've happened she musta murdered em, smothered the poor innocent lil fuckers, so Mavis showing alarm at Bim's entry onto her stage and the people telling Bim to fuck off, Go kill you some more babies, ya bitch. And the woman, Bim, reeling from the comments the cruelty, and nowhere to go from their attack. And even Jake feeling sorry for the woman she didn't look like no killer, not of babies her own babies who'd do a thing like that? and glad when someone, one of her relations, snatched Bim from further verbal attack back into the dank anonymity of mass she'd lurched from.

Kiss me, kiss me sweet, in El Morata sang Mavis back in full blossom again till some wanker stuffed fifty cents in the jukebox and out blasted a rock number. So Mavis stopped dead and so did her guitarist follow suit. And there was this young fulla hardly drinking age standing over there with his oblivious features fire-lighted in green and gold from the jukie's lights jiggin to the paid beat. So someone yelled to the bar they'd better shut that fuckin jukebox up or he'd not only shut it but the cunt who played that fuckin number you better believe. The jukie died immediately. Mavis got to finish her song.

The crowd — or that section of the mass who could see and hear her — roared their appreciation, Sing it again! Which she didn't, but she did sing another oldie favourite, Tennessee Waltz. And someone was even inspired or emboldened enough by piss to step forward and fill the gap Mavis's outstretched arms offered of imaginary dancing partner. And everyone clapped and cheered. And they yelled for more when that was finished but she got a signal that a horserace commentary was about to start on the four pub speakers so she declined. So they filled her table with jugs of beer anyway. And she smiled her big fat smile and went, Ahh. She did love a beer did Mavis Tatana. (Bet Kiri don't.)

Horses hurtling along some night track under floodlights being transposed on radio for everyone to hear and cheer on, a couple of dozen charioted nags being urged along by whip and punters' cries, and every bettor praying his bet wouldn't break regulated trotting stride, because a horse was lost once he broke stride and thus so was the punter.

They were frozen or highly animated poses and poises and postures of air-punching, yelling, tight-lipped, open-mouthed, miserable sons and daughters of bitches and bastards, yelling at their mounts to get a fuckin move on, accusing it of being a donkey, a mule, or not a horse at all but implying it as part of some form of conspiracy against them, me, him, I, personally, you could see it on their faces . . . *and it's Hel-mut's Pride a length and a half from Moody Boy and Night Spesshall coming up fast on the in-nah*, as they, the hopefuls, were caught there in some time frame of hope mixed with desperation; and outside it'd grown quite dark, and the line-up of swaying drunks with bottles at their feet kept changing as taxis swooped in to take the last of their money, sped them off into the night; then the line swelled again, but this was happening all ovah it was around this time for the ones not of cast-iron constitutions, so they had to wait till the busy period fell off again. And they talked gibberish and you couldn't understand a word they were saying, nor were their faces visible in the dullish streetlight so they were just shapes and strange callings and grunts and raspy smoker's breaths and hacking coughings in the night, shadowy apparitions in the semi-gloom of just another two-bit town in a two-bit country, but what the hell they didn't know.

And inside, at the bar servery, this young man was complaining loudly about his records not playing and the jukie eating up his fifty cents, five bucks' worth and nuthin. And what the fuck was the head barman gonna do about it? Gonna do sumpthin bout your mouth is what, the barman giving a secret signal to the bouncers to come remove this cunt. And a bouncer there in a flash, Whassa trouble, man? No trouble, bro, just want my dough back I put in the jukie. How much, man? the bouncer's tone lying to the poor fool. And Poor Fool lying: seven bucks. Seven bucks? At least. So? So whatcha gonna do about it? Whatcha *want* me to do about it, brother? call the cops? a doctor maybe? an ambulance? Come on, man . . . the Fool looking at the bouncer, trying to appeal to what reason he might have. It's the principle. And the bouncer incredulous: The wha'? The Principle. Bouncer laughing. Fool muttering to Bouncer not to treat him like a fool. So Bouncer not treating him as a fool but an enemy.

Jake catching the movement of the punch out the corner of his beady eye, thinking, Wow. Not bad for Sam. His punches don't usually hurt no one cept the old codgers. And he watched as another couple of white-shirted bouncers came a running like dogs and Sam marching the poor young prick out. Fuckim. Not my lookout. No mate a mine.

Young man was out on the street, bleeding from the mouth and aching from several other punches. His heart ached too. From cynicism. He saw the line of drunks at the taxi stand. He eyed em up first for any toughs before he vented his frustration. *Ya packa old cunts!!!* He spat on the ground at the feet of one old fulla. Hey! Go fuck yaself. Then Fool turned to the hotel and yelled, I'LL BE BACK!! and the bouncers at the big double doors just grinned and kept standing with their arms folded and sleeves rolled up high so everyone could see their muscles. So the emboldened young man repeated his promise and it echoed down the canyon of two-storey buildings, as stars twinkled overhead. And he farewell snarled at the old drunks and they did the furtive same, and the night soon swallowed him, it was only a small town.

Time. It passed so quickly in this place. One minute you had the whole sweet night in front of you, next it was nearly over. Like a weight dropping down on you. And this voice in your head, like a little kid's, saying I don't wanna go home. And you mixed it up in your (befuddled) drunk head, thinking it was some kind of joke your beer brain was playing on you. And you felt strange. Then you didn't. And the world it kept surging back and forth from darkness to light and you couldn't fuckin figure it. But you went

64

along with it because what else could you do, go home?

Change. Everything kept changing. Mood, thoughts, emotions, visual feedback, (aural) even ya fuckin ears started playing tricks on you. The pisser, your attitude's range of change seemed to bring itself out in the pisser, all of you. Feeling full of friendliness for the world one visit, hatred the next. So fullas shaking hands and putting arms around each other as well as eyeballing one another. The fuck you looking at, man? Wha'? You heard. I asked what the fuck you lookin at. At your ugly fuckin wanker face, man, that's what I'm lookin at. Yeah? Yeah. And someone throwing one and another hitting the deck, or coming back with a better one of his own. And blood all over the show, and wasn't the bouncers' job to clean it up, they never went near the fuckin toilets, not unless there was a scrap to break up and/or someone's head needing busting.

So come the end of the night the lavatory floor was near awash with blood; and sick too, and missed piss. So it stunk to high heaven, and got worse as men emptied emselves of bowels rotten and liquid with piss and pies and a lifetime of pissing up, eating junk food.

And Jake finally got his chance when the stranger with the king-hit went to use the toilet and it coincided with Jake being ready for the man, so out he went after the dude.

The two ofem standing there at the stainless-steel urinal each taking a piss, and Jake making no secret of eying the fulla's arm muscles, how they were exposed unnecessarily with the sleeves of the guy's sweatshirt cut right off, annoying Jake, presenting itself as a threat to him. Seeing the tats on the dude's (well-muscled) arms probably signifying he was a crim. A crim, eh? A bigtime crim comin into my pub thinkin he c'n blow away people and not invite some himself. Same height, maybe an inch shorter. Solid, not lean like Jake. Bit of a paunch there, so musta been outta the boob a little while to grow that beer belly. Jake fixing on that slightly fat belly, telling himself the fulla must be soft as butta. Soft as.

Asking him casually, When'd they let you out, man? And getting an instant, None a your business, bud. Jake shaking his penis. Only asking, brother. And I'm only telling — bru-tha. The guy giving Jake the real eyeball and Jake thinking, I could take you right now but wanting to enjoy it.

Whassa name, pal? What, you a cop or sumpthin? Nah. Do I look like a cop? Jake grinning at the fulla. Ya sound like one.

65

Nah, not me, bro. Y'been doin some weights in the boob? The fulla frowning at Jake, puzzled at his nerve, but not the slightest bit intimidated. (Good.) Jake feeling very nervous in his gut. A rapid sorta throbbing, but which wasn't painful. And his heart thumped. Wonder the cunt can't hear it banging against my chest.

Jake reached over and touched, ever so gingerly, the fulla's bicep muscle and went, Ooo, now that's hard. And he saw the glint in the man's eye as he must've made up his mind to smack Jake one. But Jake did it first. A left hook you woulda thought'd been made in heaven, honest to God.

Standing over the fulla — moaning the useless prick was — tellingim, I don't like heroes come into my patch, man, thinking they own the fuckin show. Jake's eyes slightly teary, as if the fulla'd really done him a wrong, hurtim. You wanna stay on side with me, man, you keep your dukes to yourself nless it's with my sayso. Then out he sauntered.

He told his table of friends, Had to give that fulla thinks he's a tougharse a tickle up in there. And they all broke out in at first a collective sigh of awe then laughter. Cept Jake, he juss stood there acting like it wasn't that big a deal. Fuckim. But his fists had that lovely tingle of wanting — aching —for more.

So the big man swept his hungry eyes over the world and hoped. For action to walk in before the morrow came.

People doing scenes all over. All ov-ah. As though last throes, last-minute acts before the curtain fell; or to complete something, satisfy sumpthin. A man could see this. But he couldn't put words to it.

Crying, bawling, howling on each other's shoulders in each other's arms; or might be slow-dancing or fast-dancing to some imaginary beat in their heads because being drunk can do that to you sometimes, make you feel sorta like you're an artist or sump-thin, a singer, a dancer, a something of special talent and quality if only life'd given you the breaks, the chances. So Jake could see some were of some skill at dancing, and the odd one real good, like that dude over there by the jukie with the frizzy hair doing a break dance. Man, was he good!

Singers too; breaking out in last-minute song before the bell'd soon start going and the bouncers start shoving em (that lot, not Jake Heke) outta the place like fuckin sheep. And the clock creeping closer to eleven o'clock closing. As people they did their thing: artisting, fucking up, arguing, crying, struggling, punching, bleeding, yelling, staring, glaring, trying to think, doing a think, trying to put words to it (thinking those flashes in their heads were flashes of, you know, wisdom or sumpthin) and you could hear those ones because they were the ones saying, Wow, I c'n see for miles, brutha. With that look in their eye that had a man wondering if they really couldn't see for miles, or were they just talking that dope shit? Then in walked the answer to Jake's aching fists.

A line-up ofem, they came in wearing their fuckin black shades you'd think the fuckin sun was shining in here at this near on eleven at night, so you couldn't see (and read) their eyes only the way their heads moved: lookin this way and that giving off that, You bedda not be in my shaded gaze, mutha, or I'll fuckin deal to you. Jake taking it as read that assumption of what the Brown Fist arrivals were thinking. (Yet vaguely aware they were just kids, really, even if they were past the age of consent.) Fuckem. Comin in here swaggering like that thinking they own the joint. *I* own it. *I'm* king a this castle. That hurt coming on.

A wide path opening up forem. Tats under the front one's eyes, stars, Jake could see; and the others the same but a couple ofem with tats everywhere on their shaded dials. And blue bandanas with white what-they-call-it, polka dots on em. And every person knew what was imprinted on their backs: BROWN FISTS TWO LAKES emblazoned in black capitals around the outer edge of a big red circle on the cutaway jean jacket. A big bunch a fives filled the centre circle. Everyone was wondering who'd let these arseholes in, complaining about the bouncers again for being useless bastards only good for beating up weaklings and old people.

A buzz that'd gone through the crowd'd turned to a low murmur scarcely believable in this normal cacophony. Jake Heke was getting madder and madder at the sight of people fallin over emselves to make a pathway for the gang members. Seven of the cunts. (Oh please, *please* come my way.) Jake not the slightest bit fazed by em. Soon, his table of mates could hear Jake's teeth grating together. And lots could see his jaw muscles twitching.

You could see the power coming off em, the front one especially. Jimmy Bad Horse he called himself. Just look at how his scowl's grown since he knows everyone's lookin atim. Jake asking his table, You with me? And instantly a murmur of yeow, bro. Warriors, see.

The Browns were all over the country and you could see they

knew it. Even the cops didn't go outta their way to gettem for anything, only when they did murder. Which was often. But so
glaringly public even a fool knew it had to be something other
than straight criminality drivin em, had to be. And they took the
rap for each other for crimes done. Even murder'd be claimed if
the fulla was a desperate prospect willing to do anything to get in.
They were also the children, many ofem, of these people, the older
ones amongst The People. Sprung from the loins and wombs of
many of these bastards and bitches. Yet they, The People, were
looking at strangers. Because you could read it on even their dark,
shaded faces the mad loyalty given to being a gang member. It
was funny, being drunk and therefore somehow wise, you could
just see why these young warriors'd joined up with the Browns: it
was love. Being loveless. As well as something else missing . . . but
what was it . . . ? sumpthin to do with race, with being a Maori
and so being a bit on the wild side when you compared with the
other race, the ones running the show. It was sumpthin closely
linked with that but damned if you could figure it.

Leader had star tats under his eyes. You could just pick em
from the bottom edge of wraparound coal-black shades. (A
middle-aged man not one kilometre distant from this distant social
world had stars in his vision as he trained his instrument, his
beloved telescopic instrument on the heavens up there, happy —
happy — with the purchase he'd scraped and saved for years to
buy; satisfied with the sacrifices necessary to acquire the thing;
deeply satisfied with its purpose and his application of that purpose. It brought things out there just a little closer to a man's mere
pulse-beat of understanding. Ah, yes, the stars, the stars. Star
stuff; from which man (astonishingly) did come, by and billions
of years by. Oh, just *look* at it out there and now at the end of my
telescope's marvellous eye.)

And the big man with the bushy beard and stars tattooed under
his eyes had the surge of gang leadership jolting through him like an
electric charge; and he felt his own star in rapid ascendency; and,
too, felt like a rough'n'tough Maori Moses, or whoever that Bible
fulla was, at the human waters parting before him. (And then
there was Dooly Jacobs, running hot with the flushes of, man, felt
like enlightenment — and he knew the word, its meaning — at
Jake Heke and then at the Brown Fists, feeling his insight spring
forth like a mushroom rising up out of his mind's deeper workings,
the voice in Dool's head going: I know you, Jake Heke. I know all
of us. Through and through your troubled bones, Jake, I know

you.) And it was so simple, or that's how it seemed to Dooly Jacobs standing there with a slight sway on but his mind as clear as the stars through the other man's telescope. (You are warrior, Jake Heke. And these arrivals, they are warrior too. You threaten each other. That is why you are maddening, O great but crazy warrior amongst us; why you come furiously from your lair. To protect your mad warriorhood without knowing that you do. You — most of you — live only in the volatile moment of warriorhood.) Whilst the man with the telescope kept gazing starwards never ceasing to wonder — *wonder* — at that unimaginable moment way back in unimaginable time gone by that did (or may have) create such unimaginably far-flung fiery space stuff which would create, in turn, the explosion called Man. He wondered hard and long about this. All this universe from a single event of supposedly Big Bang? *But how?* As an event took place in a bar he read about in the evening local (when he deigned to get the third-rate backwater rag, and when he bothered to read the sordid goings on of the court page, committing their assaults and unseemly deeds against one another, occasionally spilling their filth over into society, and mostly done by a race he, Mr Telescope Man, knew not a single member of since he perceived of their interests their miserable social condition nothing in common to his own, innocuous, mostly nightly doings.) Over and over in his mind he did ponder this question of Beginning. Nor was he of vanity sufficient to mind in the least realising that man, himself therefore, all of humanity and its ludicrous condition, was probably meaningless in the random Scheme of things. As Jake Heke's voice reverberated across the virtually silent bar of three hundred and more souls whose perceptions, sodden and weighted and yet partly lightened by what they'd imbibed, looked on at what they'd heard in a mix of astonishment and delight and fear for Jake the Muss. And his challenge echoed in their minds . . . MAKE WAY FOR THE KING AND HIS MIGHTY WANKAHS! . . . make way for the . . . oh, man, such mad courage.

Jimmy Bad Horse swung his head in exaggerated fashion to the insult; face impossible to read because of all the factors: poor light hazed by several thousand cigarettes, the wraparound shades, the dude's thick bushy beard and a similar wild frizz of hair (though some would claim they heard Jimmy Bad Horse gulp, and another that his eyes'd been wide with fear.) Halted, leader of six ofem; fuckin ugly mirrors of each other, sticking out from the subdued crowd because of the space made forem and those distinctive polka-dotted white and blue headthings, and their air of heaviness, you know, as much put on, forced, as it was anything *scary*. Though they, The People, were scared enough.

You talking to us? Bad Horse had Jake challenging the institution, clever clever. Yet he alone was a massive bulk of a man made bulkier by that big jean jacket — filthy it was too — and the tree-trunk arms sticking out from where the sleeves'd been cut off at the shoulder. Arms black and purple with tats; like a chart of his troubled childhood and early adulthood written all over him.

And Jake making a show of looking around, each side, at the floor, even up at the smoke-yellow ceiling. Back at the gang leader: Well. Paused. Well, he said, I can't see no one else round here playing like king and with a buncha wankahs withim. A titter sighing up from the crowd. Silence again.

So what's th' idea, man?

Of what, man? Jimmy Bad Horse's mouth breaking into a gappy strip of white snarling teeth. Six more doing the same, as though the cunts'd rehearsed it.

Of pushing your way in here like you own the fuckin joint? Wha', *you* the owner?

So Jake took a couple of steps forward (from his lair) as answer. And the six mirrors of leader did the same, though their leader did not.

So what's your hassle, man?

You. Jake pointed, then swung the finger of the big mit at the six-spread of young warriors (pretend ones, Jake certain.) And your fuckin — spat the last out — *pups*. Another step. But no counter.

I were you, man, I'd leave us alone. Bad Horse playing his group ace. Too soon, The People knew. Ya don't threaten Jake with his own strength, ya don't.

Jake closed the space separating him and Bad Horse and the crowd went, OOOOO! unable to contain their excitement. And five of Jake's friends stepped out from their table, stood with arms folded or at their sides hanging loose but ready. And the crowd were pressed tight against each other with hardly room to fuckin breathe. And Jake at the front there'd built to his HATE state: a steady, mad burning inside of hatred — *hatred* — HATRED! and this funny, deep-down hurt. It boiled inim. It even had these regular sounds like the crash of thunder. So it was all Jake could do to keep himself from attacking. (Easy, boy, easy. This ain't no ordinary rumble, this is revenge stuff. These arseholes'll come

70

after you with guns, remember that, Jake.) But even that was just barely enough to control Jake.

They were near face to face. And everyone in the crowd near pissing emselves with excitement. They'd never known this place so quiet. Not ever. This was unbelievable. Indescribably sweet. It was like seeing your private fantasy being acted out — it *was* just that.

Back off, man.

So Jake pressed his face closer.

I said: Back off.

Closer. A left — a *dozen* lefts — from heaven ready to machine gun in the cunt's face, a dozen rights ready to slip in between lefts (left-left and a RIGHT! And a LEFT HOOK! it was going in Jake's mind.) And so was everything else going *bzzzzzz* and thunder crashed in his inner ears and yet he could see and hear everything so clearly it was unbelievable, but then it always was this clearness that came over a man when he was in a tight, tough situation.

Come on, man, Jimmy Bad Horse in a whisper to Jake. A whisper. (Wankah. Wankah, I *knew* you had no guts.)

Jake could smell the man's breath, or feel it warm on his face. (Wankah. The wankah blew his arse.) Jake? Again in a whisper. Yet said out the side of his mouth as though he was snarlin at Jake. Y' can't do this, man. I got my boys watching . . . I lose my, uh, my pride here, man, and I'm coming back with a shotgun. Promise you, man. I'll be back to waste you, Jake. Jake shaking. With rage. And outrage: that this *cunt* should dare plead with a man to don't take away his pride then tell a man he'd waste im. Shaking. But all Jake gave away of his rage was, So you tell me, punk, how *I'm* gonna walk away from this with *my* pride? And he swore he heard Jimmy Bad Horse swallow, a gulp. Of fear. (Wankah.) Dunno, man. Thas your lookout. You the one called us.

And this whispering and low-voiced talking going on and the crowd — not a one ofem — unable to hear it. But Jake glancing over the Brown Fist's shoulder atem and seeing — being staggered by the sight, in fact — the hope on their faces, the unspoken urgings of encouragement: G'won, Jake, get the bastard. Jake saw their expectation, and even how the weariness of booze was over-shadowed by the firebright of a fight in store. And so he loved em — *loved* em all, the fuckers — for giving him their love, their hopes in an otherwise hopeless world. So. (So I could die forem.

71

I could die of just love forem all right here.) Tears in Jake's eyes. Because he (I) was their light, their hope burns eternal flame (who else they got to do this kinda thing forem?) he could see what they were thinking, they were thinking: Punch his lights out, Jake the Muss. For us, Jake, punch his fuckin lights out. They. They, The People — (the bereft, the broken of heart and spirit from all them dirty rotten homes with no love inem. Oh, Jake unnerstans, Jakey'd never leave you, People.) So Jake not budging. Not one inch. And the crowd, the grown up leftovers from the wrecked, ruined childhoods, just one big collective thought of: PUNCHIM, JAKE. PUNCHIM.

And the man with the precision instrument he'd gone without to acquire, denied himself of earthly pleasures so to gain his due reward from heaven, gazed through his beloved telescope and thought of red shifts, and blue shifts, and how, if some of the red shifts were a fact then so too was it that the universe was moving *apart* . . . meaning, that much, if not all, one day should be lost to each other in the heavenly scheme of things. A thought that gave him at the same time a sense of his own unimportance but, too, a sense of loss. Oh, almost a sorrow.

Whilst They, The Lost, waited as their Light advanced his face still closer to that of the face representing Evil and Dark, thinking: PUNCHIM PUNCHIM PUNCHIM.

The man was urinating, you could hear it hitting the tarseal street in a dull steady splash — when he started off — then he was playing the discharge with an idiot glee, laughing, and saying, I know. Gonna make me a shape. Thinking for a second. A twat. I'll draw me a twat. As he tried to form a V on the road and a woman opposite with her dog under her arm and husband walking road side of the footpath with her looked in disgust at the last of the sight of taxi-rankers. And two ofem laughing at the crude wet stain on the road. And the stars above so clear. Reflecting in droplets of urine (in the uplifted eyes of a child, Grace, laying on her back in the long unmown grass of her back lawn gazing at it up there, as her illustrious Maori warrior ancestors'd done before her) and one of the taxi-rank drunks commenting to his mate: See those stars up there, brother? Well our ancestors used em as guides, eh; navigation guides to gettem here, eh. (And Grace thinking how unbelievably vast and beautiful it was up there.)

And Jimmy Shirkey had nowhere to take his star-tatted face as Jake pressed near nose to nose with him. And Jimmy knowing the

72

wankahs all around were waiting for his blood to be spilled all over the floor though it wasn't that he minded so much (my blood's been spilling all my miserable life, my heart's bled as long as I c'n remember) it was his pride, his manhood. Then he wondered if he shouldn't take his chance, up and headbutt this Jake cunt. But Jake's rep, man . . .

Grace followed a shooting star, wheeeee . . . from first flash to white salt-pour expiry lower down in that vast black of a million bursts of light; arching her back to follow the path it traced. Thinking how *sick* of that damned Tennessee Waltz she was when her eyes fell on blocks and part-blocks of light that must be the Trambert residence. Oh far out, wonder what it must be like for them this life. What they were doing. Oh, and maybe they saw my mother, her making a fool of herself dancing with a ghost, and her face so hideous from what Dad did to her — God, I hate him. Yet Mum, she still loves him.

Claaaangggggg!! the bell for last orders went off like a fire engine'd just charged into the packed bar. And Jake he used it to tell the Brown Fist leader, You got your pride, man. But don't you fuckin come onto my territory like you the big wheel. Alright? But Jimmy Bad Horse shrugging, turned his back and swaggered off to the bar servery. Left Jake Heke staring afterim, a look of triumph on his face and The People, even in their clamour to get to the bar servery, were also reflecting triumph. Why, how many people stand up to a Brown Fist, man? And already some ofem saying how they were ready, those other goons just had to so much as blink and I'd've been in. In like a fuckin shot. Talking like this, packed tight like sardines, as they worked the seven barmen off their last ten minutes of feet.

And they downed their last drinks, and the lights got switched off at the servery, made it look so . . . ? so different, man . . . as if the lights of heaven, or the promise of it'd been switched off. And there was Grace — *wheeee*-ing at another shooting star scribing its signature across the sky. Ah, so sad really: just a brief moment in time and then gone forever. She was running when she saw it. Right in front of her. Lithe of limb and feeling she could run on and on (though not forever. Grace never saw forever in its positive sense. It was inconceivable that something *good* could last forever, or even a lifetime. A long time even. Just didn't happen to a girl from Pine Block) . . . then she was scrambling through the wire-strand fence separating her state dwelling from that stately one, the one lit up. The moon behind her; a big glowing eye in the sky. And that house just a paddock away. (I'm so *excited*.) Just standing there, aglow like the moon except parts of it snatched by the shadow of tree outline, foliage cover; an apparition, a spacecraft from outer space just landed. Oh wow. She ran. The strains of Tennessee damn Waltz permanently embedded in her mind from musta been a hundred damn times Mum played that record, and she's *still* playin it. Grace stopped: see if I c'n hear it from — Oh Gawd. I can. Turning. To see the whole rear view of houses on her street lit up, partly lit, and just the odd gap of darkness where some real odd-ones-out family must be actually sleeping at eleven o'clock Friday night. And she could see her mother, the figure of her moving across that yellow window screen (Oh Gawd help us, I can *see* her); turning back to that singular glow of light and running, running fast towards it (and I don't even know why.)

And the stars so clear, and a dew formed on the grass of Trambert's paddock, on the roofs of the beatup cars, the old cars, the hotted-up jobs, the grunt machines out in the carpark of McClutchy's bar and up the street a fair ways, and on the roofs of the old car wrecks in the streets of Pine Block where some poor kids were sleeping.

And the bells going. All over the country, in every lowdown bar in the land. Night was over.

Bouncers herding their scum customers out like sheep: C'mon, c'mon, let's have ya. Pretending to be polite, patient about it, but inside aching for trouble to break as a last bonus for the night.

And the customers lugging their bottled containers of happiness withem, hitting the cool night some ofem reeling, acting it up because they'd heard cold air and a skinful a piss was a potent mixture so there was no use in denying that scientific fact, even when it wasn't one.

And they got into their beat-up cars, they lined up at the taxi rank where they argued, picked fights, had fights, spewed up all over the road where that fulla'd tried to draw a twat (of all the things and he had to pick a twat for his artistry). And a big scrap broke out in the carpark — so what's new? — as fullas heard it and were racing to join it, as if it, the brawl, was this powerful magnet drawing em even if they didn't want to; and this fulla hopped into this car, eh, and no one in the car knew the cunt from a bar of soap, and the driver said, What the fuck? before he punched the cunt, then he and his four passengers they hauled the fulla from their car and he was struggling and saying *please, bru-*

74

thas! as they kicked and punched him senseless. Then they got back in their invaded territory and drove off, laughing, shaken a bit by the violence but also feeling *real* good about it, and driver saying: Man, who'd that cunt think he was? Yet there was another car-crasher up the street a bit who told the driver, Home please, Jeeves. A stranger he was. And the driver laughing, and thus so did his passengers, and he said to the cheeky fulla, Wha', party at your place? grinning. And the cheeky fulla said, Yeow, bro. Just like that. And it seemed like a friendship was formed.

Still others making for Taniwha Street: food. Need a *feed*, man. And the Slit-eyes waiting hungrily forem to arrive, hiding their contempt behind sugary Oriental smiles (that only the blind drunk couldn't see through) and snatched at your money, man, and the order hardly outta your mouth (and without shame, convinced it was you the shameful one); they assessed each and every customer for how pissed he was so to know how much less of something to put in his order, add it up, man, it comes to a bit you open seven days all year the cunts don't even close on Christmas day; looking at you, Maori boy and girl man and woman, brown people, all the time drunk, calculating you, giving you the Chink eye all ovah, at you, stupid drunk Maori, all the time look for trouble, why you not try look for money for a change? Ah, five thousand years of history against you, Brown People, no wonder we Chinese we loathe you. Five thousand years to know secret to life is hard work — work ethic, you hear of work ethic? But smiling at their swaying, red-eyed, foul-smelling cussimas because Chinese person he love what you carry in your pocket, and he don't mind have to work hard for it. Work easy once you decide. Watching em through their narrow slits of eyes, the customer's drunken scenes outside, his outbursts, his hysteria, his terrible things — Aee, muss be the race. Muss be. Why they so troubled? So mixed up? Yet thinking they, the prevailing brown customers, were shit, scum.

So they shook their heads, without pity, at the sound of sirens come to arrest you, take you broken and bleeding and often dying to hospital; they laughed gleefully amongst emselves at your collective stupidity, your monumental idiocy, Brown People, for helpin em get rich; they laughed even more over their woks in knowing you, your miserable untaught offspring, were their children's guaranteed future. Ah, my children they be here when these scum's children grow up: spare rib, sweetnsour pork, chow mein, chop suey, dimsims, wonton, fried wings, no matter, all

75

convert to money, and money convert to nice house, nice car, no worry, not much argument, even a holiday, happy family. So life happy, yes?

And in the early mornings when cussimas all gone to their terrible state house beat up wifes, make ruined children, drink more bad stuff, we who you call the Slits, we first prepare for tomorrow, then we count how much we take from you stupid terrible people, then we put in our secret place or we drop money in night bank deposit, then we walk out into night — oo, and very nice night too tonight — but not have to take Slit-eyes to heaven and dream bout nice things to come; we Chinese, we know from this high, heaven is what you make it. Right here on earth. Ah, Brown People, when you going to figure this?

So the parties raged, all over Pine Block they raged, man. And people, every man and woman jack ofem, they were thinking this must be life because it is life, you know . . . ? But yet something not quite equating. Ah, but who gives a fuck? Drink up and be happy. And if you wanna fight then go to it, bro. Might even join in it looks good.

And some wives screaming, or taking their beatings in pain-grunting silence. Or the sexual without feeling. Or hatingim for it. And thinking about life too: you know, how it was never gonna change, never gonna get better, it *can't* get better. Ya have to *want* it to get better first. You and your husband. Together. Maybe even your entire race.

Out in the car wrecks, or in backyard sheds, building-site sheds, under a bridge somefuckinwhere, huddled together (and some poor buggers alone) talking of their futures: Gonna be a big-time crim one day, man. Me, gonna be a Brown Fist. Nah, man, they suck, the Browns. Black Hawks, man, they the ones. And tats: Gonna get one right here, that muscle there you got it, bro. Yeow. A snake, eh. Curlin round a sword in flames. How bout you? A tiger. A tiger? With big fuckin *teeth*. Yah! Bite ya fuckin head off. Hey! Man, gonna rob me a bank one day. Know what I'm gonna do with the bread? Nah, man, tell me. Gonna buy a fishnchip shop so *I* don't never have to go hungry, and *you* and *all* our mates don't have to go hungry. Ever again. Aw, hey, bro: thas cool. Here, come and get under my blanket, it's warmer 'n yours.

Lyin there, looking up at the stars how neat they looked, about to say so but checkin emselves, no way, man. Might think I'm a wankah I start talking bout stars 'n sissy things like that.

76

Mr Telescope Man finally calling it a night: lovingly placing the cover over his precious instrument, zippering it closed. Standing there for a thoughtful moment. Smiling at himself, for the desire'd come over him to kiss the darn thing. Laughing. Derek, you're just lonely. And in his bed thinking, you know, of first a woman . . . in my arms, her warm sweet breath on me, her warmth her womanly warmth . . . ooh, darling! . . . beneath him, moaning her pleasure and he his, sighing, grunting, getting faster and faster and — Starburst. Then his thoughts returned to that Great Vastness out there; and too his marvel, at how it'd never lessened in intensity. Nor his curiosity. Thinking those unthinkable scales of distance and size, the mind-boggling enormity of it all — and how ridiculous that there should be a God ascribed to it all, let alone one with not only goodly intentions but who had to be worshipped or else he was meaningless. Not to mention vengeful. Just nonsense. Utter nonsense. Star stuff. That's all it is.

Then he thought of matter and of mattering things, grinning at the connection. But frowning when it next occurred to him: If one is blind, a sea-dweller, or a dweller in perpetual darkness, then what matter the stars? It bothered him. And he thought thus of those humans born to circumstances, social circumstances, into cultures who and which were blind to the Great Beyond. And it gave him a sense of loss, of almost a grieving. For them. The deprived. The ones with no choice; perhaps, even, no escape: you are what you are sort of thing. Then thank goodness for what I am, he said aloud before sleep came.

And his dreams were at peace with this world and that dream world. If but a little overly symbolic with his bachelor state, women in every possible dreamstate and usually naked. Ah, the lot of a man who finds that species impossible. Just impossible.

7

The Night's Last Act

. . . that house . . . that house (The Dream) Oh, not far to go now.
Glints of light, like horizontal knives slicing across her vision:
that'll be the other fence. Oh my God. Fearful and excited now.
Bladder suddenly full.

She stopped. Her breathing rapid. Wow, musta been flying.
She lifted the hem of her dress, went down in a squat; she pulled
her knickers to one side, wincing at the feel of pubic hair (belongs
to *me*?), still not sure about all this hormonal changes, turning
from one thing into another, changing and yet not changing; tried
to let it out in dignified little squirts but couldn't hold it. Ah well.
Let it flood from her, and ahhh, the relief. She shook herself,
swivelling on her heels, giggling. Like a boy shaking his thingy
dry. Ee, yuk, I don't ever want one a them inside me. I know Dad
does it to Mum, I've heardem. Uh-uh-uh, he goes. And her too,
sometimes. Like a coupla blimmin animals. Unless it's cos he's
hurting her.

Whew! I'm puffed alright. Heart beating like a jackhammer
in her chest with its budded breasts still growing. She stood.
Caught her breath, steadied the dizziness of standing from a
squat. Then she heard something amazing.

A piano. A piano? Out here? Took a little moment to sink in
where it was coming from. Now she was *really* scared: it was like
entering — trespassing — a totally different world. Neighbours,
huh? Just over the fence, eh. Yeah, another planet. She stood
listening. Adjusted to it after a while. Not altogether, but enough
to overcome the fear it created in her. So she moved on.

House looked huge up close and — Shit! She dropped to the
ground at the sight of people. Oh and what if they've got a guard
dog? Curled in a ball there in the grass waiting for some crazed
guard creature to rip her to bits for *daring* to bring her miserable
self onto their precious property. She waited for an age. And the
piano stopped registering. Took some time to come back. Must've

been me, my fear. She stood, eventually. No dogs? Listening. Heart pounding. The piano going tinkletinkle tatatata. Sweat turning cold on her. Just a tiny breeze. But everything starting to clear: my eyes, my hearing: I can see and hear so *clearly*.

Up at the sky the unbelievable cascade of the Milky Way. The formations that stood out, the Southern Cross, the Pot, the Bear, what she'd learned at school. I can hear every rustle on every leaf, over every blade of grass. What's happening to me? I can picture all the shapes the breeze must take to move around, over an obstacle, and how all those things combined must produce what we call the sound of the breeze. It's not the breeze, it's what's in the way. And she moved forward, cautiously, but with this strange confidence.

She came to the wire-strand fence, climbed through it. Easy, man. She came to a wall, she touched it, it was brick. About her lower chest height. She stood there (I feel reckless). And everything — *them* — those two standing listening to that one I can only see her hair, the big piano, even the quality of light, the brightness of *their* light they stood in, the lot as clear as day.

That piano: *huge*, man. Bigger'n even our school one in the assembly hall ole Mrs Tucker plays when we sing at assembly. It's black. Like me. And boy, is it shiny; and beautiful, somehow. The shape, or the shininess, I dunno, sumpthin. Big black and beautiful. (Well I ain't beautiful, but I'm black. Black as that sky up there. Well, not really, but I'm black even for a Maori. Hate it too. I *hate* it. Being black. Feeling out of it. And even my own, Maoris, callin me black. As if some of them can talk. My big brother (my hero) Nig, he's copper brown; he only got called Nig by some uncle of Dad's as a compliment. Man, some compliment.)

Looks like a coffin lid, that piano lid. No it doesn't. Just me being Miss Morbid again; that's what Mum calls me sometimes: Aee, Miss Morbid at it again. Can't help it. How I am. Can't run around laughing at everything when I don't find most of it funny. We have heaps of funerals in Pine Block, or people from Pine Block dying. Being killed, more like it; they don't die of old age in our area, or even sickness much. It's car crashes and fights and murders, and maybe accidents at work for those who got work. Have the funeral in their houses, most ofem, even though I know other Two Lakes Maoris they have it at their village, their pa where the person's from or his parents or even his ancestry is enough; a real traditional Maori send-off. But it's the old Lost Tribe bit with Pine Block: most ofem don't have no links with that

79

tribal stuff, that's why they have the body in the house for the couple of days the funeral lasts. Spooky too. The body lyin there in the coffin its face so cold and so *still* because even non-traditional Maoris they like to see what they're mourning over, or so I heard from someone. Classical. Is that classical the person's playing?

Grace smiled, shook her head: Classical. Glanced over her shoulder at the line-up of lights two-storey high, and thought of how these Tramberts might be fooled into thinking of them lights as homely, meaning warmth, family warmth and love, and all that stuff. Got news for you Tramberts if you do think that.

Over the brick wall, the coarseness like sandpaper brushing against her underthigh. On the other side the grass noticeably shorter under her bare feet. Mowed, of course. And now a trespasser. I could even be a burglar. Dogs . . . ? She cocked her ears her every senses. Didn't seem to be. But what about sheepdogs for his sheep? But then again they'd probably be tied up somewhere away from the house, Grace figuring. Or how'd the people be able to hear that piano with dogs yapping all night? Now reaching some kind of pitch, the piano sped up, yet not sped up. Oh I dunno bout this classical stuff.

The light from the room where the piano was fell in neat blocks onto the neat lawn. Real tidy. And the trees, the shadowy shapes ofem here and there in a girl's vision, to the side of her. The woman was tall. Oldish. Maybe Mum's age, maybe older. Yet she doesn't look older: something about her face. Lovely hair. So shiny. Good conditioner, no doubt. Mum *hates* me using her conditioner. Dad doesn't even know what it is. Think he uses soap for his hair. I know what it is: her face don't look like it's *ever* had a man's fist in it. Oh . . . ? *Ohh*, at the person playing the piano when she lifted her head. She can't be . . . she can't be any older than me! Grace astonished. Crushed. At the girl her ability. But mostly her confidence. God, to sit there and play that stuff with those two adults standing over you watching your every move. None of the Maori shyness for you, eh kiddo? No way, Hosay. Nope, you didn't inherit the ole Maori shyness neither. (Or have it thrust on you. Or catch it like some . . . like some *disease*. Oh, that's how I feel about shyness sometimes: it's a disease you catch off others. They make you like them. Or they try their damnedest to. See what these Trambert people try with their kids, eh?) Grace looking at the girl still playing and feeling more and more crushed. Massively deprived. Then she began noticing the surroundings of

80

that big room the three were in: furniture real nice, that old stuff, antiques, and paintings up on the walls, and vases with lovely flowers inem, and objects she did not recognise. And the curtains really bright with beautiful bursts of colour, of flowers, and sorta shiny, maybe silky, I dunno, I'm jussa black girl from over the way there. The state slum. And tears were in her heart. Then they were leaking from her eyes. And when she wiped at them it seemed to be a signal for em to just pour out. She couldn't help herself. Nor the sobs escaping from her when the girl ended her playing and stood up and the evident mother and father kissed her, gave her a little hug, and her smile so brilliant like on the toothpaste ads.

A girl felt more than crushed, she wanted to die.

Then her sobbing must've got away from her because the man (in the suit) rushed to the window. And Grace watched in horror at it flying open, her vision filled with the man, hearing, too: Who's there? Grace turning. Grace fleeing. Grace hitting some unmovable object in that now coal-black night. The force tremendous. The blackness darkening. The voice from afar and yet yelling at her. Like in a dream . . .

Running again. Running and running. No memory. Only instinct. Though partway in her fleeing something returned of her thoughts, her awareness. For she heard another strickened sound . . . lots and lots of running feet . . . ? She ran faster, yet she still could hear it. Wondered if she was going mad or had already reached that state. Diving over the fence into her own backyard. Up and running. *Stop! Stop!* a voice in her head telling her, you must stop now, very important. So she stopped.

Her lungs were bursting. And that damn sobbing was trying to come out at the same time. And I think I must be bleeding; she touched her forehead. Yep. Musta run into that damn brick wall. Felt the area again, pain indicating it could be deep. Sounds of a party going on inside, and anyway she could see it: kitchen full ofem. Dad and his mates. Laughter. Someone trying to get em singing. Voices loud and aggressive in that man manner. Have to go round the front door. Decided she'd sit outside a bit, wait for the bleeding to stop, clean herself up by the outside tap and go in through the kitchen, because the front door might be locked, or she might run into her father using the toilet just at that time, and if there was one thing he hated was a sneaky kid. Even just thinking the kid might be sneaky. (He thinks we're all out to get him. To spy on him so we can go and tell lies on him. But to who?

Mum? Why'd he worry about Mum? He beats her every month. Oh, I dunno.)

The stars again while she sat in the long grass; and in between them she observed the kitchen of her own house. The contrast. It didn't seem possible. From grand piano to this. Even *God* wouldn't believe it. And of course she wondered where she stood in all this, this human scheme of things.

Entering the front door, through the wash-house, into the kitchen (wow!) to a blast of sound. And smoke. And the smell of beer: in the bottle, in the glass, in the air from a thousand taken mouthfuls and a thousand breaths. Heyyy! A croaky-voiced man calling at the sight of her. It's Grace. Hi, Bully. Come an giz your Uncle Bully a hug, girl. Grace first glancing at her father sat in his corner at the table, no signal from him either way. Not welcome either. So she went over to her father's friend, gave her false uncle a hug, at the same time creating a babble of hellos and fairly complimentary comments on her prettiness, her good figure (if they weren't all so drunk) and a pat on the bottom from one ofem. Then Jake asking what'd happened to her head. Oh, I fell over. He looking at her with suspicion (and is it hate?) she back at him not knowing what her face was reflecting, but hoping it wouldn't get him wild. Where? Outside. On the footpath. Running too fast. Who from? The *cops*, who else? Bully came laughingly in and that set the others off. Except Jake. You sure wasn't someone hit you? And Grace wanting — dying — to know what if someone had? (Would you rush to my defence, Daddy?) Not minding if he did, and to hell with the violence. (I just want to know I'm loved.) No, Dad. Giving him a little (crawling) smile: who'd dare hit a Heke? Now *that* madeim crack a little smile. And his mates going, Yeow! Ain't no one'd mess with one a Jake Heke's own. Even the fuckin Brown Fists. We saw it, eh Dool? With our own fuckin eyes we saw this bastard standin up to em on his fuckin jacksy. Wasn't on his own, man, I was right there. Me too . . . And Grace was quite forgotten as the men started up something that must've happened between her father and the Brown Fists. And Grace thinking: Oo, Dad. Even you shouldn't mess with them. Goodnight. Slipping away. No one acknowledging her going, probably wouldn't even remember she'd been in the room come morning. Too interested in their fight-talk, tough-talk, man-talk; it's their love talk. Upstairs.

She checked the wound in the bathroom mirror. Not as bad as I thought. The relief of not being caught, actually nabbed, by none other than Mr Trambert. Knees hurt, both ofem. Scraped. Musta been that brick wall alright. Wonder what happened to me back there? Grace couldn't figure. Not like me to bawl just at something like that; so what the girl is about my age can play the fuckin piano? Who cares. I don't lie awake at nights wishing I could play the piano. Never even thought about stinkin pianos till I happened to be where I shouldn't and saw her. (Yet I'm still jealous.)

Past Mum and Dad's room and even with the door closed Grace could hear her mother's snoring: that fag-choked in and out breathing always threatening to die on the in. Uh-uhuh-urrghhh! (God, Mum, you're meant to be a lady.) Some lady, huh. How *could* she be in Pine Block?

Grace off to bed. Check the kids first. Spose they been wondering where I was; they got so used to me being their second mother, poor little buggers, or fuckers, as some in our world callem. Fuckers . . . Who but a Pine Blocker'd call their own kids fuckers? Huata fast asleep. Looking at the baby of the family, so sweet when he was asleep and pretty good awake too. Over to Poll's top bunk: her and her doll, Sweetie, out like lights, snuggled up together as usual. G'night, Poll. Grace imagining giving her sister a peck.

Starting to undress, remembering the door, and then the curtains, you never knew who might be spyin on ya out there. Giggling to herself. It starting to occur what she'd done. Wow, I got a look at how the other half lives tonight. Remembering her reaction, the sobbing. Stripping naked, getting her nightie from under her pillow, catching a glance of her changing physical state, of hair growth down there and the view of it increasingly blocked by the twin growths above. A woman, eh? Won't be long and I'll be a woman. Feeling scared at that thought: a sense of loss. And yes, sorrow. (I don't wanna change. I don't wanna grow old.) Into bed.

. . . 'm I dreaming . . . ? Must be. Grace could smell beer in the dream; beer breath. And fags. And there were all these men standing about drinking and smoking and talking how they do in real life — but she felt something on her leg. A touch. Then the cool of the blankets being off. Dizzy with sleep. Then this voice going, *Shhhhhh*. And the hand it was stroking her leg. (This is no dream.) Oh God, what do I do?! And totally dark. The curtains

83

across. Door closed. And a girl in her head realising: I think I'm being, uh, molested. Then everything turning hazy, and yet clear: I can figure out what's happening, but I can't work out why. I'm confused and yet I'm not. I'm scared and yet I'm scared for him too, this person doing this. This man. (What if it's my father? What if it's not and my father comes in? What if he thinks it's me doing it too?) So lying there. Not sure if she was rigid stiff or the opposite, playing dead.

The hand was probing at her thing. The beer stink rose up in wafts to Grace's sense of smell. And something else. Very distinctive, despite that stench of stale beer and fags. *Open a lil bit*, the voice whispering. (Is it Dad?) Not knowing if she obeyed. Hearing an, Ahhh. Can't tell who it is, only that it's a man. Shall I call out? I know, I'll scream. But what if Dad's gone somewhere else, to another party, and this is someone left behind? Maybe he's gonna murder — Grace couldn't even complete the thought. Squeezed her eyes shut.

Finger fiddled with her most private part. And a hoarse voice whispered, ya like that, doncha? (Oh God. Oh God.)

(I know: I'll think of something else quite different. That's what the booklet at school said if it was happening and we couldn't stop it.) But then Grace not sure if she'd read that particular advice or one of her (few) friends'd told her. The man grunting. Quiet as anything, but grunting. Everything so quiet. It's stopped, the party downstairs's stopped. Only the breathing grunting of this person, and his fingers touching her with seemingly urgency. Hurting. Rubbing her hair down there. Grunting. Saying shhhhhh, without emphasis this time. So quiet. And another funny smell.

. . . *mmmmm!* through her clenched teeth at the intrusion — the pain of something inside her. Working its way in. Roughly. The breathing quite loud now. (Oh God . . .) — *mmmmmmm!!* once more at the probing really penetrating. The man panting now. And Grace thinking: Think of something else . . . think of something else . . . I know, think of them, the Tram — no! Not them. Hurts too much. Them and this man what he's doing to me.

Mum? She could hear the faint muffled sound of her mother's distinctive snoring. *Mum!* in her mind, thinking of mental telepathy, communication between mothers and daughters in trouble without screams or words. Just come, Mum. Oh please come. But not daring to scream in case.

The night lasting on and on and on, and Oh God, it *hurts* so.

84

And (why — *why* — is he doing this? What've I done to him?)
And the man breathing his rotten fumes all over her, his whiskers
harsh on her face, going: mmmmm, as he kissed her. And she
lying there with lips shut tight but not daring to twist away, or
even indicate she was awake. And that smell stronger. And kind
of knowing what it was . . . that it was somehow self-familiar,
something sexual, an off-giving, except this sensed as somehow
corrupted. By him. This man. Raping her. She wanted to vomit.

Out on the street. Seems so long. Parties going. What time is it?
A car growling into her hearing, and coming to a deep rumbling
halt alongside her. A voice: Hey! Whatcha up to, darl? Laughter.
Then another voice: Hey, man, let's split. It's one a Jake's kids. Oh
wow. And the car gunning off into that streetlamp-lit night. A girl
crying. With hurt and physical pain, and love (or thinking it was
love) at her father's dreaded rep getting her out of (another) sticky
situation. Moving on. I know where I'm going.
   A dog barking. A big moon right there. It'd moved. Gat going
nearby; where all the lights are on. A lot of houses in darkness. But
a lot still lit up with noising life. Car-wreck outlines on darkened
lawns. Car-wreck bodies clear in pools of light from partying
kitchens, partying sitting rooms, partying open front doors spilling
a kind of lonely light onto em. Grace knowing which wreck she
wanted. That one, the one with the bonnet all alight from the
half-open front door.
   Toot? You there, Toot? Waiting. The gat going full bore in
there where Toot's pisshead mum and dad lived and Toots wasn't
allowed because, well, they didn't like him, too cheeky, sumpthin
about him, they dunno, juss that every time they look atim they
get wild. So Toot, he knows when he's not wanted, so he made
the car wreck home. Why, sometimes you could see his parents
come home from the pub, carrying crates of beer, staggering up
their footpath having to go pastim, up to their front door, opening
it, bringing light upon their own son's cobwebbed miserable car-
home: and not so much as a kiss my arse, nuthin.
   Toot? It's Grace. Wake up. Wake up.
   In there withim. Oh Toots. (My just about one and only
friend.) Whassa madda, Grace? Oh Toots. Here. Come and get
under the blanket. (So nice in here. And warming.) And me and
Toots, just us against this rotten fuckin world. Got anything to do,
Toots? Wha', glue or that? Anything. No glue left, Grace. Grace,

you don't do glue? Do ya? I might. Nah, Grace, it's no good. Stay
away from it. Well, you do it. Nah, it sucks, Grace. Honest. So
why do you do it? I'm, uh . . . I'm different. Oh Toot. Well, I
ain't got none left. Whassa madda anyway, your olds been at it
again? Yeah, sumpthin like that. And staring into the semi-gloom
and the silence and that funny sumpthin that only they could feel
because they were, well, you know how it is, kids get to know each
other. Specially sad ones.

Cunts, aren't they? Yeah. Who needs parents, Grace? No one,
Toot. Fuckem. Yeah, thas what I say: fuckem. That silence again:
their own world. This is ours, this is us, ya can't take this little bit
from us. And Grace feeling something sorta dribbling out of her,
like her period or sumpthin, except she'd had that only about a
week ago. Hey! Whatcha doin'? Sorry, Toot. Holdin hands . . .
We're *mates*. Know that, Toot. I juss felt like, you know — Sorry.
Aw, nemine saying sorry. Wha', you wanna hold hands? Nah. Not
now. C'mon, I don't mind. Yes ya do. Don't. Ya do. Grace . . .
Well, you pulled away from me like I got some disease or sumpthin. Well you ain't. Here. Now hold it. Toot taking her hand,
squeezing it. Grace feeling the warmth travel right up her arm,
spread into her chest, go down into her tummy, down her legs,
back up her spine. And finish in her head, somewhere deep down
and satisfying in her head.

Toots . . . Wha'? I told you sumpthin, would you — Nah, G,
ya know I wouldn't. Who've I got to tell anyrate? Promise? I
promise. Wha', ya been stealing? Toot chuckling away beside her,
she unable to see his face because he was right back in the seat,
legs up over the front and covered to his chin with the blanket.
Not stealing, Toot. You know I don't steal. So whassa big secret?
Well, I . . . I, uh, I . . .

And inside, hardly a stone's throw from the car wreck, a party
that'd been raging began to break up. To fuck up. People, they
were starting to argue. Dunno why. No one did. Only that it was
one of those things they accepted. The dream — nah, not the
fuckin dream, man. We don't call things dreams, only winning
Lotto, and before that it was the Golden Kiwi. The party is over.
That's what, and that's all it is: party's over. Same place, same
time, next week.

8
The Visit

Beth was so happy. Oh, I haven't been like this in God knows how long. Proud of herself too, for not drinking in thirteen weeks. Not even a sneaky drop. Smilin to herself, And look what it got, feeling tingly all over as she did a last-minute check in the bathroom mirror — Yeah, yeah, yeah, at the car horn tooting on the street below. I'm coming. As she fussed at her shoulder-length hair all done up, thirty flippin bucks it cost. But worth it, I guess, but not quite sure of herself; feeling a bit self-conscious, a standout, as if people'd think she was trying to be up herself. And I ain't; just wanna look good for my boy, that's all. No make-up, other than lipstick, and even then she wasn't sure if the colour suited her coppery complexion. People said she didn't need make-up, had good smooth skin (if ya don't mind the scars from a hundred hidings, that is. Oh, but even that was alright. Today it was.) and besides, Maori women don't hardly suit make-up, dunno why, but they don't. Scarlet lipstick? Smacking her lips. They'll have to do.

She smiled at herself: Ahh, good teeth, even with all those years of smoking, I got good teeth. Look after em, that's why. Mind you, front one left side is capped. From who else's fists? ACC, they paid for it. Otherwise they've stood up to everything he could throw — Oh, don't be thinking of morbid things, Beth Heke, you're sounding like your daughter, Miss Morbid Grace. Off I go.

Out to a glorious day you wouldn't believe, not for winter almost started; no clouds up there, no breeze (to muss up a woman's flash hairdo) just glorious warmth. Jake tapping his fingers on the steering wheel to a pop number playing on the car radio. The rental car radio. Look atim, you'd think he owned the blimmin thing, Beth getting in beside her husband, smiling to herself. Clicking her tongue, Where's the volume control? Too damn loud. Making out she was still the same old Beth, flash rental or not. And pretending to be confused: All these damn gadgets everywhere. You worked em out, Jake? Looking at him, and he was acting up himself, real casual like: Yeah, sure. Piece a cake. Doing a fancy flick of the volume and the tone controls. And Beth thinking, This is gonna be one beautiful day. Calling to em at the back, You all okay there? in a cheery tone. And them answering, Yeow, Mum! This is *choice*. Though Beth didn't hear Grace's voice in that lot. Only Abe, Hu and Poll. Kid'd been even quieter than normal lately, Beth couldn't figure it out other than putting it down to teenage stuff. Growing up. And hormones and that. Thinking that Grace better not go and spoil this day. No one'd better. Let's go, she smiled at her husband and he back at her in his gruff way, but not so that she missed seeing the happiness in his eyes.

Food in the boot. Heaps of it. Ah, what you can buy when you got the dough. The way life sorta opens up when you haven't the booze or gambling on card games to worry about. The *surplus* that builds up, Beth was staggered to discover of her abstinence.

Whole rotisserie-cooked chicken from the supermarket deli (Jake not knowing what a deli was, let alone a rotisserie-cooked chicken. Beth laughing atim, Man, where you been? But in the good spirit that'd been ruling the house ever since she told everyone of her plans.) and a whole lot more food besides. For our Boogie, who they got under welfare authority care over in Riverton. Riverton Boys Home, that's where we're headed for the day, O Heke family. With the exception of Nig; he wasn't hardly ever around these days. I got roast pork in slices, cooked silverside, a heap a boiled eggs, you name it. Even cheeses. And Jake saying none a that fuckin cheese for him, no way. It's Pakeha food. I ain't eatin Pakeha food. Beth not bothering to tell him that most everything they ate was food introduced by the dreaded white man Pakeha Jake seemed always to have not far from his mind. I got salami. Salam-what? Sal-arm-ee. Huh? Having to explain to Jake what it was, in terms he'd understand not get anti: sausage, it's only a fancy name for cooked sausage. Oh, and a few spices thrown in. Cured sausage. Cured of what — disease? Jake'd joked. Hahaha, very funny, Jake Heke. Had to check herself: she'd nearly called him dear. We can't have that; not as though all of a sudden I got an angel on my hands. (Yet when he'd smiled down at her from his magnificent height, Beth'd felt the power of his physique, his great fighting physique, coming off him like rays. Made her feel slightly weak with . . . well, desire, she sposed, but having to act tough, asking him: And what's that smile for?)

Now, I'm sat in a nice car, my husband at my side for once acting like one, my kids in the back, or four out of six, and the fifth coming up, with a boot fulla picnic food and even a purse with a few bob for extras. What more could a Pine Block mother want?

People they knew did double-takes, they waved, winked, frowned, stared with naked jealousy at the sight of the big Ford Falcon rental cruising so slow down Rimu Street they may as well be walking. With Jake playing the part to the full: half-lidded eye-balls, arm out the window, bent at the elbow, fingers only lifting in cool greeting to a face he knew; or he'd give a wink here, a chuckle there, hit the horn when it was one of his mates, or hit it harder at those he hated. You'd think he'd just won the Lotto. But Beth enjoying it too, don't worry bout that. Go down Alligator Street, Beth instructing (meaning Matai but so named because it was a kids' myth that an alligator lived in the stormwater pipes there). Show off to Maggie. Beth's sister. The one she hardly saw except at the card schools Mag ran every Thursday and now was accusing Beth of being up to something why she wasn't coming to her card games anymore. But Beth realising, with her abstaining, that her sister had all along measured Beth's worth in how much she lost at Mag's card schools. Fucker. Look at me now.

Want me to stop? Jake at Maggie's house. But Beth seeing her sister's car wasn't there (the car that's been too good to come pick me, her own sister, up in take me shopping, save her sister a cab fare and luggin all them bags with her.) Fucker. Oi, the language, Jake laughingly got back on Beth for earlier chiding him for his language, telling him to try just for today to, you know, act nice (civilised). She smiled at him (oh Jake); it was all she could do to stop herself reaching out and stroking him . . . his, you know, his thingy. Hasn't touched me in weeks. (Maybe he's got a bit on the side.)

Alright back there, kids? Mum, you asked that about three powerpoles back, Abe telling her. Alright, alright, only makin sure. Poll, you okay? Yes, Mum. Hu? Choice, Mum. (Grace? Why is she so quiet this last few weeks?) Grace? Grace . . . ? But no answer. Answer ya mother, girl. Jake growling. And Beth regret-ting singling Grace out. Forget it, forget it. (I'm not having this day spoiled.)

Jake driving all over Pine Block, playing it to the full. And laugh? Never heard him laugh so much. But then they came within directional sight of the Brown Fist headquarters (They'd been given a complete two-family double unit for their own use by the Housing Corporation, and rumour said they didn't pay any rent because the government agency was too afraid to send someone to collect it.) and who should be standing outside the high iron-clad walls, none other than Nig. Made a mother's heart fall. And she shot a look at Jake: he'd seen Nig alright. Jake had a smoke in his big left hand as quick as lightning, drawing at it the way he does when he's trying to hide his anger. (Oh please, don't let's get off on the wrong foot.) Then the little ones crying out, There's Nig! didn't help. Beth feeling the car slow.

Jake . . . ? looking at him. Jake, please don't . . . Her pleading tone surprising herself, she was no crawler, she was no anything weak, refusing to eat humble pie on account of even him, Jake the Muss. Except today. (I tried too hard, I've wanted too much for this day to spoil it with my stupid damn pride.) And Jake flashing a look at her, then back out the window at the tall figure of their seventeen-year-old messing about with a couple of other Brown Fist prospects, not even giving them even an accidental glance. Jake said nothing. Just turned the wheel to get them out of Pine Block and drew hard on his fag. (Thank God for that.) Beth loving her man just that little bit more for showing surprising restraint. And she knew, within her bones, that this was gonna turn out a very nice day. Smiling at him (I can just tell).

Past the vacant land and Jake saying whyn't we take a cruise round, and everyone in agreement, why not? long as they got to see Boogie sometime. This flash car a sorta corruption ofem all. Though Beth shot constant weather-check glances at Jake, wondering and praying he'd stay as he was. And she called again to her kids: Ya lookin forward to all that grub, kids? Was able to pick out the yays, with Grace's the missing prominent. And a little bit troubling. Turning to Jake: Say, salami, Jake. Grinning atim. No way, sista. G'won, say it. Giggling atim, and the kids with their half-suspended giggles ready to go either way depending on their father's subsequent reaction. Slami, Jake shot out in a mumble. What was that? Beth cupping her ear. A good sign of a chuckle from Jake. Again: Slarmi. Slarmi, eh? Well, whatever, cos I ain't gonna be eating it, no way. Jake with a grin, that laugh of his starting to bubble up from him like a spring just started. So everyone (even Grace) rising up with him, like a little orchestra of laughers or sumpthin. And the rest of residential town going by out the windows.

90

Now the whole car rocking with laughter at Jake turning the tables on Beth, getting her to say, writing; because Mum's r's more like w's, and so Dad teasing her with: Witing? witing to who? or you mean waiting? She means waiting, kids! Laughing. Laughter rocking the car. Rocking it. (Ah, but I never been so happy.)

Nothing down Taniwha Street on a Saturday morning other than a few window-shoppers; couples, lone ones, and a drunk staggering down main street from no doubt a party. A Maori. And Jake yelling out: Hey, bro! Go getta rental! So laughter again filling the nicely upholstered world. More when the fulla stopped and gave em the fingers and Jake just laughing and not doing anything, like stopping and punching the fulla.

Past a young couple obviously in love, and Jake saying: Ah, to be young an frisky again, eh dear? Taking Beth by complete surprise, specially the dear bit at the end. (I feel like —) but nope, she wasn't risking it: not even a touch on his leg. He doesn't like a woman starting things, even hinting. It don't matter, anyrate; I'm happy as can be. (What's sexual satisfaction got to do with it?)

Down main street, cruisin, cruisin . . . no shops open, not till the first of the Chinese takeaways, a big late-model car parked outside, a whole pack ofem busying away inside the shop. Same at the second Chinese. Bringing a comment from Jake: Them fuckin Chinks, man, they live for work. And sounds of disgust from everyone.

Down at the lake, getting out, taking a walk; kicking at autumn leaves, looking at the unruffled waters of the lake, and Abe wondering aloud if their Maori ancestors'd had any big rumbles out on those waters, in canoes, them fuckin big carved jobs, Jake saying, Yeah. Sure they did. Your ancestors, boy, they were fighters. Grinning at Abe, face suggesting the fighter was still present in some ofem (us — me, Jake the Muss). And Abe going, Aw, Dad, and giving his father an Ali shuffle, dukes raised. And Jake winding up a Bolo punch special, a Sugar Ray Leonard special, with his left going round and round winding up then shooting out with a straight right instead. The two falling over emselves with laughter. And a mother and a wife wondering if Jake wasn't in some state, maybe he's started smoking this dope stuff. Because never had she seen Jake like this. Not in sixteen years. Well, maybe fourteen of the married sixteen years. Oh well, enjoy it while it's there, Beth shrugged.

Jake calling out to Grace: Hey, not too far, not too far from our car. With a half-grin, Someone might steal it. Kick a few more ole leaves, imagine your ancestors of old when they were racing their great war canoes across them waters, armed to the teeth, mad as anything with the fury of war, and doing battle with the enemy. Then Jake suggesting the best residential area in town, Ainsbury Heights, as next visit.

But who knew where to go? Ainsbury Heights was just this thing in their heads, a name given to an area where posh people lived. But the actual getting there was another story. Grace piped up: I know. And everyone lookin at her, specially him, her father; Jake twisting round and lookin at her. How come you know, madam? Grace shrugging, cos I've been up there. Added, obviously. And the word immediately echoed several times sarcastically by others in the car: Ob-vee-us-lee. When? Jake demanding. Oh, a few times. After school. How'd you get there? Not far to walk, Dad. Ain't it? Dad, it's Two Lakes we live in, not Auckland. And Jake missing her point: So when've *you* been to Auckland? I haven't, Dad. Well you said — I only said it's Two Lakes. Two Lakes is very small, Dad. So it's not hard to find your way around. And Jake looking at his wife, shaking his head: She's pretty smart for a thirteen-year-old, isn't she? What'd a Pine Block kid want up at this Ainsbury Heights anyway? Jake unable to figure. Same as you, Dad, Grace coming back with — To gawk. And the others smiling nervously. And Jake unsure of where he'd go, but opting to laugh. So all ofem following suit, sweet suit. Day still alive. With hope. Even promise.

Grace directing her father to Ainsbury Heights.

Hey, where's all the houses? Jake to everyone in joking tone. I c'n only see trees. Nuthin but trees. At the prevalence of long-established trees fronting each and every property they were slowly driving past, and one side with an elevated view of the township, the glistening silver of lake, the green hills beyond. And snatches of big houses through the almost leafless trees. And Jake saying, Man, those aren't houses, they're fuckin mansions. His voice shot with envy, and perhaps hatred too. So Beth countering: Well, I don't think they're all that hot. Thought they'd be newer than this. Some ofem look like they're half fallin down. But Jake: Only thing fallin down, woman, is you. Giving her a nasty look. So Beth not willing to push it, afraid she'd bring it right out his old hatred, resentment of anything had white skin, had a job, owned a house, had a car.

Time we were heading to Riverton anyway. But not Jake. Hold on, hold on . . . staring all over, out his window, out front, out Beth's side. We'll be late, Jake. Says who? We got all morning yet. Beth sighing. (Letim be. He wants to go off the deep end at these people up here having plenty and us having nuthin, letim. Juss as long as he gets it out ofim and we can get back to being one big happy family.)

Then from Grace right behind Beth: Oh man . . . to live up here, eh. Beth snapping at Grace to be grateful for what you got. Grace asking, And what would that be? (Never known her so cheeky. It *must* be growing troubles.) Jake adding his weight to Grace's argument: Yeah, you tell me what we got to be grateful for? Jake, turn this car round and let's do what we sposed to — visit our son. It's been over three months. Don't even know what we're doing up here in the first damn place. Beth getting irritated. Fretful that it was all going out the damn window.

Jake kept driving; slow hugging the kerb, eyes going up every driveway, and muttering from him about how many fuckin cars did these greedy honky shits want, about a Jag costing, he heard, a hundred fuckin grand and yet here were they with not one lousy hundred between em. Let alone times a grand. And Beth biting her tongue. And the kids quiet and knowing in the back.

Jake stopping the car. Looking at Beth. Back out his window. Big mits coming up off the steering wheel in question. But only, Man . . . coming out. Shaking his head. Sick. He looked sick. Hands rising again, The bread, Beth. Where do these white shits get the bread from? Looking pained now. And pointing up the driveway out Beth's side: Three cars. *Three.* How do we know it's not just visitors they got, Jake Heke? But Jake refusing to entertain that idea. Nope, it'll be their own cars. I just know it. Three fuckin motors, Beth, and here's us, this dumbarse Maori family from Pine Block, with nuthin. A fuckin *borrowed* rental, thas all. And tomorrow, Beth? It goes back tomorrow. And then what we got? Aw, Dad. Abe from the back. No big deal havin a car. Oh, ain't it? Jake swinging angrily in his seat, Beth catching those eyes flashing murder. And his confusion. (Oh Jake, it's not just the car and cars, is it? It's more. If I'd've thought you were gonna be a better man, a happier man if only you had a car, I'd've worked my butt off till we got the bread to buy it. Swear I would. But it's something else; maybe it's us, Maoris, our whole damn race, we're just a bit lost when it comes to this money thing, how to get things, how to go about borrowing the bread, mortgages and that, to get them. Maybe us Maoris got caught with our pants down and it's just taking a while to gettem back up again, I dunno.) Beth rubbing her forehead, closing her eyes. (And maybe you, Jake Heke, maybe you're just another of the wild ones, the Maori wild ones, who can see things not equal, not balanced, that you can't put into words and so you do the only thing you can do — strike out. Swear and curse and get furious at not being able to do a damn thing to catch up. Maybe you just want some of their material action — why you started off so happy with this rental — to just have a *taste* of what it's like not to have to live from hand to mouth, from one government benefit day to the next. Poor Jake: this rental car fooled you, didn't it? Had you feeling like you kinda owned it. And now, like the kid you really are, you realise it has to go back tomorrow. Your dream's been spoiled.) But what could a woman do? say?

Finally Jake restarted the engine. Let's get outta here before I see one a these white shits and punchim. And they drove out of the tree-studded street.

(Surprise, sweet surprise) at Jake eventually breaking out in a chuckle and saying, Who'd want a big house like that anyway? Ya'd spend half ya fuckin life mowing the lawns and pickin up leaves. Eh kids? Laughing. It echoing back. (Thank goodness.) And we all know it wouldn't be your old man pickin em up, mowing the lawns, eh kids? Aw, Dad! Going along with his act, like the experienced little actors they were where their father was concerned. Then they were heading north to Riverton, the sign saying it was left turn 500 m on, and Beth wondering when Jake was gonna slow to make the turn. Jake . . . ? at him going straight past the turnoff. The car smokey with Jake lighting up yet another fag, even Beth not matching his puff rate. He's upset still. So where you taking us? Around the lake. Jake, come on. We got the morning, woman. Then we c'n spend all afternoon with Boog. Eat up all that grub you got. Slarmi, and rotiss-a-sumpthin chook. Eh kids? Chuckling. Cleverly bringing em in. Okay, okay, Beth sitting back. May as well enjoy havin a car while we can. It occurring to her that they'd soon be going past the village she'd been raised in, Wainui pa. Haven't been back since Mum's funeral. That was, what, four — no, five — years ago. Dad's the year before that; and everyone saying Mum, poor Raita, had died of a broken heart, that she'd given up because life without her man, Bunny (Kupa) Ransfield, wasn't worth living. Except Beth knew it wasn't the truth. Mum died of cancer. Lung cancer. From

94

smoking these things, Beth looking frowningly at her cigarette before her body had her sucking at it for what it offered. And love, thinking about love between a husband and wife, and how her father never showed his love to Mum because he was of that school of being gruff, tough, manly — *manly* — and happier when he was around his mates, drinking with them, laughing and talking their men talk, and drinking. Beth further realising that drink played a big part in all their lives; her parents', her husband's, her friends', herself (till three months ago), everyone she knew. Shaking her head at that, thinking it was such a shame and a terrible waste what drink did. And then they were slowing for her pa, as she knew Jake would. Smiling at her.

It's changed, Beth at the old dirt road leading off this main, now sealed. Jake saying, Ya reckon? Looksa same to me. But he wouldn't know; every time he'd been here he was drunk. And bits of the meeting house, the wharenui, its carved gables visible through the skeleton trees. Houses — and new, some of them — off to the sides of the big main community building, and not traditional but modern. Beth thinking that maybe the 1980s had finally reached her home village. Feeling nostalgia growing.

The lake there, a sliver of it beyond where a girl'd swam, played by, the usual things. Well, well, well, eh. Beth clicking her tongue. Never thought I'd be here today (or many other days, for that matter; maybe a funeral here and there as the old ones dropped off). Sighing, and hearing it emerge laden with emotion which had her thinking maybe it was her period coming on or maybe this day was too much for a hardened Pine Block house-wife, wife of Jake Heke, to expect. Beth informing her kids to their questions of why they'd stopped, the younger ones, that it was where she grew up. And your relations, some ofem, live in there. Looking at her kids for their reactions, three of them showing genuine interest, the fourth, Grace, not giving one thing of what she might be thinking, and Beth getting more and more pissed off with this quiet, still waters running deep attitude of her daughter's, it'd gone on too damn long. But checking herself despite that. The day. Can't spoil the day. Then Jake coming in: Relations. Thas all every Maori thinks about. Relations. Ya meet someone in the pub (of course the pub, Jake Heke, where else?) and the first thing he asks is: Whas your name? Then: A Heke, eh? Oh, you muss be related to so-and-so. And ya try and tellem you're not, they don't wanna know. Juss wanna shake ya hand: Here, put it here, cuz. You and me are related. Then they ask who your old man is, ya mother, ya fuckin grandparents, every fuckin person ya know. But who cares about who ya related to? I sure fuckin don't. It don't buy ya three fuckin cars and a big flash house, does it? Jake gunning the engine, taking them away from here. With his legendary farewell, Fuckem, to the fast-fading stopover in the windscreen mirror.

Now Beth getting testy: Jake, let's head off to Ri — Fuck Riverton. I tole you, we got all morning. Only takes half an hour to drive right round, Dooly told me. Anyrate, Boog's probably been let off whatever shit jobs they getem doin in these joints with us coming to visit. Means he'll get off a bit longer, was Jake's very own logic.

Hey kids. Know what I inherited as a Maori? Jake asking out of the blue, as sheep and cattle countryside sped by on one side, the lake in bits between trees the other. A freshly lit fag in his big left mit. Slaves. (Oh?) Taking the big motor around a hard bend as casual as could be, right driving elbow out the window, big fingertips just controlling the wheel, and a wife thinking her husband, for all these years of being carless, could sure drive. Wonder he'd even had a licence when she went to hire the car, but he did and it was up to date. My family were slaves. Beth waited for the joke. Aw, Dad. It's true. What you mean, slaves? Slaves. Like I said, kids; slaves. Ya haven't hearda slaves? And everyone gone quiet. My branch of the Heke line was descended from a slave. A fulla taken prisoner by the enemy when he shoulda — he *woulda* — been better off dyin. In the fight. Beth hearing the rustle of the kids coming forward in their seat.

Yep. Slave he was, this ancestor of mine. And Beth getting worried by Jake's tone.

When I was a kid — me and my brothers and sisters — we weren't allowed to play with many other families in our pa. No way, not the Hekes, man. Don't play with them, you'll get the slave disease. Thas what they used to say. Jake drawing on his fag, inhaling deeply, blowing out a jet stream of smoke. And Beth in total confusion, wonderment: I ain't ever heardim mention this before. See, kids, to be a warrior and get captured in battle was the pits. Just the pits, eh. Better to die. So us Hekes — *innocent* — having to cop the shit from being descended from this weakling arsehole of an ancestor. Jeez . . . Shaking his head, and everyone able to hear his teeth grating together. Five hundred years, that's

96

what they used to tell us Heke kids. Five hundred years of the slave
curse bein on our heads. Teeth clacking together, jaw muscles
pulsing out and in. (You never *told* me, Jake. You never told me
. . .) As for the kids related to the chief: if we went within a
hundred fuckin yards ofem they'd be throwin stones, yelling and
screaming at us to get away, go home, you Hekes're juss a packa
fuckin slaves. Ooooo! Jake letting out a kind of growl yet sounding
half like a moan. (Of hurt, my husband? Oh, poor Jake. I never
dreamed . . .) Bullying us. Picking on us. Hitting us. Beating us
up — Dad! No! Abe in outburst. How *come*? How come what,
son? How come you got beaten by them? Only when I was little,
boy. Jake chuckling grimly. Not when I got to about your age. No
fuckin way. Eh son? No fu — no way, Dad. And Beth telling Abe,
Lucky for you, boy. And Jake going, Aw, Mum. It's only a word.
We all use it. Even the Maori's got it in his language: whaka —
whatever. It comes natural to us. Maybe so, Jake Heke, but I ain't
having it come natural to no kid a mine till they're old enough.
And that's final. Poll saying, Dad, but you're not a slave now eh?
Nah, girl. Do I look like one? And the three of them: No way!
Their laughter with an edge. (Poor little fuckers: only defending
their father, the family name. And who blames them? Oh, but I
wish a man'd told me; mighta been able to, you know, help in
some way. Or at least understand him better. Oh but maybe he's
tricking us.) Though a look at Jake told Beth no such thing.

So that's *your* family history on your father's side, kids. So Beth
informing them all: Slaves, kids. Us Maoris used to practise slavery
just like them poor Negroes had to endure in America. Surprised
at the passion, the emotion in her voice. Yet to read the
newspapers, on the TV every damn day, you'd think we're
descended from a packa angels, and it's the Pakeha who's the
devil. Clicking her tongue: Just shows, we're all good, and we're
all bad. Thinking, Slaves . . . (How dare they bring my husband
up believing he was a slave.)

Then it felt like an electric shock had hit her. It went racing
up her arm from her fingers, into her tummy (where all my little
ones got carried, seeded by this man, *my* man) and tears just
sprang from her eyes. At Jake's fingers warm on hers.

The road followed the lake all the way, in a big circle. The kids
chattering away. Their father coming in with the occasional crack
that had them all in stitches, even when it wasn't so funny. And

teasing each other about I ain't being no slave to *no* one, to their
father urging them on, You got it, kids. Don't let no bastard treat
ya like a slave. Then he was telling them stories of his childhood,
of growing up in a small forest settlement way out in the
wopwops, but very traditional in their ways. Why the Hekes were
treated like shit, I spose. So all us Hekes — even my cousins and
uncles and that — all sorta shunted into this one ole shack
because, well, you know how people are when they're being you
know, singled out, they stick together. Jake pausing to expel a long
sigh. Cept it ain't natural, is it? What isn't, Dad? For people to
live together in one little ole house, not sort of, you know, loving
each other. And drinking. Living only to drink. Working in the
forest only to buy beer. Jake sighing again, but smiling too. Oh
well, with a shrug. Guess the drinking part weren't so bad. Once
ya learned. Chuckling. Magine some fucka telling your old man
he's a slave, kids? *Nooo!* And Beth sure even Grace's voice was in
that outcry. Anyone tried that on me now and I'd fuckin deal to
im, eh kids? *Yay! Deal to him, Dad!* Fffff — him! and all a giggle
at that. And cruisin, just cruisin. And such a lovely day outside.

Sign said a hotel was coming up, and Beth looked at her newly
bought watch (from the second-hand shop in town) saw that it
was just after eleven. The sign had a big picture of a beer mug
foaming with beer. Said it was 300 m to go. Beth saw Jake lick
his lips. She tensed. Relaxed when he drove straight past the place.
Well, well, well. Now she *knew* everything was gonna turn out
today. She knew.

Back in town. Once more cruise down the main street, eh
kids? Yay! And the place busier. Kids everywhere. Lunchtime
movie. And the rear windows going down, and the kids calling out
to others they knew. (But not Grace.) They got plenty of pointed
fingers from Pine Block kids who knew they were a carless family.
Looks of disbelief, like they'd stolen it. Jake tooting the horn at
them: Eat ya fuckin hearts out! He turned the volume up on the
radio. They got the red at the first set of lights, and he waited
patiently; drumming fingers on the windowsill, head moving in
time to the music. Green.

Stopping at the pedestrian, even though he could have driven
through. Smiling at Beth: No hurry, no hurry. She back at him.
Kids crossing the zebra pattern and Jake telling em watch out the
zebra don't up and bite ya ankles!

No shops open. Not in Two Lakes. The rest of the country all
adopting Saturday morning shopping but not Two Lakes with its

white-dominated council, Beth understood, being of a religious persuasion and thinking Saturdays were as near sacred as Sundays. Sumpthin like that. Not that it mattered to Beth. How often've I got dough left come Saturday morning?

Past the Chinese grabbing a bit of lunchtime trade. Then Jake swinging left, and the first thing catching Beth's eye was the red neon sign. McClutchy's. Spinning a look at Jake. But him apparently unaware of the sign advertising his first home. Or he wasn't showing anything.

The taxi rank: how strange it looked without its line-up of usually older drunks standing there swaying, with packets and crates of beer at their feet. Beth looking at Jake again, Jake . . . ? Hey, hey. Jake returning her look. It's alright, it's alright, even though he was slowing. Just gonna pull up so someone can see us. Grinning like a little kid with a new Christmas toy. Fair enough.

They sat there, engine idling.

Radio belting out some pop number. No one entering the bar that Jake had a desire to toot at, show off his twenty-four-hour status to. Beth asking the kids if they liked this rubbish playing on the radio and getting a strong reaction in reply that they sure did and where was she living, it sure wasn't 1990. No way. So she grinned and said no more. Feeling nicely at peace from that deep throb of engine idling, nice-vibrating beneath her. Sky still clear outside but with just a touch of cloud building up on about the Pine Block horizon, where she guessed Pine Block'd be. Otherwise still lovely.

Two fullas walking down on their side. Stopping. Peering at the car. At Jake sitting there acting like what's the big deal? But his stomach shaking with suppressed laughter. The two stepping off the footpath and coming round to the driver's side, Hey, it *is* Jake. Stepping back in that exaggerated fashion only Maoris can do, asking Jake where'd he pinch the car, and didn't he know the penalty for car theft? And Jake giggling. Like a little boy. Then one of them asking, Well? Ya comin in or not? And Jake looking at Beth but she shaking her head, No . . . But her tone not too strong. And Jake raising one finger to her, Just one? Dear?

The dear winning her, and probably the slave thing too. Okay. But just *one*, Jake Heke. And one of his mates chuckling, One dozen you mean. But no. Jake promising: One, Mum. Promise. Then he was gone.

Go get yourselves an ice cream, Beth told the kids. But don't get yakkin to your mates anywhere. I want you straight back or we'll leave you behind. Sat there thinking about Jake and this slave tag he'd apparently had to wear his entire growing up. And how unfair it was that one lot got to inherit slave status while another inherited chieftainship. How the Maori system worked. And the English one, come to think of it. Maybe life works like that: you cop what the cards fall for you. And then she thought about drink, being reminded of it sitting out here, how she didn't miss it, hardly a bit. Surprised herself. Only made a fool of myself, or got Dutch courage with Jake and got belted for my troubles. Nah, who needs it? But as for smokes. She lit up. Ahh. No way could I give this up.

Kids came back eating ice creams. Grace, as expected, the odd one out with nothing at all. Grace handing her mother her change, Here. What about you? You wanna be one a these anorexics or sumpthin? Beth unable to hide her irritation. But the girl shrugging. And Beth telling the others not to eat those things in here, eat it outside. Thinking of the nice car, of saving its nice condition, not havin Maori kids getting food all over. And that damn Jake, how he was sure managing to make *one* jug of beer last. Half an hour now. She told Abe. You can drive, Take the car round to the carpark, but careful. You ain't licensed. Beth not wanting to be sat out here for all the busybody McClutchy's world to know her business. She went in after Jake.

It was a world she knew so well. Yet it felt unfamiliar. Jarring on the senses. The three-month sober senses. Hell, just on one o'clock and already some ofem pissed outta their little minds.

The poor light, the permanent haze of smoke that even to a smoker was yet thick in here. That old BLAST of SOUND hitting a woman in her ears. Been here, done it all. No more. Her name called several times from all over, Hey, Beth! Long time no see. We heard you'd turned Churchy. That kinda shet. Didn't worry her. In fact, I feel almost superior. Looking at people she knew well, not so well, the all ofem suddenly lighting up in her mind as kinda lost. We're a lost race. Then the thought was gone (I just want my husband and out of here.) Made for Jake's corner.

On the way being stopped by someone, kissed, hugged, asked what she was drinking, being welcomed like a long-lost friend. But no thanks. I'm off the drink. And getting a few funny looks

100

and reactions for it. Who cares? A race commentary starting up.
All ears and eyes on the ceiling speakers, and the bookie's big
ghetto blaster radio on his table. So what's changed?

At Jake's table, Oh hello, Mavis. Kissing the huge fat woman.
A real friend. Could sing the pants off anyone too. Whatcha
having? Nothing, Mavis. I'm off it. Ah, good for you. Come to
drag it out of here? Looking at Jake with his ears and eyes glued
to the horse commentary. Chatting to Mavis about this and that,
the big woman quietly but surely downing beer after beer. (Like
I used to.) Beth feeling pious, if she knew the word. Someone —
Sam the night-time bouncer, one of them — putting a full jug in
front of Jake. Fuckim. Jake? Not even a look. Jake! Still nothing.
Come on, dear. But Sam just shouted me a full one, he managed
to get out before taking his concentration back to the race in
progress. And when it was finished and she could see he'd not
won, as usual, Beth thinking it'd be wise to let him finish that
second and probably a third jug. But tapping her watch pointedly,
and saying see you to Mavis, and going out. The bar three-
quarters full already.

Out in the carpark and the first thing Beth noticed was the
number of kids running around. And she clicked her tongue, some
younger than her little Huata. Running wild or hung all over
bombs of cars bored out of their poor little minds waiting for
parents that weren't gonna emerge for some many hours. Poor
buggers.

When's Dad coming? Soon. Aw, I bet he's there to stay. The
hell he is. I bet you ten bucks. You ain't got ten bucks, and if you
have I wanna know where from, mista. Abe. Getting a bit too
smart for his boots. But Beth starting to feel a little uncertain of
Jake too.

Car pulled up. A typical heap of rusted junk. Kids spilling out
of it. And a mother and father. Mother going, Here. Giving her
oldest-looking one some money. Thas for fishnchips, and don't
come askin for more cos there ain't no more.

A mirror. A fuckin mirror of all our lives. Maori of course. So
Beth got out from the front, opened the back door, on Grace's
side: Move over, honey. Grace looking astonished but, Beth hoped
she hadn't read wrong, rapt as well. She put an arm around
Grace. Alright, kid? You been quiet lately. And Grace smiling her
smile at Mother and twisting away from her arm, but not so hard

that the arm fell off. As a mother knew it wouldn't. Hu asking his mother could he go play with that new lot just arrived, and Beth saying no. You stay put. In here with your family. They're scum. Just scum. Even though she knew she shouldn't blame the kids it was hardly their fault, she had to fix on someone. And as the parents were gone . . .

Mavis, all plus-twenty stone of her was making fun of her sex life. My non-existent sex life. Laughing that way fat people do, has you following suit because ofem jiggling up an down and the laughter rooooollin out. And someone saying that if she had babies, Mavis, it'd be a whale that came out, and everyone roaring with that. But the person, Willie someone, going on that Mavis'd have to take her kid to the zoo — no, one a these aquariums, or the thing'd die. And everyone in stitches at that. And this Willie fulla still not finished, telling em or it might come out a fuckin *elaphint* and Mavis'd have to *donate* it to the zoo! Rolling all ovah at that. And with that experienced bar timing, someone saying, Who's buy is it anyrate? just when the laughter was subsiding. And someone else (not so experienced, or maybe just kind) saying he'd buy but Beth sticking her face in, No way, mista. My buy. Pulling a wad of ten-dollar notes from her purse, holding it aloft telling them triumphantly, This's what you get when you *dis*-ciplinc yaself to stay off the booze for awhile. Then leaning against her husband, telling him: Had the hots for you, dear. All day I been hot for you. Leering at him. But not knowing she was. Not as bold and bare-faced as that. And swaying a little. Not used to the alcohol in her three-month dry system. But Jake leaning away from her, telling her: Alright, alright, thassa bout the tenth fuckin time you said that, woman. Aww, hun — N'mind the fuckin hun, neither. If you're buyin, then buy. Juss don't talk that sexy shet. Giving her one of his snarls. And asking one of his mates, Eh Bub? My own fuckin missus and she's comin on like a fuckin hotpants or sump-thin. Lookin at Beth. With that look.

Up at the bar. Standing there. Jake's voice, his cruel tone echoing in her ear. His face like it was still there in front of her: snarling, lip-curling at me. (Oo, I fuckin hate him sometimes.) And head not quite right. Spinning. No, not spinning, but getting mighty close. And hurting in her heart at his rejection; wanting to tackle the problem head-on before it overcame her. The way she mostly did with problems: head-on. But all the noise, the jukie, two, three gats goin, and that constant hum of people. And the word: Kids, appearing in her mind, her half-mixed-up mind. Oh, thaz right, my kids're waiting for me. Yeah . . . (Not only me. Not me to start off with. *Him*. It's all his fuckin fault.) Okay, okay, after this round we're off. Still time to have a good visit with Boogie; and I got enough dough to extend the hire. Go seeim again tomorrow. And if Jake won't come then I'll get Abe to drive. He c'n drive. They c'n all drive these kids nowadays. I'll tellim to drive slow. Still time for *one* more. Hahaha. Good enough for the goose, good enough for the gander. Fuckim, eh Beth? Having a little giggle to herself. Thinking about how well she'd done, considering . . . how much dough I put aside for this day . . . my boy his picnic, his VISIT. Oh won't be long now — the clock in front of her — a fuckin great big one at that — announcing the unbelievable. — to *five*? Ten to fuckin *five*!

But this could not be. At her watch — I haven't looked at my new watch since I came in here. Same time.

Panic welled up. She felt sick. Then like hitting someone. Oh God . . . Standing there, rocking back and forth on her heels, her half-hour-polished, almost high heels, trying to set herself, steel her insides against the pain come crushing in.

How many, Beth? Uh? How many jugs? Oh, uh . . . (Come on, woman. Get yourself to*gether*.) Make it six. Yeh, six'll do. What of, Beth? Eh? What beer? Oh anything. DB. Anything but that lager pisswater. Giggling. But thinking, That wasn't funny, Beth. Oh who cares? We'll visit soon. Tellim we got a flattie. Two ofem.

Carrying the jugs in two trips back to the table. No one so much as sayin a thank you, kiss my arse, nuthin. Hurting a woman: (I saved for this. Went without. Kept myself at home. And for what?) Stood there feeling hurt. Then it occurred to her: I know. Told Mavis she'd be back in a minute. Went out.

I *know* that. But ain't me, it's your father. (Oh but how'm I gonna explain the picnic food?) Your father's run into someone. What with, his fists? Grace the first to show the waiting'd got to her. Beth trying to focus her oldest daughter, to line her up so to chide her. But she couldn't. Grace all blurry. Beth shaking her head. Even slapping her own face to gain some clearness of bloody vision. (Jesus Chrise, the hell's up with me?)

Tomorrow. We'll go visit Boog tomorrow. And Grace really

putting the boot in, sarcasming her mother's funny r's: Tomowwow. Exaggerating Beth's drunkenness: Tomowwow, kidsth. We'll visit tomowwow. You wouldn't talk like that your father was here. Well he *ain't* here. And he's *never* gonna be here. And you know it and so do we. (My God, this girl ain't stupid. So who'm I tryin to kid?) So Beth turned to Polly instead, asked if she wanted to add her two bobs' worth while Grace was at it. Poll shaking her head, Just wanna go and see Boog. And Abe, he was staring daggers and so was even little Hu copying the mood. Making a mother mad. Not my fault. But them just looking at her, like it was her fault alright.

Your father's fault. He's the one wouldn't come out. But four sets of eyes accusing her. (*Me.*) Then Polly asking, When're we gonna be eating the picnic? Put the fear up in Beth. Uh, tomorrow. But, Mum, it'll be stale by then. And rotten. No it won't. And if it is I'll buy a whole new lot. How's that? Beth feeling treacherous. Smiling through her teeth. And she dug into her purse. Here. Gave Grace a twenty. Go buy sumpthin to eat, and you can go to the pictures after. Catch the bus home. Grace looking at her mother one last betrayed time.

A woman sitting there watching her kids, four ofem anyrate, troop off into the dusk. The fast-gathering dusk. And all she can do is sit here feeling like nuthin on earth ready to pounce on that picnic soon as they're out of sight. And kids runnin around the place. Little buggers. Horrible little buggers. Least mine've got a decent mother who . . . who *cares* about em. (I do. I truly do.) But feeling as if she was being driven by some force greater than herself. Watching . . . watching them disappear so she could jump, like a thief in the night, the almost night, onto what was theirs, her children's, their food, their treat, sposed to be their day. (Oh, but we Maoris are cursed.)

At the table with the borrowed from next-door's chilly bin on the table. Here! Playing the conjurer with plastic-wrapped parcels of food. Now, this'll be — looking at it as if she didn't already know every lovingly wrapped goodie backwards — roast pork. And everyone going, mmmm. Waiting for the next. And this'll be — (wait for it) — Oh, now *this* — smacking her lips, smiling like she had sumpthin over them, their peasant limitations. She grinned over at Jake, asked him: You tellem what it is, dear. But Jake snarlin at her. Turned away. Salami, Beth announced. Smiling when half of them went, Wha'? And just into telling (these ignorant) them what salami was when Jake piped up, Get on with it, woman. In that drawling dismissive manner of his. (Spoilsport.) Beth thinking it was Jake's own ignorance on the subject had him testy with her.

So out she came with six hard-boiled eggs in plastic wrap, and someone saying, Ooo, now what would *they* be. Laughing. (At me?) Beth confused, not sure, but being driven on. Hauling out a lettuce. The wit saying, Far out, a lettuce. Onion rings. Oh wow. What about a whole cooked chicken done on a rotisserie? Beth like she was running an auction. And being asked, On a *what?* Beth smiling. Another urging her, Oh come on, honey chile. *Ej*-acate us. Beth missing the cynicism, their world-weary McClutchy bar hardness. (Man, we only wanna fuckin feed not a lecture.)

Then Jake leaned over and grabbed up the chicken, tore one of its legs off, took a big bite out of it. And it seemed to be the signal for everyone to dive in. Grabbing at parcels, pulling frantically at the plastic wrap, stuffing things into their mouths and going mmmm, not bad, not bad. Smacking their lips, makin sucking noises, eating with their rotten fuckin mouths wide open (in case there's sumpthin else they see to stuff in); and Beth watched, in a growing despair that'd started off as pride these — animals — consuming her hard-won, worked-for pride and joy meant to be for her family, her Boogie, herself. She picked up her beer glass, filled it to overflowing and downed it in one gulping hit. She lit a smoke. No ahh, nuthin. Felt terrible, tasted terrible. She had another glass of beer. But still she felt dreadful.

She looked around her . . . at them, the feeding animals gorging on what felt like her very own body, such a violation did it feel. Her eyes found those of Mavis (Oh Mavis . . .) the huge woman's size seeming to symbolise something (greed?). No, can't be greed, she's the only one not eating. She's standing *away* from the rest ofem. (Oh Mavis!). She looks like a queen; like she's gazing down at this rabble and hatin em for their peasant condition. Beth stepped toward the giantess. Come on, honey . . . The big arms went out and the rich voice beckoned her.

. . . *was my Boogie's picnic!* Beth bawling in Mavis Tatana's arms, and Mavis patting her, There there, honey. Mavis unnerstans. And Beth sobbing. And Mavis telling her these people are our poison, Beth. They the scum a the fuckin earth. Clicking her tongue. Patting Beth's back. Stroking her hair. But they're ours, whether we like it or not. They're our people, Beth . . . Beth wondering what Mavis meant.

And then night came. And The People they'd grown mindless — or their minds'd been transported — and soon — too damn soon — the bell clanging like a fire engine'd crashed into their world to tell them the dream was over. *Brrrrr! Brrrrrr!* — why they *do* that every fuckin closing time, every fuckin last-ten-minutes-to-go time?

Spilling out onto the street, the taxi rank, to cars where children were slept huddled together for warmth but mostly love, it half suggested to the drunken parents, but halfway ain't enough, man, it ain't; milled around the carpark talking last cries and mumbled jumbles of shet, and hoped for a fight to break out as a last bonus for the night; into rust heaps and grunt machines and vehicles really shot they headed to parties, somewhere in ill-lit houses in ill-lit streets, but who gives a fuck, man? it's where we're sprung from, eh, we're jussa pack a sewer rats headin back home; and a scuffle turned into a beaudiful big rumble, hadem running from their cars, their halted cars, their just-about-to-enter cars, and fists cracked and glass tinkled, and it was because this fulla, eh, he gave this other fulla a smart look, eh, so the fulla went up to him and asked him whassa fuckin look for, cunt? then the one who started it, the one with the smart eyes, he pushed the other fulla, eh, and then it was on, eh.

And so the beer from the broken bottles ran, eventually, from the carpark to the street gutter where it shone briefly and dully in the streetlight and the flare of a drunk at the taxi rank lighting a fag, it picked up a snatch of the low, angled moon hovering up there, a crescent, a slice a fuckin gold, man, just sat there in the black and you could even pick out the tiny pinpoints of starlight reflected in the draining beer if you were observant or stoned enough; and there was one fulla, eh, he could see his own blood, wisps of it as it dripped outta his smashed nose mixing in with that draining beer . . .

And down the street juss around the corner, on main street, waited the slit-eyes, hungry as ever for your arrival, confident in your arrival, laughing inside, smirking to each other over their soon-to-be-frantic woks at you — yes *you*, missa Brown Man and oh even your woman. For you we wait.

And the tall one, the one with the magnificent fighter's physique, muscles's hard as stone, fists like hams, he had a small crowd gathered round this flash car, eh, this was after he'd joined the scrap and smacked a couple ofem down just for the hell of it, laughing and askin em, What ya think? Making out it was his very own car, makin a neighing sound as if to suggest it was a win on the horses got him this, but not so drunk he didn't think to cover his lie: Mind you, dunno if I'm gonna keep it. Too big, eh. Fuckin bastards ta park these big muthas. Nah, might get rid of it on Monday. Thinking he hadem fooled and none of em in fact the slightest bit believing of him. And him missing their disbelief telling em, Too fuckin flash for Pine Block anyway. Eh folks? Laughing. (He'd been laughing near all day long. On and off.) Those Pine Block kids'd have it stripped in a hour. So who wants a ride before it goes on Monday? And Jake lookin around at the faces and pointing, Errol, wanna ride, bro? Yeow. Kingi, hop in. George, my ole mate George, you c'n come. Oh, but watch out for Beth in the back there. At his wife sprawled out unconscious in the rear seat. Beyond even dreaming.

Oh, and this poor kid, eh, the one in the Boys Home up in Riverton, waitin all day for his visit. All day. And the housemaster on the evening shift coming up to him: Mark Heke, it appears your visitors are not coming. And the kid saying, Yes they are. Yes they are. How kids get when they won't face the truth. And the house-master reading Boogie (Mark) all wrong, thinking Mark Heke was trying to get out of his evening cleaning duties, so ordering Mark to work, and yelling at him for being such a sook at a mere thing such as work. Any fuckin wonder these kids grow up with chips on their shoulders, eh? Any fuckin wonder they grow up still mostly a kid in their hearts; it's because people, adults, the fucked-up society they come from, don't take any notice ofem, they don't have dreams — *dreams* — for their kids; and when they get sent away to these Boys Home places for being bad, the people working there think the first and only thing they gotta do is straighten the kid out. Straightenim out, fa fucks sake. Yet they wouldn't treat a dog like that a dog was sent to em been kicked and abused all its life and carrying on the kicking but under a different name, and expect the dog to not wanna bite em. Now would they?

107

9
Loveless, She Stumbled

Ya stick the tube at the bottom, ya close the top of the bag, ya hold it for a bit till the fumes build up, then ya stick ya face in and *breathe*. Then Toot snapped his fingers — wasted. Ya *way*-sted then, G. Grace giggling and pulling the blanket higher over her and Toot goin, Oi! Ya wannit all? But laughing. Then telling her, But you ain't gettin none a it. Aw, Toot! I said, Ya ain't gettin no glue. But what if I *want* to do it? Don't care. Ya ain't tryin it with me. And that's final. Grace going, Awww, Toot, snuggling against her friend; and he coughing, then sighed, then wiggled a bit to make out he wasn't cool about this, you know, being snuggled up with a girl sposed to be his friend, and the trouble she had a while back there with bein, you know, messed with her private parts by some arsehole cunt, but thinking oh well, guess she needs it and so puttin an arm around her.

Toot smiling shyly ater in the light spilled from the upstairs window of them, his olds, finally gone ta fuckin bed forgot to turn the fuckin light off too fuckin drunk as fuckin usual; Toot hopin one ofem'd left a smoke burning and that it'd catch their bed on fire burnem all up cos, man, I sure won't be yellin Fire! Fire! no way, I'll be off down the street laughin my fuckin head off, man and — Oh, and I'd grab G here, a course I would, she's my only real close friend — and we'll find somewhere where we can sit down and laugh our heads off at them up there burning, burning . . .

But I'll let ya have a smoke with me ya want. Oh choice! Ain't that good, G. Ya reckon! Ya tried it before, G? Yeh, course, man. Ya haven't, have ya? I have. When? Oh, a long time ago. Long time ago? Well, you ain't 'xactly *old* now, girl, so ya musta been, wha', bout fuckin *six* when ya tried it? Chuckling at Grace, as he fiddled around rolling a joint in the dark.

And the smoke began its work. And it was good. And it got better. So *gooooood*. (I don't want this to end.) Toot? Wha'? I never want this, you know, this feeling to end. Never. Yeow, G.

Never. Never, never, never (never, never . . .) And time seemed to have stopped. And pain had ceased to exist. Well, maybe just a niggle there, why she asked Toot: Toot? Does glue getya more wasted than this? Yep. Honest? Too wasted, G. Ya don't wanna try it, I'm tellin ya. I might, Toot. Nah, it sucks. So how come you — To get wasted, G, but y' know . . . It ain't a good way to go . . . But does it take you out of it more than this dope, Toot? Take ya right out, enda fuckin story, for some ofem. What, like in — I mean dead, G.

Then the darkness returned, and it was funny: ya head clears and it gets darker. In ya heart. Saying to Toot, Member when I told you bout, you know . . . ? Yep. Oh don't say *yep* like that Toot, like it's sumpthin happens like every damn day, like it's sorta *normal*. Or like it was *me* did it. G, I never said I — Well, it sounded like it. Sorry, G. That's alright. (My it's dark. So dark everywhere.) Well, Toot . . . ? Yeow? It's, uh, it's been happening again. Oh, Grace!

And the silence of the old car wreck so complete, like the dark inside and out. Toot saying how he c'd *kill* people like that, and no more because, well, we're only young, we don't have words only feelings, and we sposed ta have dreams, you know, like the white kids, most ofem anyway. But we're just Pine Block Maoris, there must be Pine Blocks all over this rotten country, ya see it on the TV, hear it at school, read about it how we're the ones doing all the bad things ending up in jail and places like that: Boys Homes, Girls Homes, Borstals, Youth Detention, Youth Prison, Mount Eden, Paremoremo, Mount Crawford, Waikeria, see, even a thirteen-year-old kid knows this. Ah, but what to do to do to do . . . ?

. . . can't tell my mother, I just can't, Toot. But why, G? She's a choice mother, int she? Yeh, she's alright I spose. But I can't seem to get through to her, I can't kinda like talk to her . . . (I can't I can't . . . I *can't* go on like this) . . . as for him he's the worst old man in the fuckin world, I had a gun I'd shoot him stone fuckin dead I would, Toot. I know ya would, G. And I'd help ya. Would ya, Toot? Course I would, G. You're my best friend, aren'tcha? Oh, Toot.

. . . had some more a that smoke. Yeah, me too. You got any glue, Toot? Told ya, no. And I did you wouldn't be gettin none. We could *really* get wasted then, Toot. No way, G. Oh, maybe ya right, Toot. And spose it wears off, eh? just like this smoke? And, you know, fuckin *life* comes back stinkin as usual. Gotta go now. Shrugging out of the blanket. See ya, G. See ya, Toot. Hey!

Whatcha doin'? Gonna give ya a kiss, Toot. No way, Hosay. Aw, c'mon, Toot. Just a little kiss good night. Nope. See ya when I see ya. Yeah, bye, Toot.

Standing there . . . in the middle of Trambert's paddock, the one backing onto the back of Rimu Street; hardly any lights left on in Pine Block, the Trambert place in darkness. Not sure where she was. Yes, I am sure, but I'm not. The two opposing thoughts feeling quite natural. Grass damp with dew between her toes. No shoes: wanna be quiet. So quiet they won't know I exist. Cloud crossed over and covering the slice of moon some time ago. So hardly any light. No breeze. I can't hear the shape of the wind, the noise of the obstacles it'd have to move around and over and under. But plenty of stars up there, in between patches of clearing from the cloud. A guitar playing clear as clear, yet the voices accompanying it muffled, deep, tired-sounding. Must be four or five or even six in the morning. Am I still stoned? Oh I wish I was. Grace centring on her head, her brain sensations for any lingering effects of the dope. Nothing. Gone. Like everything in this life that's nice or pleasurable or, you know, has meaning — gone. Then she began walking.

Toward that dark shape of house and tree outline sitting like a huge ship anchored in the night.

She'd been over this same ground before; earlier, when she'd walked home, left her siblings to take themselves to the pictures. Depressed. I felt depressed. She'd dreaded them having got a dog this time. But they hadn't. She'd climbed a tree. She'd watched them, the Tramberts, from her perch like they were a film, a TV show; the eatings and goings-on of the other species. Ten ofem there were. If you don't include her, the girl. The fuckin self-assured has-to-be-smartarse girl who can't be any older than me. The pianist. Eleven if you do. And they sure had counted her as one a them. Consumed a girl with jealousy she had, that Trambert kid. The way she, you know, con*duct*ed herself amongst all those people. Daring to not only talk but *converse* withem, as if she was not only a confident child but their equal. Not only that, she seemed to think it was such a big yawn.

For hours this show went on: each person seeming to take a turn at talking (*taw*king) how they do, holding court as they'd say in English at school, then someone replying or responding or no one saying anything at all, just resuming their eating, their wine

110

sipping, their dabdabs at their mouths with serviette, which a Pine Block girl knows're called sumpthin else except she doesn't know precisely what.

And the woman, she musta been Mrs Trambert, with her shining lovely hair getting up every so often but not before giving em a beautiful smile with the tiniest of nods, and sometimes her daughter had got up after her, and they came back after a bit carrying plates of food and wearing smiles, handing em around ever so graciously, and everyone not touching their grub like a Pine Blocker would, not till the Mum and her spoilt little bitch'd sat down. Oh, and there woulda been five — *five* — courses. Compare with Pine Block where it's one course and it lasts as long the food does not a moment longer or sooner.

Nibble-nibble-nibble, then down'd go their knife and fork or whatever it was they were eating the course with, V-ed points in on the plate, dabdab with that bit of cloth at their dainty mouths, picking up their glass of wine, which'd started off as white and then the mother and her husband'd come along and filled more glasses with red wine; it had to be red wine unless it was something else a Pine Block girl didn't know about just as she didn't about red or white wine, only that she'd figured it from TV. Each course taking an age to eat.

And she could see the lights of *her* world from her tree perch. And she'd look through the foliage at the row of lights of home — back into the room of other species — so nicely dressed: the women with, oh, just indescribable dresses, outfits, and the men with a tie and a nice jacket. Grace looking back again, at home. Then down into that room. The feeling that something, someone had *done* this to her; this sense of having been not deprived but *robbed* of a life, growing stronger in her more and more tormented mind.

Ideas, notions, concepts kept zinging back and forth across her vision of thoughts, like flashes of light trailing a message but going too fast to catch the words. So it was just the row of lights and faint sounds of a car revving a snatch of group singing. A real-life TV scene down there, in that sitting room, or dining room, or whatever the hell they call it I don't know I'm just a . . .

The departure of the people. The visitors. Mrs and Mr coming outside withem; the front door — big woodpanelled thing it coulda been the courthouse — light flooding the area, the cars, the suited men, the smiling laughing women, the girl-bitch so fuckin confident in herself; their goodnights, their we must do this more

111

oftens, their oh yes, we musts, ringing so clearly to a trespasser in a tree. Their accents, their demeanours, their *soberness*, their every communication so so different.

The red eyes of tail-lights disappearing into the night and a girl betting those cars wouldn't have to be returned in the morning; lights disappearing like everything disappearing: stars, moon, day, picnic, mother, hope.

A girl thinking: What if you people came over to our world, joined our party? What'd happen? Imagining the novelty of havin not just Pakehas in their midst but posh ones at that; all over em, breathin beer fumes over em, gettin over-friendly the way they do when they're drunk, askin em stupid questions, rude questions, insulting questions. Eyin em up, the men, for trouble to pick. The women for what they — Oh can't even think about it. Then sure as eggs (fried eggs) someone'd walk up to one ofem and ask: The fuck're you lookin at, cunt? Then, Tramberts and friends, they'll punch the shit out of you, kick hell out of you, spit on you, scream abuse on your bloodied head. Then they'll party on, inspired, spurred by the beating they have given you. For they know it is the only taste of victory they get from life.

Feet freezing. Solid blocks of ice. Oh, but what does it matter? And she climbed her shivering form, step by painful barefooted step up the tree. (The girl, the Trambert kid, had done the act: just that simple kissing of her mother, her father, goodnight.)

This high enough? Looking down, hard to tell in the dark and no moon up there. No. I'll go higher. (And the mother and father they'd gone back to that big room with the big table. Sat down. Sipped at their red wines; she smiling lipsticked lips at him this nice complimentary scarlet: everything fitted. Everything. They'd talked a bit. Grace couldn't hear a word, only see her lips moving and his profile in animation but mostly still. Controlled, see.)

She stopped. She bounced her weight to test the strength. This'll do. She unwound the rope round her arm. (They stood up, she stretching, and seeming to giggle at him smiling funny at her. She had her arms up and he walked over to her and they started pashing. Wow. As old as that and pashing. Then they broke away and they left the room, holding hands. Pop! they went like that in a disappearance of love stepped into the dark. And Grace left there. Lonely — lonelier than ever.) She tied the knots with a practised skill; jerking on each one as she went. (And the front entrance light went out. Then an edging of light speared alight on her left. Stayed on for some time. Then it too popped out.) Wow. Just me now. Me and the dark. Me and —

Felt so strange, the rope around her neck, tickly against her throat. Strange and this calmness. As if it really wasn't going to happen, that it couldn't possibly. And yet . . . nothing there, in the background of vague thoughts and blurry pictures and this odd buzzing sound, to say this is *not* going to happen. Because it was happening . . . I'm testing the rope.

Potential. It popped up in her head, an old familiar word, concept she'd latched onto. From a magazine it was; about everyone having the right — the *right*, it said — to realise their potential. POTENTIAL.

It sat there in her mind as clear as a neon sign. Like the McCLUTCHY'S one. No need for on/off blinking. Not when it was what everyone knew. No need to blink on and off.

Then her breathing quickened. In and out in and out, rapider and rapider.

Then she jumped.

. . . so she could not hear the sounds from the row of two-storey lights over yonder field, of song in mass rendition, a party trying to surge back to life. And succeeding. And remarkably in tune . . . (and thas even tho we pissed as, man. We — huh! — we c'n still sing tho. Issa . . . issa . . . issa *potential* of us, eh. Comin out in us because we're pissed. Drunk as. Issa potential us Maoris got for singing — oh not juss singing, neither. Iss lotsa things we got potential for. Lotsa things. But singing, well, thas our best potential, eh. Oh, and fighting too. HAHAHAHA! Thas why we don't wanna go ta bed: because we, you know, are re-a-lising our po-ten-shall. Ya realise that doncha? HAHAHAHA! gotta laugh, eh, or we'd cry. No we wouldn't, we'd fall over flat on our drunken backs and go ta sleep. But not forever, no way. Juss a few hours. Because there's tomorrow, eh. So play that gat!)

But eventually there was no more light along that back view of state houses. Only the stars, as always, up there shining on. Though a man in town owned a telescope and had much learning, he could have told you that even they, the stars, go out. So what's a life? (Potential, sir. It's an unrealised potential.)

10
They Who Have History II

And now the second day . . . And tomorrow (tomowwow, kidsth . . . Remember that, Beth?) tomorrow'll be the last day. Beth looking at the face — Tomorrow, and you'll be gone.

As if you were ever here in the first place.

A constant, low wailing from an older woman sat at the end of the coffin. And people all around, backs against the walls, sat on mattresses, and out in the centre of the vast room they were sat on woven mats; and the elders, men, sat on bench seats.

Beth touching the face (I still don't believe it) so cold. So utterly, unfeelingly still. Still in disbelief and yet nothing could be more final and absolute as this. And an elder rising to make yet another speech in a language a mother did not understand. (And yet he is part of me, my heritage; probably related to me. Yet he speaks his tongue and I understand only another. Yet they are gathered here . . . ? to help a mother farewell her tragically gone daughter?)

Beth not understanding. Not the language, not their insistence that she bring her child home for proper farewell. Beth half resenting the male elders, their privileged position, their secret language that only they and a few others knew; remembering that this very place, its cultural practices, had always been a mystery to a young girl growing up: a males-only domain. And only certain males at that. From certain families. From chiefly lines. And to hell with the rest, you're here to serve us. That's how a girl'd felt. And growing up to the knowledge that as a woman she was never going to have the right to speak publicly, as this man now was. Not ever. So Beth had to draw a deep breath to stop herself crying out to the speaker to shut up if he wasn't going to speak English. But courtesy. And lifetime fear instilled. And a woman knew her grieving had her in a state.

A single-roomed building of huge dimensions: forty metres by thirty wide. Steep-pitched roof giving the inside a chamberlike effect; a speaker's voice tended to echo somewhat, despite the absorbing presence of two hundred and more people.

Walls of woven and rolled plant, decorated with simple geometric patterns of traditional design.

Every pace a carved wooden slab of wall column, depicting an illustrious ancestor, the legends of the people; the lore of the tribe etched out in intricate (but secret) detail. Warrior figures with huge tongues poking grotesque defiance at the imagined (and assumed) enemy; three-digit hands holding a weapon, and perhaps an animal depicted at the warrior's feet, a lizard, a whale, a bird. And the odd woman was depicted too; you could tell by the two droops signifying breasts, as well the chin and lip tattoo.

Ceiling a rib-row of rafters painted in traditional fern-curl or geometric pattern. Two main centre support poles, each an elaborately carved totem of massive log. A bookless society's equivalent of several volumes. If you knew how to translate it, that is.

Outside, the doorway framed in more elaborate carving, the single window frame, the gables the same.

Atop the apex of iron roof a wooden warrior with legs astride, spear in hand, fierce face wild-eyed and tongue-ejected at all would-be enemies. Wainui. (Where a girl once roamed and had dreams.)

Over by the wall on the right as you entered she lay in state. Ancient feather cloak draped over her from breasts (buds cut short of their prime) down. The lid to her last residence stood on its end directly over the coffin. You could see her (sad) reflection in the highly polished wood: just a face framed in white rayon.

All the people except the male elders without footwear. Black the predominant colour worn by the women. Beth on Grace's left; her children, Abe, Polly and Huata beside her; opposite her an aunt on her mother's side; and beside her, Maggie, Beth's sister, for once looking genuinely of pity. Down from the aunt a disgruntled paternal aunt, put out and making it known her slight at not having prime position up there with the mother. Giving smouldering looks at every opportunity her usurper. And at meal breaks telling all who'd listen that it wasn't right, you know, the auntie on the mother's side to have head position over the auntie

115

on the *father's* side. And everyone going, Yeah, yeah, Auntie Tare.

Jake, the father, doing his grieving at where he felt he belonged.

Light rain pitterpattering on the iron roof; it'd been like that all day. Ah, the sky weeping. A sure sign from the heavens of exceptional grief. And rightly so. In the, uh, you know, the circumstances.

The older women taking it in unspoken turn to maintain the formalised wailing: a haunting, sobbing sound that never let up, and it'd rise and fall and rise again to such an extent it had Beth's hair standing on end. Chilled a woman. (But I done my weeping.) No more to cry. Only guilt left. And a slow-building anger — no, a rage. A rage building up in her. (Wasn't me who killed you, girl . . . Wasn't me who made the circumstances that had you go and do this. It was your father. It was *his* fault.) Yet not sure. Not yet. Too soon. Beth afraid of judging too soon.

The speaker intoned on. And it, his voice, sort of moved in and out of a woman's hearing, like a tide, a wave lapping the shore, ebbing, coming back again. A rhythm. No denying that; there's a definite pattern of beat in the way he's talking. But that rage also creeping over her. And the nagging thought: (Oh please don't let it be . . . ?) that her race, Grace's facthood of being Maori (deprived, I don't know . . .) might have been the cause? The speaker ending his speech.

Cigarette smoke wisping up from a score of sources. And Beth struggling with her thoughts: (What damn use your formal speeches, elders, in a tongue most of us don't understand and never will understand even though they're drumming it into us from everywhere, on the TV, the radio, the papers, this kohanga reo stuff, what use when a race is tearing itself apart?) Easy, Beth, easy. Grabbing a handful of black dress and squeezing till it hurt and her rage'd subsided. Then another elder stood. He coughed his throat clear. And off he went into a foreign-languaged speech whose only quality Beth could hear was that eerie clicking pattern of rhythm.

Beth wanting a smoke. Badly. But not proper. Not right beside the body. The face . . . always that face . . . can't get away from it. One more day. (Sorry, darling. Not that I want you to go. But you're sending a mother mad.) Beth buried her face in her hands (and everyone thinking it was her grief, her love for her tragically

116

self-taken daughter. Ah, such a terrible shame, eh. And so young.)
The speaker breaking into a waiata, lament for something precious
lost. Others joining in. And so collectively compelling they had a
wretched mother's head lifting . . . Drawn to it.

. . . three, four . . . eight ofem. Chanting. The notes hardly
changing. Yet as sad as anything Beth'd ever heard.

Melancholy, that's it . . . Beth listening quite intently now
. . . *Hei tuupoho ake te wahine a tangi aurere nei: Making glad
the hearts of women who bitterly lament* . . .

The line of bare lightbulbs glowing brightly down the centre
of the room, strung over the cross-members. A kid bawling loudly.
The kid being hushed. The waiata continuing its rolling rhythmic
throb. Quarter-tones. That's what a woman remembered from
somewhere as this style of singing. So *moving*. (Have to get a grip
on myself or I ain't gonna last. Gonna crack.) Be strong, Beth.

People came; they stood in their little groups before the coffin
with bowed heads and just the wail of formal weeping. Then a
speech of welcome from a host elder, followed by a reply from the
visitor leader. Then around the room rubbing noses in the old
way: hongi. Getting to Beth and embracing her, sobbing over her,
patting her back, mostly wordless, and then gone. Ghosts. Just
nice ghosts being kind to a woman, not because they knew her but
because she was one of them.

This occurring more and more to Beth, their kindness.

They'd take their leave and there'd be a break in the speeches,
so a woman'd be left with only her thoughts and that quiet sobbing in the background, and her daughter laying there speaking
— calling — from her tomorrow's grave: (*Mum, I am wronged.
I lie here because I have been wronged.*) But a mother unable to
figure, for the life of her, how great the wrong to have Grace do
this.

And her remaining children — what remained of them, with
Nig still not shown up and the welfare not having brought Boogie,
so with half the offspring she began with — stunned and not able
to find much comfort from Mum (Oh I'm sorry, kids) only take
them in her arms now and then. (But what to say because what
use words?)

So the hours passed, another hour gone, one more hour closer
to a girl, a life, a supposed *potential*, gone forever. And, sometime
in the haze, a buzz going up at the entrance of a man, and Beth's
aunt, telling Beth with a reverence: It's Te Tupaea, paramount
chief of the tribe. But Beth giving the man only a glance, So what?

117

He wasn't tall, nor particularly distinguished. Just an ordinary man who'd been born with chiefly status, was how Beth gave her cursory interest when the man stood began his speech. And even given the Maori he spoke in, Beth was thinking the chief as ill-suited to the role, and thinking it was proof of this inheritance thing that you can't make a leader from poor material to start with. Then Matawai, Beth's maternal aunt, began what Beth presumed was a translation, perhaps it was rough outline of what the chief was saying.

. . . his whakapapa, Matawai was saying, he speaks first of his genealogy, as the chief rapid-fired in a half-whisper a complex and endless mouthful of names, words . . . His ancestry — your ancestry, therefore, Beth, and mine — he recalls all those tupuna long gone yet still alive in the heart of every true Maori. He is saying, Beth, that we are what we are only because of our past . . . and that we should never forget our past or our future is lost . . . Beth wondering if perhaps that was what ailed her people: their lack of knowledge of the past. A history.

Now he speaks of an ancestor who was a great poet as well a great warrior . . . of the great poems he composed for his loved ones lost in a great storm whilst at sea, fishing. Now, Beth, it is a master carver he speaks of. Ah, and this time — Matawai chuckling — it is of a great lover ancestor who had many many wives.

And as he spoke, so too did Beth pick up that his voice was rising. Nothing loud, emotional; just a gradual increase in intensity. (I know: it is confidence his voice rings with.) Then out from the row of seated men he came.

One minute an ebb and flow of tidal verbal force, next a rapid-fire ejection of emotionally choked formalised fury. Then he'd shuffle forward several steps in dancing warrior fashion. Bring to a halt. (Alright, so he's interesting, Beth conceding.) An arm sweeping theatrically before him. His movements dance-like: a hand slicing the air; a hand fluttering like a butterfly in motion; a hand shaped like a bird beak; both hands quivering rapidly and rolling back and forth across his suited chest. And so *dignified*.

He'd come to abrupt halts of voice or posture: eyes fixed intently on some unknown point, perhaps a place in the mystical universe of his mind, or it might be a mentioned enemy from the historical past, perhaps a sight of visual wonder, or a recalled historical incident requiring fixed attention; his head might cock to one side like an alert bird, which'd suddenly launch into symbolic flight with an outspread of dark pinstriped arms, and a flash

118

of gold cufflink. Yet he didn't seem to belong to this century, nor of the culture whose attire he'd assumed.

Talking, rapid-fire then cut — shock-still. No voice. Not even a breath from him. Completely motionless. Only the breathing of the people in awe of him. Then on he'd go, in that lilting rhythmic speech, the Maori tongue, with its every word ending a vowel, aiding the flow; a hand on a hip affecting a casual pose which'd dramatically switch to a fighting posture of legs apart, hands at the ready, jaw thrust beligerently forward. Then he could just as easily turn, walk away, muttering. Plainly this was the stage he'd been reared for.

From out of nowhere a handclub. A mere. White. Whale-bone. A reincarnation of murderous days gone by. (Who says they're gone?) Te Tupaea using the weapon with delicate skill, subtlety. A swishing, slicing, thrusting, (throat) cutting aid to the speaking voice. And Auntie Matawai resuming her translation for her niece's benefit . . .

He is speaking of life . . . how precious it is, how sad to see the young tree cut down before its prime. His weapon quivered out in front of him, went behind his back, still quivering, he still talking — speeching; the mere returned to his front; it twirled, it thrust out and danced threateningly for a while, came quiveringly back. And he came back with it: dancing on back-heeling highly polished feet. He stopped. The weapon froze. He resumed moving. The weapon resumed its threatening. Whatever he commanded, his weapon and his body did.

Now Beth no longer trying to kid herself with token looks of disinterest elsewhere; eyes only for the man in the pinstripe suit and the dark skin and the gold cufflinks and the gold pocketwatch that danced and jumped whenever he did, yet stayed secured by flashing gold chain.

Now his words alight with passion and flying spittle. Drops flew from his teeth-bared mouth, flashed briefly and frequently in the naked bulb light. And the whalebone flashed white as it arced this way and that through the air; you could feel the wind of it, imagine the finality of it bringing your life to an end.

It went up over his head, tipped blade downwards, shook rapidly in quivering hand; his tongue stabbed and emerged a purple and red swelling of meat, wet glistening meat thrusting out of a salivating sheath. He came stomping forward . . . two . . . three . . . four . . . five big steps he took toward the coffin — came to a halt.

119

He went up on one set of toes, the other leg bent behind him, weapon held high above his head, a stream of utterances coming from him — suddenly he faced the other, in a deft movement of swivel on the back heel. Down on the front knee, weapon quivering, always quivering, its threat. And face a picture of absolute warriorhood. Had applause been permissible he'd've brought the house down.

Up on his feet he did a slow turn back towards the coffin. He began speeching. Matawai followed in whispered translation . . . an ancestor whose child was accidentally drowned . . . blamed his wife, was going to kill her for her neglect . . . the tribe with him . . . wanting to kill her. But not so the great chief . . . he told them no, they must wait . . . discuss it first, your anger, and let the fire die down before you start talking of shedding your clothing. They did talk. For many days they talked. They decided it was all their fault . . . since the child belonged to the whanau, them as a whole, it was all their responsibility. So the chief asking them: Now tell me who dies?

Then the chief in the suit ended his speech. Left a mother a little less of her grieving, a little more of her respect for a people she did not really know. Then Te Tupaea began a waiata tangi: lament for the dead.

The elders rose as one, came forward to join their chief. Their great chief (who'd inherited his title). Then several women (they knew who they were; who was permitted, who wasn't) also stood from their floor-seated positions and joined their men. And their chief. He who had greatness expected of him. He who thus delivered.

The air resonated, *thrummed* with the song of thirty and more voices: . . . *As I slept I was walking in the underworld with plumes in my hair. The tokens*, ee, *of my gannet feather that I allowed to leave me. My heart string is quite cold — she is taken from me!*

Aee, Beth, my niece. I cannot keep up with it; my heart it fills too quickly with, you know, emotion.

Beth nodding across the face, the perfectly still face of her child, at her aunt: It's alright, Auntie. It's alright. (I feel so much more at peace now.)

Verse after verse. Legend after legendary ancestor they did recall on the roll, the incantation of chanting cry . . . *Raangaitia atu to noho* (Arise from your rest . . .) *Kia whakamau koe ki nga whetu o te rangi* (And take your place amongst the stars of the sky . . .) (Oh yes, look! The stars, girl. The Milky Way.) (Hey, bro? See them stars up there? Well, our ancestors, boy, they came to this land by the lights of them stars.)

Now they were sending one of their number back via the same stars.

The women gave it higher-noted poignancy, more emphasis on the emotional inflexions; though their men had a distinct tonal sadness their own in the way they sucked in breath and quickly resumed the waiata tangi, as though afraid of not contributing, or as if the emotion got checked partway through.

Ah, would ya look atem: raptures. They're in raptures. Half ofem with their eyes closed. In joy, pure joy at being Maori. Oh aren't (they) we a *together* race when (they) we're like this? History, thas what they are. They are history and therefore so are we, and who needs anything else when you got the strength of history supporting ya? I mean to say.

On and on and on, a reincarnation of what was, a resurgence of fierce pride, a come-again of a people who once were warriors.

Then it ended. What was the last line, Auntie Matawai? Why you ask for that line? I dunno. But tell me what it was. Well, it was . . . it — well, first they asked what does it really matter this lament, and then they said because our Grace'd never return.

The cultural journey was not finished: all hell broke loose as the thirty and more men and women launched into a haka, or peruperu, as it was properly known and informed by Matawai to her niece.

A roar from the chief began it: *Aa, toi-a mai!* And thirty voices answered: TE WAKA! they were crying to their chief, urging, haul up! The vessel on which their ancestors had once sped to war; the blood still running strong with those ferocious genes.

Thirty and more right legs rising as one then *down* they came to the floor, shuddering the very building. Uuup again, *down* in a one-note thud of shoed and stockinged and bare feet on bare floorboard. Arms going out, feet coming down, arms coming in, legs raising. On and on this beat. Hands ringing slappingly on elbows, on chests and unflinching breasts, on thighs, in great muscle flexing movements of self-induced fury. Words exploded forth: *KAMATE! KAMATE!* each line, every encrazed utterance a spit-laced outpouring of *WAR! WAR! WAR!* And inwritten with this (atavistic) beat, this terrible animal rhythm of yet the highest order. Man, it was a beautiful, crazy war-dance; like a mad fuckin ballet, man; like they were risen from a swamp. (A primeval swamp.)

And the sweat dripped — it flew — from them, men and equally encrazed women. And still their fury unleashed itself: RISE UP! RISE UP AND FIGHT! *AND FIGHT!!* Arms thrusting in striking unison. Thirty and more sets of hands slapping on unfeeling bare skin. Thirty and more tongues spewed forth in maddened defiance of this imagined enemy. Gone they were. Quite gone of this century and much of the last. Oh man. And a woman feeling, you know, her heart just *racing*, and proud. (I feel warrior too.) Inspired. (I feel as my ancestors must've felt.) Skin alive with power, stomach on fire with jolts of electric excitement. At the sight. This sight of what (she) they all must have been. Her mind no longer able to think — not in words. Filled that she was with this, this sense of . . . STRENGTH. (Strong. I am made strong again.)

(And why, perhaps, the boy Nig — Nig Heke, eldest son of Jake the Muss — was right then asurge with the flexing of his own muscles as he prepared to do fistic combat with another. Just another prospect Brown Fist hopeful being pitted against his own kind to do battle until one was no longer able to lift a fist in defence, and even then it might continue, if leader Jimmy Bad Horse said, Carry on, kick the muthafucka's head in.)

As his blood relations, his kaumatua, his kuia, were joined as one in dance of war; and their spit flew (as the boy smacked a left into the other dude's face) and the sinews on their necks stuck out like picket fences (a right, another left) and tongues jabbed from maddened wet lips (and blood belched from the other prospect's nose) and the war encrazed people roared words of urging, verses of inducement (and the Browns with membership roared with delight) this formal expression of war (a rumble) expressing itself (doin it, man, *doin* it!). Then it was over. (Ovah. Man, that dint take long. This Nig, man, he c'n *motor*.)

And The People sat stunned. Stunned beyond all comprehension. You know, knowing they'd witnessed the profound, and knowing it was, you know, it was somehow *emselves* they'd witnessed. Emselves but with a different force behind em. History? Man, sumpthin like that, I juss dunno.

Two hundred and more chests heaving with getting breaths back. And when, eventually, they had, you coulda heard a pin drop, eh. And just the wind, moaning up there like a distant dog howling. Up in the ceiling, eh, the rafters, or up there somewhere. Kinda spooky too, eh? Like your ancestors'd sent a sign, eh? A sign to you, those of you who don't know your own culture, you better get your black arses into gear do sumpthin about it. Before it's too late.

And Grace's face there the picture of death. Death absolutely not moving. Whilst life — *Life*, man — it was seething the opposite in the two hundred and more inspired living around her.

And the rain then: running all over the roof like ten thousand mice goin pitterpatter faster'n you could say. All day they'd been going like that.

Wasn't a person in the bar hadn't gone ovah to Jake Heke, expressed sympathy, deep condolences, the loss of his daughter.

They'd shook his hand: Man, dunno what to say, eh. I'm sorry to hear the news, Jake. You know how they are these bar people, awkward till they're fulla piss. Some were pissed, so they'd come to him bawling, weepin, carryin on (ya'd think it was me who fuckin died) makin fools of emselves and him, because he was never at ease in anything but a scrap, a good rumble, or the promise of it.

They'd embraced him, kissed him, slobbered all ovah a man; said stupid things (inept), stood before him like a kid before the headmaster or sumpthin, shufflin about and not knowin what to say (don't care what ya say, just wish you'd fuck off, leave a man in peace, to have his beer in peace, keep to his own circle.) Though the real genuine ones made a man feel really bad like he could just bawl his eyes out — cept he couldn't. Not Jake, the Muss, Heke. So any wonder a man just wanted to get drunk.

All the day they made the beeline for his table where he always drank at. Always. Trekkin over to a man to pay their respects (man, funeral's juss up the fuckin road. Why can't they go there and pay their respects to her. She's the one dead. I ain't.) Jake only too aware that they were honouring him first; him, the fighter, before it was the father of the suicide girl. Yeah, leavin their cards of sympathy with a man, it's not really her, Grace (poor Grace, Jesus Christ, but *why?*), they've never even met her, most ofem.

And he had his understandings, Jake, that this was another event in their lives, just another thing they could fix emselves to till they'd sucked it dry, then it'd be on to the next thing. He saw it brought em all closer together, as if by sharing each other's miseries, tragedies, it sorta made their own less. Sumpthin like that; Jake didn't exactly string his perceptions together in one long, reasonably articulated sentence. Just that he did recognise

123

when grief was drama, and what drama was for.

Only one'd made Jake really cry was Mavis when she'd only found out the news when she came in: the look she'd given Jake, of — (I dunno, a sympathy that was sorta *pure*.) Then she burst into tears. And even Jake'd started then. Holding each other. Man. She got a taxi went straight to the funeral at Beth's home village. A man hadn't seen her since.

That first day, man. Heavy stuff. Cops knockin on the door, a man wondering what the fuck he'd done he didn't remember when he was drunk, then the cops askin him did he have a daughter about thirteen, fourteen, fifteen, around that age? Jake findin out they'd gone door to door all over Pine Block tryin to find out who the kid was found hanging from a tree over at, all places, the Trambert place. Deepening the mystery to Jake. The confusion makin it worse. Beth still half drunk from the night before when everyone'd ate her picnic up and she'd got real upset at that, yet she was the one brought the damn thing in, having to get her out of bed (after checking Grace's bed and the *fright* a man'd got to see her bed hadn't been slept in) and tellin Beth what the cops wanted. Both ofem going down town in the cop car (and people in Pine Block pointing at us like we'd been picked up for sumpthin) to the morgue. And . . . Well, it was Grace alright.

Bringing her body back to the house in a borrowed van from a mate, and forgettin they had the rental car, and Beth (and me too) confused about it, not knowing what to do. Gettin Dooly from up the road to take it back. So confused you know. Takin the body, the coffin into the sitting room that the kids'd cleaned up from the party Jake and the boys and a few sheilas'd had after the pub (and a girl out there while we were, you know — oh Jesus, it don't bear thinkin about — while we were havin a good time a man's own kid was killin herself) and the neighbours arriving with flowers, which made it a bit better but not much, a man still felt as stink as he'd felt in his whole fuckin (rotten) life, but what to do but stand there as people from all ovah Pine Block came in and out, shakin a man's hand, huggin im, havin a cry, stayin or not stayin long. Man. Man oh fuckin man.

Then this old Maori dude comin and shakin Jake's hand then goin over to Beth and havin a long talk with her, then goin out but back in a tick with these other fullas, not a one of whom Jake recognised; all ofem shakin his hand, tellin him they were related to Beth from her pa, Wainui, and that they were taking Grace for a proper funeral, a dignified one. Didn't even ask a man was it alright. Not that he minded. In fact, it was a good excuse to get outta the place, go somewhere different so he wouldn't be so reminded of himself, what he'd been doing whilst his kid was taking her own life.

But all that culture, man, had a man feeling so outta place it was worse'n home, Rimu Street. So he hadn't stayed long. Told Beth he was goin for a walk. That was two nights ago. (Yeah, yeah, know it's wrong. I do.) Jake dialoguing with himself. (But I don't like that culture shet. I mean, what'd it ever do for me? Same sorta people tole a man and his family when he was growin up they were just a buncha slaves. So fuckem.) So he'd filled in the time drinking. And sleeping the nights at Dool's. Good ole Dool. What would a man do without his mates?

Drinking with Dool, asking him, Dool, have I been a bad father? Nah, man. I don't think so. But Dool's tone not sounding right. Well you know. I ain't sayin I been the father of the year, not sayin that. But . . . And lookin at Dool. And saying, You tell me what father in Pine Block is a, you know, like a — like a *proper* father. You tell me that, Dool.

Know what ya mean, Jake. Know what ya mean. Not that any of us is great at this fatherin thing, eh bro? Both ofem chuckling at that, just a little uneasily too. But ya don't see any other Pine Block kids goin and killin emselves, do ya? Nah, man, ya don't. So why you think she did it? (Because honest, man, I'm so confused.) Man, I dunno. Dool liftin up his hands, Leave me on that one, Jake. It's too heavy, man. Sorry, but it freaks me out, eh.

So Jake having to drop the matter, leave a man in the dark without a fuckin light.

Wakin up, Where am I? I'm at Dool's. That's alright then. Was having a bad dream . . . these dudes all kicking and punching me and I couldn't hurt em with my punches back, like my fists were feathers. Sumpthin else too — oh shit. Grace. They're buryin her today. Gotta get up, get myself cleaned up. Man oh fuckin man, she's dead . . . one of my kids is . . . dead.

Happy. I'm happy as can be expected in the circumstances, Beth looking at the big man in the suit and especially the one beside him

125

(Oh, hasn't he got tall in just those few months!), wanting to beam her pride, her love for him, but I can't. Not here. But when he ghosted a smile of acknowledgment her way Beth nearly fainted with happiness (and guilt being lifted too). It hardly mattered, even, the reason he was here. (It don't matter; he's my son. I'm the one who borned him. I'm the one who *owes* him.) Mum, it's Boogie! Mum, he looks . . . *different*. And *shush!* to young Huata and Polly from their Great-Aunt Matawai, Don't you know where you are? (No, they don't, as it happens.)

She could see he was nervous; he kept shifting his weight from one foot to the other, in contrast to the imposing figure of the child welfare officer, Mr Bennett, standing huge and unmoving with head only just bowed as if impatient to get on with something. Perhaps a speech, Beth thinking. The host welcome from one of the elders; a reply in turn by Mr Bennett. And a very rich, commanding voice he had too. And for those who understood these things it was plain the big man was well versed in these matters of culture and protocol and that sumpthin else extra, hard to figure, that goes with these traditional Maoris.

Then Bennett began a waiata, and immediately his voice seemed to fill the room. The timbre in his voice. The self-assurance. Then the boy beside him joined in, and The People, they made an involuntary exclamation of surprise and delight at such a young man versed in such matters. And Mummy, she was just flooding with tears as the ancient lamentation went on, the young harmonising the older. And Auntie Matawai telling Beth of the words: *Girl, prepare yourself, get ready your spirit . . . for the journey to the Spiritworld, it is yours, girl . . . your journey alone* . . . Aeee, as a mother listened and wept, and understood that Grace was not alone. For she is accompanied by all the warriors and warrioresses who have journeyed before her. (Aeee, my girl, I weep and laugh all at once for you.) So.

So the man and the chanting boy were joined by the great chief and chosen others; and so the air was afill once more with thirty-two and more voices in rhythmic chant-note; decreeing themselves on the notes of history. And oh with such magnificence you could not believe of the same people that they moved through greatly troubled waters. Oh but you could not.

A mother looking through her tears at how proud, how ramrod-straight this teaching had made her boy. And thinking of how he yet belonged to the state, was still a ward of Them, and yet looked so . . . so *free*.

126

And the hour drew nearer, and the hearse drew up outside, and an air of urgency grew, of pain, love and final farewell, climaxing, so did a stranger arrive in a nice car and walk the distance to the meeting house, where he stood awkwardly, alone, not knowing what to do, the protocol (these people are sticklers, I'm told, for protocol); dressed in a suitably dark suit, black tie; people milling around outside the carved-gabled building, a man'd never seen one so close nor realised how magnificently complex was the art of a people he knew, not socially, a single member of, some of them just sat around, on the parapets either side of the entranceway, kids most of them, and fooling around like kids all over do, except they imparted this rather patent air to the visitor (one can't help it) of laziness, slothfulness; as if all their drive was channelled elsewhere, perhaps bottled up for ill-directioned expression, was how Mr Trambert saw it, he couldn't help himself; then spotting the man in a sort of quaint uniform, like an old Home Guard from the war days or on that comedy TV programme, looking very self-important and giving the white stranger a sly look that said he was aching to be asked something, have his position confirmed. Uh, excuse me — Yep? This funeral, am I — Nope. Oh, I see. You coulda come earlier. It was in the paper what time it was. Yes, I'm sorry, I — Wha', can't ya read or sumpthin? Gordon Trambert just smiling at the man then, thinking, Oh well.

Having to stand there as a light drizzle began to fall, *hating* himself for not plucking up the courage to come earlier so he might pay proper respects to a girl who, after all, had hung herself on his property (like my Penelope . . . A mirror, God, a bloody mirror of my own daughter) and that official giving a chap the bad eye with inordinate emphasis, and stand amongst slothful kids and (one hadn't noticed before) ill-at-ease adults who looked as much out of place as he felt — (Pine Blockers, see: with none a this cultural learning, no social precedents, rules, no regulated teaching that'd givem the means to pay their proper respects. So accidentally rubbing shoulders with a man whose sheep they'd stolen, crept out into the night, the drunk and hungry night, and slit the creature's throat, he won't know, he's got thousands ofem, and who cares if he does) — whilst inside the mighty strains of now three hundred and more voices were joined in last hymn.

And the lid to her last residence was on and screwed tight shut forever (or as long as it takes for the, you know, the worms to break in) no longer that which you could see, take from the sight of whatever you would or could not help but take from it — Just a Weight.

A Weight in a shiny box with six handles on it waiting to be lifted by four strong men and two of the Weight's brothers.

The hymn, adapted to Maori wording, but well chosen for its minor noting thus its strong emotional appeal to an emotional and musical people; and this big fat woman, Mavis someone, doing the lead because, well, the mother of the dead girl had asked the chief that this Mavis be allowed to sing, leading each sad refrain and being answered by the swell of The People. And man, could she damn well sing.

And the harmonies taken up by The People just a natural arrangement. Uncannily so; from inside an overwhelming force of deliciously melancholy sound. Outside, and one was able to pick out the several different harmonies and be amazed at how well placed they were, the balance of no harmony dominating the main melody, and in particular that solo woman voice (I'd've never believed it possible were I not here to hear it, Trambert thinking) and in perfect tune and pitch, and Gordon Trambert comparing it to his Russian choral music recordings (perhaps this a little on the rustic side, though nothing that good training wouldn't fix), Trambert having difficulties reconciling the files in his head of newspaper readings and TV programmes and TV news figurings, of this race being a people in such trouble, spiritually; and even the culture meant to be shaky, or so he understood. (Really?)

Trambert scarcely able to believe his ears, the *quality*: it had him, the hymn, to having to bite his lip, but still his eyes misted over. So he bowed his head.

. . . and the Weight was lifted, and borne to outside waiting hearse. And by, and last sad speeches and tears, by, it, the Weight, was lowered into the space created for it. So the earth bore the Weight, and the preacher he said it was where she, the Weight, was sprung from, and that he was handing back the child to where . . . dust to dust . . . that sorta message. (Poor bloody kid.) . . . *Why?*

Sextons having their lunch sat on a concrete tomb and notice this kid coming out from behind the line of pines over there on the lakeside boundary . . . Huh? Walkin a queer way. Watchinim. I think the kid's zapped. Yeah, looks like it.

128

Watchin the kid stagger drunkenly towards the mound of dirt ready to be shovelled in after lunch. Watchin him stop there, stare down into the hole where that suicide kid was, the girl who hung herself at the rich farmer's place, there musta been sumpthin goin on there — He'll fall in he doesn't watch — Hey! Hey, you! Watch ya bloody step! The kid swinging his head the sextons' way — Oh man, I think he's been on that glue they use. I reckon. Watchin the kid with real interest now.

Toot had a flower in his hand; picked from the bed ofem scattered all around G's grave. And there she was, down there in that wooden box — Man! Man oh fuckin man, I don't believe it. Then a cupla fullas'd yelled at him. Fuckem. I ain't doin no harm. Just wanna say goodbye to my mate, G. Starin at her coffin coated in flowers. Lookin at the one he'd picked up: red. Like blood. Which brought emotion hurtling up from inside him. And he went down in a huddle; embracing himself. Howling like a dog to a full moon.

I think we'd better leave the kid, eh? Yeah, think we better. Maybe he's not zapped after all? You know, maybe it's just the grief. Poor bloody kid.

Watchin the kid. Feelin forim. But what can ya do?

A light drizzle starting.

11

The House of Angry Belonging

YA GOT THAT! YA FUCKIN *GOT* THAT CLEAR IN YA
MUTHFUCKA HEADS, YA *GODDIT!!*
Yeow, Jimmy. Have, man. Nig Heke shuffling on his feet,
head goin from side to side, dunno where ta fuckin look. On the
floor'll do. (The filthy floor.) What the other pros was doin, who
cared. I mean this is heavy as, man. Waiting for Jimmy Bad Horse
to bellow his squeaky high voice at a fulla and thinkin: All I want
is in, man. Nuthin else maddas. Nuthin.
  Then Bad Horse sayin to the others all around: *Whassa* FIRS'
RULE, bruthas and sistas? Whassa *firs'* rule in this family? A roar
erupting: BROWN FIST-SSZZ FIRS'!! THE GANG BEFORE
ANYTHING! THE BROWN FAMILY FIRS'!! BROWNFISZZ!!
BROWN FISZZ!! BROWN FISZZ!! (Oh, man, juss, you know,
overwhelming. Kid c'd hardly think.) Yet Nig desperate for a
break, an opportunity to ask Jimmy Bad Horse sumpthin, Sumpthin really urgent, Jimmy'd understand. But the big leader with
the funny high voice walkin up and down and Nig despairing of
getting his question asked. And the fuckin time marchin on. Any
other day but this, man.
  Even yesterday, when Jimmy Bad Horse'd turned up and tole
Nig he could be in, but that don't mean a patch member, just, you
know, takin the first step through them big black-painted gates.
Like gettin an invite ta heaven, eh Nig? Bad Horse chucklin away
in his evil style. Tellin Nig he had a dude arranged to rumble with.
It was outta him and this other pros from town sumwhere. Man,
just point me to im. Even though Nig'd been just about to go to
the tangi, Grace's funeral, when Bad Horse showed up.
  The rumble turned out a breeze. (Freaked out to start off with
till I connected with that left. Then I was right. Wasted the cunt.
Man, I moved like I was a boxing champ. God, I was good.
Though I didn't like it Jimmy tellin me to carry on, kick the poor
fucka's head in. But I did. And now look where I am: I'm standing

smack in the middle of the Brown Fists' house, man, thas where it got me.)

Bad Horse had em all chanting about Brown Fists coming before even ya own family. That *this* is your family now, to Nig and another pros, Warren Grady, who Nig'd grown up with, and wanting the same membership for as long as he could remember. Now here they were.

About two dozen ofem; two dozen crazy mad heavy dudes, bout half a dozen ofem sheilas. *Who-are-we?! Who-are-we?!* Jimmy hadem goin. Had Nig all astir inside except for that feeling of Grace, her funeral. (She's gettin buried today.) Made him wanna piss himself with the urgency. Yet overcome by this sight, this noise-force in front of him: everyone wearin a scowl (I practised my own for years) and those shades, man: cool. I mean *cool*. Wraparounds. Make ya look meaner'n a snake. And tats, man, everywhere tats. On faces, arms, hands, you name it. Got my own share ofem. Done em myself. Dint make a sound neither when I was puttin em on. The cutaway woollen gloves — brown for Browns. Man, make ya hands look like clubs, or like chain mail what ya see in comics. Heavy as. (Oh my old lady, she can't stand the Browns. I told her and told her they're only trying to look tough, thassa whole idea to look tough, to look mean. But they're not bad when ya get to know em. And when you're in withem, as a member, then it's heaven. Nig convinced of this.)

But Grace, her face, nagging away in Nig's mind.

Then Bad Horse was right beside Nig and hissin in his ear: We let ya in, man, and *this* is your family. Nig nodding, I know that, Jimmy. I accept that. Bad Horse stepping round in front of Nig: Ya bedda. Bad Horse resumed his pacing. Nig sorta sussed that Bad Horse hadn't said the same message to Warren.

The leader'd walk all the way through where the wall'd had a big hole knocked out of it into what used to be a next-door neighbour; from kitchen to kitchen. Then he'd pivot on his heavy (kicking) boots and come back. And the bros and sistas standing there waitin on his next move; a stereo goin in the background but quiet because he, Bad Horse, had said turn it down till he'd finished. The leader'd come right past near a kid's nose on his return: stridin out, his big bulk massive, man (And yet a Heke boy wondering why his old man'd told him this fulla Jimmy Bad Horse had no guts. Didn't look like he didn't.), and them fuckin arms like tree trunks. Man a fuckin alive, who'd be crazy enough to mess with him?

131

The picture of Grace grew more urgent in Nig's mind; so he took a deep breath and got Jimmy his next time past: Uh, Jimmy? I, uh, have to go to — My sister, she's, uh — But Jimmy cut him short by stopping dead in front of Nig and turning his vast, Brown Fist emblazoned, back. And Nig heardim in a sorta whisper: Wha' sista's this? Uh, you know, my — Grace. (Hasn't he heard about it?) The big frizzy head with its blue and white headband going from side to (worrying) side, Nope. I ain't heard a no sista called Grace in this family. Then he turned.

And he was looking up at Nig's several inches taller face. What sista called Grace, man? Man, I didn't mean — But the leader turning his back again, and pointing. You mean her? At this skinny bitch, Nig'd seen her around, mean as. Hidden behind her shades she looked meaner'n some a the dudes. Her name ain't Grace. (I never said she was.) And she's a sista. Nig twigging at that. (Oh man.) The half-gloved hand swung to another: Thas Mullah. She ain't called Grace. And *she's* a sista. The head going slowly round at all the faces, Nope, Nope, at each sheila. No Grace here, man. Sorry. But Nig wanting to go see his sister off. Uh, just the way she . . . you know, how she, uh (Can't say it, man. Can't say: died. I can't.)

The face again. Big beard. Bit fat face. Big explosion of wild hair. Shades not giving a kid a chance to know how he was goin, where he now stood, now that he'd seemingly broken some code or sumpthin. Oh man, we *know* bout your *sis-ter*, Nig. Clicking his tongue. (No eyes a kid can read. For a clue.) Her's was a, you know, a *hea-vee* trip, man. It was. Then — (shit! the fuck's happenin?) at chairs scraping, fallin over, boots stomping towards him it felt like the fuckin world was comin to an end. Yet a voice in Nig's head tellin him: Keep ya eyes open, man. And keep ya head straight. Don't madda *what* they do to ya, just don't show fear.

But the banging and crashing and stomping and wide arc of denim and eye-shaded advance hard to stand fast against. Nig wanted to piss — nah, *shit*. Just let his bowels open and let the fear flood out. Felt his mind shut off.

. . . Bad Horse saying how he, all ofus, brutha, were with Nig on Grace . . . (this a trick?) man, we know who she is — uh, was. Eh, family? And murmurings of yeah, they knew who she was. Seen her around, you know? . . . not that we actually sorta *said* nuthin to each other, I don't mean that . . . I mean, man, her age, eh, she was only, what, thirteen? That right what they say her

132

only thirteen? Oh man, we can dig the heavy trip she musta been on . . . Looking up at Nig after shoving his shades upwards on his head. First time Nig'd ever seen the man's eyes; Nig surprised at how sorta ordinary they looked: just bloodshot brown eyes, nuthin special, nuthin evil *bad* about em. But then Nig's blood ran cold at Bad Horse sayin: Ole man like you got, man . . . Sorta shruggin with his lips how they do. Chuckling. I think anyone'd wanna commit, you know, sideways, they had ta live withim.

Nig not sure if he felt defensive or hatred for his old man. Maybe both. Jimmy still talking: Yeah, we seen her around, knew she was your lil sis. But she weren't one of us, eh. I mean not like we thought you were one of us . . . y' know, hanging out as a pros all that time. But had to learn to trust you, eh Nig. You know, ya mighta turned out sumpthin we, uh, didn't like. I mean, we ain't what you'd call geniuses. Eh Nig? Laughing. Hahaha! geniuses. Man, we ain't even *average*. We're just a packa dumb Maori fullas — oh, and a few sistas — got together. But we got sumpthin most people ain't, Nig. Know what that is, man?

Staunchness, Jimmy. *Staunchness*, Nig. You got it, bro. He's got it, eh bruthas an sistas? YEOW! Their affirming cry lifted Nig's spirits.

Staunchness, Nig Heke. For each other, man, we'd . . . we'd die. (Oh I'd die, Brutha. You just gimme the fuckin word, man: I'd die for a fellow Brown.) We might — Jimmy cocked his head to one side, acting funny — we might even — HAHAHAHA! — even — HAHAHAHA! — you know, *loooove* each utha. And laughing so hard it made his shades drop back down to near exactly their right position. Man. Tongue licking out over the mo part of his beard, Well . . . Dunno whether we'd go *that* far. Laughin again. And everyone laughin withim; and that word: *loooove*, echoing over and over from em, the mass, The Gang, as they said it in a dozen different ways: you know, tiptoeing it out, lettin the word sorta plop out, or teasin it out, or spittin it. Like it was some kinda bad-tastin medicine, sumpthin like that, they knew'd cure em. But damned if they were gonna take it, fucked if they were. And Nig could hear the change when their leader yelled: More like *belonging!* Eh people!

Next Jimmy was shakin Nig's hand, tellin im, Welcome, brutha. Welcome. And a boy's heart filled with that sense of the word Jimmy'd used before: *belonging*.

Somehow, with all the members comin up to Nig shakin his hand in the Brown Fist way of receiver holding the right thumb up to be taken in the full hand of the giver, releasing and giving each other a light tickling touch on the palm, somehow Jimmy Bad Horse managed to find Nig's ear tellim: *This* is your fuckin family. From now on, *this* is where you're at. So I'll leave it up to you. Melting back into the crowded room. (God in heaven, but I can't go.) But no time to think. Party time, bruthas and sistas! Jimmy announcing. (I'm sorry, Grace. But what can I do?)

Clink of beer bottles rattling in their wooden crates, a kid — every kid and adult in the room — had heard it all his life. It'd become the music he wanted to hear himself when he was old enough to play it. Crates and crates of the fuckin sweet stuff bein lugged in dumped on the floor, hands grabbing at the contents; decapping with teeth, a ring, cap to cap, on the edges of anything sharp, a belt buckle, a knuckle-duster, a fuckin big knife, man, bigger'n Crocodile Dundee's, and one mad dude just smashing the top clean off and guzzling from the broken neck. Oh man. Heavee. (Grace . . . Grace, Grace, they're burying you. I'm so sorry . . .) Can't think bout that. Not any more. To much happenin here.

The stereo turned right up. Can't hear myself think. Drink up, Nig. Drinking up. Marley and the Wailers. Oh man. SOUNDS, bruthas! Sounds. And just the hint of things in the movements of hips, hands, groovin bodies. But too soon yet. Too soon.

Smoke got passed around. Big fat joints half a fuckin yard long. Heads. Sins, man. None a ya fuckin weed for the Browns we *deal* in it.

Smokin, guzzlin, faggin, rappin, bigtimin, hate-talkin, smokin and guzzlin some more. And the music, man, expanding to ya ear . . . hearin it so clear ya felt ya'd composed it yaself, or so clear ya understood the, you know, the creative whatsit behind makin the recording. Oh you know. Smokin, ahhh, but that is *gooood* shet, man. Guzzlin. Like our olds, eh? Haha, finding it funny now, after all this time, your olds boozin their lives away and now you doing the same. Man.

The SOUNDS, keep on callin to a man, tellin im sumpthin, I dunno. Sumpthin about himself, I dunno . . . Like the art, man: I c'n dig the *art* went into this music-making. Why they started looking at each other with that mutual recognition goin snap in their minds: Hey, we're at the same place, man!

Guzzlin, smokin, rappin, *listnin* — (So much potential . . .) — startin to groove in time to it, or move to the offbeats; unnerstandin, mirrorin each other's movements with sly smiles; flowin *flooowin* to this whole new unnerstandin in their heads. Then suddenly droppin it.

Talkin tough and rough, we ain't groovin to no sensitivity, whatever ya call it, it *sucks*. So then their sentences had little length. Short spurts. More like grunts. And curses. Fucks. Cunts. Wankah. That sorta thing. (Yet inside all this unspokenness like some uncoiled spring of beauty, unnerstandin, just achin to unleash itself).

Eyes hardly stayed in contact with each other — those that weren't hidden or lurking behind the shades — just a flicker, a stolen glance, a shy dart of vision that they, none of em, could hold. But things started expanding again.

The music did it: brought em out, flowered the little buds in their funny little brains, had blossums bloom in their dirty little ears. The music, man. It loosened em. And when a bad dude gets loose he releases sumpthin.

All that Pine Block growin-up bottled all them years, havin to act tough and only tough or ya die, man, I'm tellin ya; all them years of learnin to be a supposed Maori, man, what it must do to ya, you know, ya actual *potential*. Ah, fuck the potential. Only joking. Only joking. But no sooner said than a dude got taken by the SOUNDS again, or else it was whatever it was in his head been set free; so he was walkin down main street of Kingston, Jam-ay-kah, with Bob at his side, and the other cats really thinkin he was hot shet.

Then the collective mind shifted again: Volume. We want more VOLUME. And *fuck* the neighbourhood, makin it out as an act of stroppiness, or gang-power display, when truth was (any kid could see) they wanted to hide in the volume of music like they were always hidin behind their shades or in the dope and the booze and the fags; they juss wanna drown out the, you know, the upbringing. The stain of growin up a Pine Blocker. Of growin up havin to fit a role, a race role, man, and thassa fuckin truth you know it and so do I: havin to turn yaself into sumpthin ya mightn't be. Yeah, thas what bein a Maori is for a Pine Block Maori. Gimme more smoke.

Passed around again. And again. It'd stone a fuckin elafint, man! Music vibrating the whole fuckin house, all two storeys and two full homes of it. And the truth out in the open now: gonna strut my stuff, man, an I don't care *who's* lookin.

Dancin. Movin this way — that way — cut this way — hey-hey! — spin — *hooold*it — now turn. Yeow! Turnitup! Turnitup!

135

Gimme a beer, gimme a beer!

Movin with mah groovin this is a *cinch*, man, a breeze, a doddle — *Lookit* me. (Yet weighted, I dunno, hard ta explain when ya jussa Pine Block nobody who only went ta school to beat up the honkies and feel their sheilas' twats up. Childhood. I think it's to do with childhood this weight thing.) Why so many were doin their thing with eyes closed, as if they were scared of the discouraging adults, the arsehole parents who were always tellin em ya gotta be this, ya can't be this, don't be that, juss a wantin to shut out the voices of authority in ya head, the mystery of ya mind tellin ya ya ain't nuthin but a little cunt no madda *how* hard ya try not ta be — Oh gimme another beer.

Swallowing some more courage, see if tha'll do the trick, shut out that fuckin *voice*'t stays in my head. Nother one. Ahhh, that feels bedda.

Swaggerin, staggerin, actin up, actin out, showin up, playin who cares just don't let the Voice come down a bummer on my, you know, my expression. Juss wanna dance . . . (with my darling, to the Tennessee Waltz — !?) Oh fuck that, man, thaz a *oldie* numba. Member em doin that, man? Our fuckin olds, man, they *love* that wankoff song. Another shift.

Rumblin, man. LOVE IT. Rumblin. Talkin about it — interrupting each other, climbing all over each other in their haste to get the password in. And havin this unnerstandin of sumpthin else about rumblin, the rhythm of it. Rumble in the jungle, member that dude? who was he again? Ali. *Ali*, man! What a fidah! Oh yea, what about Sugar Ray then? *Sugah Ray?* O far out! but he's the — And that dude foughtim that time wouldn't fight no more, what's his name ag — Duran. Roberto Duran, man. Know what they callim in his, you know, wherever the fuck he comes from, language? Hands a Stone. Howzat?! Oh wow. Call me that, man, I'd love it. I seen tha scrap on my brutha's video; man, what a fuckin rumble. He ain't no wankah neither that Duran fulla. No? No, man. Well how come Sugar Ray wasted the cunt? Sugar Ray'd waste any cunt. I mean, he's the *ult*imit rumblin machine.

Actin out their fistic hero's movies: Hey-hey, watch me, watch me, this is Sugar Ray's Bolo punch . . . ooooooo! ca-boom! HAHA-HAHA! In stitches. In an uproar. At the act bein so, uh, so *true*. Hey, what about this: *ba-boom-boom-daka-duk-duk-kapow!* A Leonard combination, pictured in their minds with all the exclamation marks, the *sounds*, juss like out of a comic.

Watch me, watchme: a blurring combin-ation — a pause of

posy arrogance — nigger cheek; flickin out a lazy left and kapow! comin over with a big right. Bobbin, weavin, bouncin, Ali-shufflin, Bolo-punchin, shoulders goin whiff-whiff-whiff! like *oil*, man . . . (I) he moves like he's got oil in his joints. Eyes goin all poppy: chin juttin out, shoulders going yahyahyah — kapow! Gotcha! Laughin. Like this, like this: . . . Oh just mirrors, man, of what they'd seen of the world, the creative world, the achieved world doin its stuff, struttin its stuff, on the TV, and every right to, man, cause others'd TRIUMPHED ovah the, you know, the odds. (Juss one fuckin win is all a kid, a man ever wanted. One single victory ovah sumpthin, someone.)

But then a lull comin down onem. This slowly descending lull. And with it: Truth.

Truth. Zingin, pingin, a crackle, a sparkle of electric zaps. Man, is it the dope doin this . . . ? Truth about what? Truth about us, that's what. Why, what we done? Nuthin. It's jussa, you know, a process ya go thru. Didn't last long though. Truth doesn't. Truth ain't a continual process; it ain't a game that has a set time length. It's just a zap. A mili-sec buzz. A (uninvited, unwanted) disturbance of ya thoughts, like God or sumpthin has stuck a mirror in front of ya when ya weren't expectin it. Nah, it's just a small-time, short-moment hurt that goes, man. Promise ya. Here, drink up. Drink and be happy. A shift again.

Fulla went out back to the kennels, came back with a trio a dogs. More like tanks, ya mean. Bull terriers. Built like fuckin tanks. Black and white tanks, HAHAHAHA! And everyone pattin em, strokin, ear-ticklin, sweet-talkin, or steerin clear ofem. The bro bringin em over to Nig to take a sniff atim, the bro tellin his tanks, Is alright, he's one of us. Pat em, Nig. Nig patting the dogs in turn.

Air thick with smoke. Dope and fags. The music loud but the ear adjusted to it. The other music of more beer arriving in crates, brought in by more gang members and hanger-on associates, the ones with a bit more bread. Man, must be fifty ofem in here now. (Grace.) Can't hear myself think. (But sorry, Grace. I'm thinkin of ya, honest. Gonna make a special trip to your grave. Gonna buy a big buncha flow — no, a wreath. I'll buy her a wreath. It's dole day tamorrow. Tomowwow, as Mum'd say.) Nig having a private little giggle to himself and this sheila comin up to him and askin: Whatcha laughin about, man? And not a bad looker neither. (Man, I might be in here.) Oh this an that.

Nother fulla came in with two more dogs. Rotties. And he

137

wasn't wearin a Brown Fist patch either. Other bro with the three tanks goes up to the associate asksim: Ya reckon your dogs c'n beat bulls? And everyone goin, oooooo! And the dogs started barkin at each other, and straining on their leashes. Dunno, man. Mine're mean fuckahs. So're mine, man. Nah, I like my rotties. Don't wannem, you know, damaged or nuthin. The Brown lookin at the dude, Okay, man. Spose I'll have ta damage you then.

Real casual, eh. Like tellin the fulla his name.

Fear on the associate's face. Real fear. Like he'd walked into a nightmare and only just realised it. Nig feeling sorry for him, Okay, lettem fight, the scared fulla agreein. The Brown givinim a wicked smile: Thas cool, man. Make it in half a hour; give my boys time ta warm up. Chuckling at the scared dude. C'mon, boys. Pulling his three dogs away. Y'c'n have ya suppa in half a hour. Laughing.

Whaddid you say your name was? Nig to the sheila who'd come up to him. Tania. The sheila givin Nig the Brown Fist hand-shake. And Nig thinking he might be in here.

Up the street, around the corner and down that street a bit, at Number 27 Rimu, several cars were pulling up outside. People gettin out and takin crates of beer up the footpath withem. Went on for about fifteen minutes, this car and beer arrival. Neighbours across the street all eyes between their dirty venetians.

Wash-house stacked high with the stuff, and inside the kitchen where the late afternoon party was startin up, the fridge chocker with beer too. And back in the wash-house a fulla'd filled the stone sinks with cold water and filled em with beer bottles. Full ones a course.

Jake in the kitchen sat at the table sayin, Comin, comin, to all and sundry like he was a fuckin king or sumpthin. Which he was.

In they trooped till ya c'd hardly breathe. But it was good like that: ya seem to have a bedda time when there's a lot of yas packed in a room tight. Long as there's plenty of beer, that's the main thing. Oh, and smokes. Nuthin worse'n runnin outta smokes. Seen ragin parties just go dead when the smokes ran out. Dead.

Anyone bring a gat? No gats, man, this is a, you know, a housestamping to, you know, scare away the ghost of the departed. Oh yeah, thas right. Forgot that. Everyone goin all falsely quiet for a bit in respect to the girl. The one who killed herself. Jake's girl. But it didn't last long before they were back to their normal buzzing volume, having already been half-tanked up at McClutchy's beforehand.

Jake was really enjoying himself: being surrounded by so many people he hadn't had a party as big as this in years. Made him feel popular; and better too. In his heart. The heart sposed to be grieving. (Well it is. But I ain't no sook about it. And that's how people expect of a man. Of me they do.) Besides, he'd had an awful lot to drink the last few days, so his head had this nice permanent buzz to it.

So where's the mother? a woman askin out of the blue. She'll be here, someone answering on Beth's behalf. What about the Maori priest? the woman wanting further to know. Jake peering through the crowd to see who it was askin these questions. Askin her: What's with the Maori priest bit? (I know who it is, it's Nicky. Silly ole Nicky Hodge.) Well I ain't touchin a beer till you had the house done, Jake Heke. Huh? Jake standing up so to be eye to eye with this bitch. What's gettin the house done got ta do with — Ya gotta get it stamped of the ghost before y'c'n start boozin, mista, you oughta know that. Ah, shuddup, woman. And siddown. Okay, Jake Heke, it's your house. The middle-aged woman sat herself down on a beer crate.

Everyone back in the swing again, guzzling, burping, laughing about that, so someone dropping a real clanger of a fart. The house shakin with their laughter. And people thinkin that why can't life be always like this? you know, with everyone happy because they got, and had, plenty to drink and smoke, to laugh about. Oh, and sure, it was a terrible thing this girl a Jake's doing what she did. But that aside, man . . . I mean, life has to go on.

So when's the Maori priest comin? Nicky Hodge again. Shuddup, Nicky. Won't shuddup. This ain't right. This — Then fuck off! Jake getting annoyed with Nicky's persistence. I ain't. Not till the house is done. Jake up on his feet: Done? *Done?* Done fuckin what? Everyone going quiet. Oh-oh, Jake is off.

Done the fuckin spirits, that's what. Spirits? Where, Nicky? I dunno. Why ask me? I ain't a fuckin cop. I only know they exist and they have to be done by someone who knows what he's doing. Like a Maori tohunga. And I ain't touchin a drop till one comes. Jake outraged at her insistence, and the fact that she was a mere woman. Tellin Nicky, Ya weren't even at the funeral. Realising too late — And nor were fuckin you, *mista*. And I ain't scared a you.

139

Jake lookin at everyone, Listen to her, would ya? (Oh they were listening alright.) I don't like all that speeches and singing fuckin hymns stuff, thas why I wasn't there, Jake hearing himself explain without consciously deciding he would. Adding, All that bawlin, howlin stuff. Tapping his chest: Ya think that's for Jake Heke? He nearly'd said, the Muss.

Mista, that's what they have a blimmin funeral for — so ya c'n cry. What, ya can't cry, ya can't show ya not tough at your own kid's tangi? Oh man . . . Jake close to steppin over and smackin Nicky one. Ah, fuck you, woman. Sitting down. Lighting up. Trying to dowse his anger straight from the bottle in one long guzzle. Cept it didn't work. Nicky'd got to him; sumpthin about her tone, and the way her eyes seemed to know sumpthin that he oughta know but didn't. Dunno. Can't quite figure it. Oh have another beer, Jake. Drink up and be happy. Givin that firmly seated and non-drinking figure of Nicky Hodge a bad-eye glare. Fucker.

Nicky sat in the gutter outside the house when Beth arrived in a taxi with her kids. Asked Nicky what's wrong? why're you sitting there like that? Nicky tellin Beth (with pride too) that she wasn't gonna be like the rest of those animals in there drinkin, partying when the house hadn't been done by a Maori priest. Quite right, Nicky, the newly converted Beth agreeing with her friend's stand. He'll be here any second now. Beth marching up the footpath to the house.

They — every man and a few women ofem — with looks of disbelief, outrage, anger and even hurt at Beth's storming into (my own) the house, the kitchen, ordering em out. The lot of you — out. Jake jumping up and tellin em, Don't listen to her, she's, you know — Beth, c'mon, dear. These're guests. Only reason he was being reasonable because of Grace. Not my guests. Now go. The lot of you.

And this societyless lot, this structureless pack of arseholes not budging, just making out they were moving by milling about without actually making a single step of progress toward the door, unable to bear the thought of being banished from a promising party: and all that *beer* not yet touched. Then Nicky walkin in and all ofem turning on her: Yeah, it was you, ya bitch! Ya shit-stirrin bitch, whatcha been tellin Beth? Poisoning the lady of the house's mind! (The lady of the house now, eh?) OUT! at the lot

140

ofem, hating them for their lack of order, discipline. Their mad love of drinking. Mad because it was ruining their lives (killing our children) driving kids to joining gangs and then hurting and killing each other. And they *cannot see it.*

Rid of them finally. Just Beth and Jake. She staring at the man — So where was my daughter's father when she was buried? Told ya, I hate that — Get out, Jake. Oh shuddup, woma — *Get out!* Okay. Jake shrugging. It's only cos a Grace I'm lettin — And don't you come back, mista. What? Ever.

Jake laughing, HAHAHA!!! Bending over holding himself with laughter.

And when he rose, Beth spat full in his face. Then closed — or half closed — her eyes waiting for the retaliation. (But it's worth it.) Up his arm came, except it went no further. His jaw was trembling though. And Beth's insulting discharge was sliding down his nose. Jake shaking his head, Gonna get you for that, woman. I am. She standing there, feeling . . . feeling almost *exultant.* Go to hell, mista.

Neighbours across the street watchin Jake walk fuming down the footpath not long after the main lot'd come unexpectedly out; followed him with their eyes, striding up the street. To his second wife, Dooly, I bet. It's Dooly Jake shoulda been married to, not Beth. Cos that's who he spends more time with.

At cars pulling up, except when the people got out they didn't start cartin in crates a beer, nope. So who are they? Oh, must be Beth's people. Man, they well dressed for Pine Block. Well dressed for Maoris, fullstop, eh? Hahaha! they'd better watch emselves, the people round here might think they're rich and rob em.

Beth waiting at the top of the path; a great big fulla in a suit leadin the cupla dozen men and women no doubt come to do the house. That's Bennett. The welfare officer. So it is. What, he's a tohunga? Must be. Well I'll be. Watchin through their sly slits of dirty venetians. Oh and that's the one got sent away by the court a few months back, what's his name again? Boogie.

Boogie, that's it. Funny thing, I think it was that Bennett who, you know, did the damage in his report that sent him away. Now they're walkin side by side. Well, well, well. Mind you, someone was at the tangi yesterday and seen Bennett and the kid, Boogie, doing one a them whatyoucalls, the old chants they do. A waiata. Yeah, that's it. Said the kid was neat too. She heard, this woman

141

at the tangi, that Bennett spent two full days at his place with that kid coaching him to do the waiata, and hardly any sleep. Well, I'll be . . .

Watching with increased interest now. Oooo, he's got tall since the last time I seenim. Who's got tall? The kid. Jake's young fulla. Though I heard he's a proper little sook, eh. Is that right? Clicking tongues at that. Aee, such a waste of a good build too, eh? A waste alright. The oldest one, Nig, he's a Brown Fist now. Aee, another one joined up with them mongrels? But you wouldn't think Nig'd turn out like that, eh? Why, what's so different about him? Well his mother . . . she always loved that kid. All the years I been here I never saw a woman so much as lift a hand to that boy. Such a nice boy too. Tall, gotta good build like his old man, but oh, I wouldn't a thought he had his father's wildness. Not to up and join the Browns. I mean to say: they *mean* bastards. Maybe he is too. Nah, I don't think so. Oh well, he'll find out he's in the wrong league then, won't he? Spose so. Unless they, you know, change him.

What about the girl? Grace? Oh my daughter goes to — used to — go to school with her. Said she was a proper little stuck-up. Always wanting the, you know, the *bedda* things in life, according to my girl. Said she was always on about potential, some flash word like that. Said she wanted to realise her potential. What fuckin potential, livin here in Pine Block? Only potentials here are jailbirds. Hahaha! Have to laugh. Wonder why she did the deed over at the Trambert place? Yeah, I been wondering about that too. Spose it was to show us peasants sumpthin or other. Spose it was. Unless there was some funny business goin on, eh? Lookin at each other. Waitin, *hopin* for the snap of same conclusions to time in, go *zing* between their eye contact. Wha', like they had sump-thin goin . . . the girl and . . . Sumpthin like that, Mabel. Funny you should be thinkin the same thing. Well, it was obvious when ya think about it, eh? Guess it was. Guess we'll read about it some day in the paper: you know, farmer hangs himself on same tree as Pine Block girl — Pine Block waif — waif then. As waif was found hung on. I betcha.

Still staring out the gaps in the blind even when the visitors'd all gone inside the Heke place; speculating on why the partygoers, then Jake, had come storming outta the house like they did. Not that ya see Jake Heke in anything but a wild mood. Well, one day he's gonna get his beans. Who from? His missus? Laughing, hahaha! now that was a joke. Or the girl'll come back and

142

hauntim. Or he'll get stabbed in one of his bar brawls. Or . . .

And the light dying outside.

And cars — wrecks, grunt machines, gang growlers, beat-up jalopies — going past, roaring past. And kids, some ofem hardly walking, out on the footpaths, wandering about with no one carin, runnin wild. (And growing up loveless.) Another prospect taken the place of one of the two who got the big nod today. Another tryin to get up the courage to declare the same hand. A dead girl's spirit being helped on its way to the Spiritworld. Oh, juss another night in Pine Block.

She led him by the hand. C'mon, I ain't gonna bite ya. Giggling, tugging at him to follow.

Up the stairs; incredible noise behind em of dogs goin mad, their audience goin mad. Screaming, yelling, egging the fighting creatures on; stomping heavy-booted feet in time to some crazy beat one ofem'd started. The fuckin stereo at full blast, Marley, who else. Din partly muffled at the top of the stairs with a layer of floor between em.

Hey, where we goin? But she juss smilin atim, making her beauty the more (wasn't for the star tats under each eye, though). Leadin Nig by the hand past a replica of home, but I guess every home in Pine Block is a replica, yet still noting to himself that this'd be the old's room . . . then mine and Abe's, and next door where the littlies sleep with — No, forget about that one. Just think about the girl, this girl.

Passing directly overhead the sitting room where all the noise was comin from: Wow. Ya juss wouldn't believe it. On through another crude-cut opening in the wall to what used to be a next-door neighbour till the Browns moved in. Took the fuckin lot. And rent-free! And Tania tellin Nig that the hole'd been cut by Jimmy Bad Horse with a fuckin chainsaw! The two in hysterics over that. Down the passage, a bit quieter. She squeezed his hand, he squeezed back. (Gonna fuck her *slooow*, man. Ain't gonna rush it. I'll get her worked up first.)

Came to an open door, he followed her into the room, kicked the door shut behind him. Quite quiet. Least they could talk without havin to shout. Just the thump and yelps and barks and reggae beat sorta in the distance. She looked different in the quiet. (Maybe she's changed her mind?) Or maybe she's a cock-teaser, Nig thinking. Oh well, she's smilin at least. Pity about them tats:

143

can't stand a tat on a woman. Make em look cheap. Like they're a slut. Though Nig hardly expecting a virgin.

Pale skin, almost white. You a half-caste? She frowning. What the fuck's that got ta do with — Brung herself to a halt. Stared at him. Only askin. Alright, I am. Satisfied? Nig shrugging, No big deal, sista. No big deal. Good. She stepped up to him. (Now *this* is better.) You're fuckin tall as, man. (Put a fulla right off.) Put an arm around his waist, the other held off there somewhere, a fulla couldn't figure it: she either wanted it but was just a bit shy, or she was a teaser. Oh well, have to see.

Nig rubbed her rump through her tight jeans. Firm as. (Oh man.) He had to bend at the knees to kiss her — her kiss immediately rough: lips tight, pressing too hard, no movement, no softness. (So what gives?) Then she started moaning. (No way, man.) It was wrong. Her timing. Not as if a fulla'd done nuthin special. He eased away, but she went, *mmmmmmmm*, and pressed harder her lips to his. It fuckin hurt. He went to pull away with more force this time, except she stuck her tongue in his mouth. (Oh well, in that case . . .) But then she started up with that mmming again. Oh but then she rubbed his penis through his jeans. And Nig no longer had the ability to be discerning — Till her rubbing hurt him. (Jeez, she's got no fuckin idea.)

Then she pulled herself away from him . . . walking backwards to the bed (there were two ofem, and both in a filthy unmade state. My old lady'd freak out if she thought I was gonna be in one of these.) He followed her.

Well I'll be: he could see the Trambert farm out the window. Had him thinking of Grace. (Sorry, Grace.) Tania was taking her gear off; having a job with the tight jeans. Red in the face. Nig turned away to lessen her embarrassment. But she said, And don't look, neither. So he did look, in time to see her naked form diving under the grubby grey blanket (and no sheets?!) He took his clothes off, back turned. But only so his excitement wouldn't, you know, freak her out or sumpthin. He got in beside her — quickly.

Up on one elbow to talk a bit. But she pulled him down onto her, somehow rolled under him. Started that damn kissing again. He reached down, felt her, but she shoved his hand away. Mmmmmm, she went. (Jeezzz.) He tried to enter her, but she kept clamping her legs — no, her thigh muscles. Ya'll have ta help me, he told her. No. Jus get on with it.

Eventually he got inside her: she was barely damp. And it hurt like hell to start off with. He paused during it and she was straight

144

away asking him, Ya finished? He shook his head, no, into her hair. Least that was clean. He flooded inside her. She nibbled at his neck then, giggling. Gonna give ya a lovebite. He asked why. Huh? Doncha like em? Promptly sucking at his throat. He told her: don't see the point ofem. So she stopped immediately, rolled on her side, Only tryin ta be nice. I know, I know, Nig pulled gently at her to face him. (Man, this bed *stinks*.) Keenly aware of the quality of bedding now that his urge'd been satisfied, if nuthin else.

So how long ya been a Brown? What does it madda? You a fuckin cop or sumpthin? Bitch was sulking to the wall. And drop this, you a cop shet, Nig felt like givin her one. A backhander. Teacher to talk to him, a man (or near enough) like that. I thought you wanted to talk? he gave her a chance. Who said that, man? Aw, c'mon. Ya got whatcha wanted dintya? I thought you wanted it too? Well, maybe I did. Maybe I didn't. And she shrugged, Oh, wasn't nuthin anyway. (Nothing?) What, havin sex? Nig was amazed. Yeh, whassa big deal about havin it? Because it's . . . it's, you know, it's kinda special. Oh yeah? Yeah. For fullas it is. And for sheilas too. Bullshet. It's for fullas; all they think about, most ofem. Well I don't think about just that. O doncha just? No, I fuckin don't. Good boy. Very good boy, Nig whatever ya other name is. Go to the front of the class — Then Nig slapped her.

Hey! She was around in an instant. The fuck ya think ya doin! Don't talk to me like I'm — Her eyes blazin at him: Tell ya what, busta, I only have to give the word to them downstairs and you are dead meat. Ya got that? Ya dead fuckin meat. Her eyes on fire. And I mean, busta: dead-fuckin-meat. (Dream's turned into a fucking nightmare.) Okay, okay, forget it. Nig went to get out of bed, but she grabbed him: Stay. Looked at him with big brown eyes. Stay, eh? He shrugged. Okay.

They lay there for a bit. Listening. Calming down. Dogs'd stopped the fight, no more cheering and yellin. Wonder who won it? Ah, the rotties, easy, she was certain. He said, Nah, the bulls, man. Ain't nuthin can beat a bull in a scrap. And the music pounding away beneath em.

So tell me about your sister. Took Nig by surprise. Poor thing. Tania looked and sounded genuinely sympathetic; the first show of real humanity Nig'd seen in her. Was she pretty? Yeah, pretty as. Oh, Tania's bottom lip dropped. She looked like you then? Dunno. She must've. Oh, she went again. Nice, you know, nice-natured? Nice as, Tania. Honest. I ain't just sayin that. Nig felt the emotion welling up in him. He brought it under control, thinking: I'm nearly a Brown now.

Tania askin a heap of questions about poor Grace. What kinda hairstyle did she have? Did she have lots and lots a friends? Nope, hardly any friends, Nig tellin her. And she looking all hurt and astonished at that. The *poor* thing. How old was she again? Thirteen. Thirteen and killed herself, eh? Clicking her tongue. Staring into space, up at the ceiling, eyes misted. (Man, she's got heart after all.)

Dunno why Jimmy didn't want you goin to her funeral today. He coulda picked another day to bring you into the Browns. Not as if we got, you know, other things on. In life, I mean. Well, it was to put me to the test, Nig'd convinced himself. But she sneered at him: Yeh, some pass. Pass what? Of the test. She rolled on her side again. Hey, come on . . . I'd've gone to the funeral I wouldn't be here now. And, man, you don't know how I wanted to be a Brown. Couldn't it've waited, though? Yeah, but he's the leader, right? Sure, but he ain't fuckin God. Some of the seniors said he shoulda let ya go. But Nig only shrugged. Them's the breaks.

So where're you from? None of your — Come on, Tania. Okay, I come from Mangakino. Where's that? Bout fifty k's from here. Middle a fuckin nowhere. It *sucks*. Place *sucks*. So what's your olds like? What's *your* olds like, busta? Old lady's good. Old man's a wankah. Yeah, well, I don't know who my old man was, and my old lady's a cunt. Yeah? Ya bedda believe it, busta.

Used to leave us — me — on my own, go drinking. Yeah, well . . . What could Nig say that they both didn't already know from experience. Ya never see Pakeha kids like that do ya? Dunno. Never thought about it. Well I have, and I c'n tell ya, they don't go leavin their kids to fend for emselves while they're pissin up. Ya don't see Pakeha kids in hotel carparks do ya? No. No, come to think of it. And you know, how ya read in the paper about some poor kid's been left in a car while its olds are in the pub drinking and it, the kid, got holda some matches and — and . . . well, you know. Tears in her eyes, she wiping at them with her tattooed hand. Uh, that happen to someone you, like, know? Yeah. It did. Wow, that's a hea-vee trip, sista. It sure is. Like your poor sister. Oh man, Nig, I think you shoulda gone to her funeral. Tania, I couldn't. You coulda told Jimmy you're goin. Like it or not, I'm goin. Nig sighing, Maybe I should've. Ya got any smokes?

They lit up. Smoke driftin, the foul odour of the bed, its bed-clothes, sort of gotten used to. The music never stopping except for

146

a tape to be changed. Just a cupla kids sharing the mirrors of their life experiences . . .

. . . only twelve, jussa bit younger'n your poor sista, havin to look after my kid two brothers and a baby sis. Four of us. And four different fathers. Can ya believe that, Nig? Four different fathers. And not a one ofem still around? One day, eh, she went on one of her binges, left me with the kids, nuthin in the cupboards ta eat cept a packet of Weetbix, not even milk ta go withit, y' know?

. . . She didn't come back that night; I was awake half the night worryin, you know, ghosts, burglars, perverts. Even the dark was freakin me out. All the next day — it was a Sunday — waitin, waitin . . . my lil bros and sis crying all damn day, starvin. And still the bitch wasn't home. Then my brother, Mark — Hey, I gotta brother called Mark. Yeh, yeh, alright, alright. Sorry.

Mark found five bucks down the back of the sofa. Thought we were made. A sign from, like, heaven or sumpthin. This was about six. At night. I thought, neat, we'll have some fishnchips for our tea. You know, with this five bucks we thought God'd sent us. God . . . Tania's jaw muscles clenching and unclenching (like my old man). So. Sighing. A long sigh.

So I told em, wait for me I won't be long. Sucking in breath. I, uh . . . Sucking in again. I was so . . . so happy, you know, with Mark findin this five bucks just when we needed it most . . . And uh, uh . . . Well, I came back and . . . and the house it was, uh — *The fuckin house was burning!*

Okay, mista, I had my cry. Tania wiping at her face. So. So ya wanna do it again? What? You know, what we did before? Her eyes moved off to the ceiling. Nah, I don't. And Tania sat up at that: You mean, doncha fancy me? Not that — Fuck you, busta. (Bitch's gone and got wild again.) Took Nig some talking and gentle touching to get her back in a reasonable frame of mind.

He traced the shape of her breast with a finger. Ya like that? I might. Come *onnnn*, Nig chuckling at her nipple hard to his touch. So ya do want to? she seemed unsure. Oh I might, he teased. And tried to concentrate, not think of burnt children and a dead sister with a broken neck . . . You're pretty experienced for, what, seventeen, eighteen? I had a girlfriend. What, at seventeen — At fifteen. Oh. Ya still with her? Might be. Nig laughing at Tania pulling away from his touch. Might not be either. So you an her you do it, eh? Used to do it, yeah. What, lotsa times? Sure.

147

As often as we could. So whassa big deal about it? What, sex? Well we weren't talkin about fishnchips, mista. It's good. It *feels* good. Nig stroking her, rubbing against her skin. Skin to skin.

You have, you know, orgasms? Or-what? Orgasms. The hell are they? It, Tania. It's an it. So tell me. Well, it's coming — Don't be disgusting. I'm not. Ya are. And girls, women, don't come. Who told you that? I know. Ya know nuthin, sweetheart. Don't call me that. Ya know nuthin.

He moved his hand down. (Give her the flutter-touch) going on an older past-companion's teachings. Ya like that? It's alright. Only alright? Yeah. How about this? Mmmm, nice. Her inner thigh muscles relaxed in his fingers. The smell of her sex wafted sweetly up to him. Ya wanna try and come? Can't. She shook her head. Ya wanna try? Told ya I — Just try? Well, alright. But don't expect nuthing.

So nothing took place from Tania's part. But I enjoyed it, Nig, I honestly did. And they smiled at each other. And below them the music had mellowed: Wonder. Someone's got Stevie Wonder on. *I love you*, Tania taking over the last of the chorus line, but so shyly you'd think she was suffering from sumpthin. A disease or sumpthin. Let's go down and join em. I'm dyin for a joint. Juss wanna spend my whole life *outiv* it. A madness in her eyes. Or maybe it was sadness, Nig didn't know. (Can't be thinkin now. Gotta go with the *flow*.) He shifted his thinking as he and Tania went hand-in-hand down the stairs. Then Nig thought he'd better ask: Ya not taken are ya? And she smiled at him. (Oh man, she's beautiful. Even with the tats, she's beautiful.) Nope. Looking at him, Not unless you . . . ? left it hanging there.

Into the double sitting rooms: no more a place of anger and yelling for the blood of the rotties, just belonging. Dancing, or sat back stoned and drunk, and belonging.

Out on the floor (the stage) doin their stuff to the (muse) beat in their head, the sweet-high brain with its amazing at-oneness with the music playin, man. Amazing.

Hitting all them steps (inherent) in the sounds, struttin their (choreographic) stuff. Dancin with arms around each other. Or standing there talking, rappin, you know, about how he and the other Brown Fist dude they were bruthas, man. *Bruth-ahs*. And *fuck* anyone else outside this house, this world of our belongin. Juss us, bruthas and sistas, but mainly the bruthas, man, cos fuckin sheilas, man, even Brown Fist ones, they're not, you know, as *real* as us dudes.

Then half ofem breakin out in a cheer at Nig and Tania walkin in, teasin em, Yah! Must be love, eh? Love at first sight! Laughin at that, fallin about emselves at the fuckin joke .of it: love. Oh man. It's more like, you know, belonging.

Yet when Stevie got to the chorus of his *I just called*, it was when they sang loudest: . . . to say: I LOVE YOU!

12
Visits

Fulla answered his door, Ye — What the — at the sight, gotta be, of two Brown Fists standin there.

Jimmy Bad Horse stuck his hob-nailed boot in the doorway as the fulla tried to close it. Chucklin that way of his, and tellin the dude: Your friendly ree-possession agents, cuz. With that high-pitched laugh. Shades, beard . . . a winter night. Aw, c'mon fellas, — No come ons, man. Jimmy held up a piece of paper. This is official, man. We come to getta a TV, a colour one. Less you got the three months' payment you're behind. How do I know you guys are — Here. Jimmy thrust the repossession form at the fulla, told him to read it, then read what it said himself, off by heart: Says you are in breach of a hire purchase agreement between you, Daniel Toby Hohepa, of this address, and Star Appliances of Taniwha Street, Two Lakes. And ya read down at the bottom, cuzzie, it says that me, J. Shirkey, is *au*-tha-rised to collect either the security — the TV in case y'as stupid as ya look — or the payment arrears. Chuckling. Oh, and plus the costs of bein here, tapping a cutoff woollen glove on a brown leather jacket: Mine and my associate's here, thumbing at Nig Heke.

Look, you guys, I'm a Maori, just like you guys — Man, don't care if you fuckin Chinese. Jimmy lookin at the guy. I got a wife and five kids — Man, don't care if you got *six* wives and a *hundred* fuckin kids. The TV, cuz. Thas what we came for. Or else the three months' payment arrears. Fullas, I haven't got a penny! Then you bring that TV out here, man. Fear on the fulla's face. I, uh, I haven't got that either. You see I — You hear this dude, man? Jimmy to Nig. Yeah, heardim. Nig playing it tough, but feeling sorry for the guy. He woulda been fifty if he was a day. Fulla says he ain't got the bread and then he says he ain't got the *TV*. Man, what does — But Jimmy didn't finish. He swung and drove a punch into the fulla's gut. The fulla went *ooooff!* came over doubled and Jimmy smacked an uppercut into him. Caught

150

him with another punch as he fell forward. So Nig threw a wild right at him and connected somewhere just before the fulla hit the deck. Nig felt he'd bedda put a cupla boots in too. Just to show Jimmy Bad Horse he was bad himself.

They helped each other haul the fulla to his feet. Jimmy did the talking. Back tamorrow, cuz. TV or the bread. Or your fuckin head. Ya get that? He let the fulla go and punched him again. Then shoved him backwards, stumbling, bleeding, moaning, falling down in his own passage. Nig followed his leader off into the night.

Next night they were back. Mob-handed. Three carloads ofem, and gang-dressed up to the shaded fuckin eyeballs.

Woman answered the door, but only after Warren, the other pros given his probation entry the same time as Nig, kicked and pounded with his half-mitted mit on the door: Ya bedda answer it! Scared out of her wits she was. Where's ya husband? He's not here. Oh please, boys, I'm just an — The fuckin TV, lady. Or else the bread. And don't forget the extra thirty bucks for our collecting fee. But we don't have anything. *Please.* (And Nig wanting out.) So ya husband left ya to cop his shit, did he? No, he — He's a fuckin wimp. What else ya got then? Nothing. Honest to God we have *nothing.* No fridge? freezer? Warren swinging a smiling head at Nig beside him: No *jewels?* Laughing. Just like a version of Jimmy Bad Horse. We own nothing, sir. (Sir? Nig wondering at that.).

So Warren shouldered the woman aside. Left Nig standing there not sure what to do. The other Browns came marching past Nig. He followed them. Watching how they swaggered and had that sway the way they do, but Nig horrified that it was in another person's house. And this woman following up behind em bawling her eyes out and beggin please don't scare my children. And one of the brothers telling her, Lady, we'll *kill* the lil fuckas ya don't shut ya mouth. Heavee.

Then another bro must've smacked the lady one because when Nig turned she was on the floor bleeding. And all these brown leather jackets and Brown Fist headbands and boots and filthy jeans and shades . . . (Man oh fuckin man, what've I got myself into?) Banging and crashing goin on as Warren threw things around, yelled, threatened the woman; and then her kids startin up, cryin and screaming (no fuckin different to my old man goin

151

off his face when I was growin up and so were my kid brothers
and sisters tryin to do the same: just grow up. In peace.)

Into the sitting room, Warren lookin round the joint. Nuthin.
Just a few ducks on the wall which he, Warren (the kid turned
into a man I don't recognise. And not even a patch member yet.)
tore from the wall, one by one, chucked em at the wall opposite,
one on the fireplace, the other through the window. (Jesus Christ
. . .) Nig unable to believe his eyes. Man, these cunts've got zilch,
man. I mean, zilch. Warren's breathing all funny. (Nig feeling
helpless; lost, sad, an invader. Helpless.)

Right. He marched out of there, up to where the woman was
still sat against the wall bleeding, and bawling her poor eyes out.
All these heavies lined up down her hallway. And all over a lousy
fuckin TV; and not as if it was *their* TV, the Browns', it belonged
to some white prick with a business in town gettin dumb Maoris
to do his dirty work forim. That's how Nig Heke was fast seein it.

Warren standin over the woman. (What's he gonna do?) Man,
man . . . Nig starting to tell Warren to lay off when Warren up
and kicked the woman in the face with his heavy boot. Nig heard
the pop of her face bursting. And he had to close his eyes. And he
thought of how it was like being back home, you know, with his
old man beating Mum up. But he never kicked her. (I never saw
him kick her.) Warren did it again. And again. And Nig having
to close his eyes or he was gonna murder this cunt he was, Brown
brother or not.

Back at the gang HQ, and Warren and Jimmy Bad Horse in a
huddle, talking quietly. And Nig standin around with some of the
bros and a cupla sisters, and Tania one ofem, but he couldn't look
at her, at anyone. Just in a daze. Numb all over. Then Jimmy
called him over, Hey, Nig. Here.

Whassa fuckin story, man? About what, Jimmy? Bout you
lettin Warren here do all the work? (Call that work?) Not my
scene, man. Wha'? Jimmy's mouth dropping open. Beating up on
women, man. Nig shaking his head, Not my scene. Oh, is that
right, angel face? Jimmy steppin up to Nig. So what *is* your scene,
boy? Nig embarrassed; not wanting to be singled out. So he just
shrugged, dunno. How you think we live in this world, man? Ya
think the food falls outta the fuckin sky? Eh? Ya think maybe one
of your angel *friends* drop us our groceries just whenever we want
it? Do ya? Jimmy flicking a finger under Nig's jaw. And Nig

thinking: Back off, man. And wanting to warn Jimmy to back off, leave him alone. But he couldn't.

Then Jimmy punched Nig, a roundhouse right which Nig saw coming from a mile, but what could he do but wear it? He staggered from the blow. And Jimmy was telling him in that high-pitched squeaky voice that didn't really sound, you know, a leader's voice: Ya gotta lotta makin up to do, Nig. A hell of a lot. (The dream'd turned to a nightmare. And so soon.)

13
Letter from the Grave

. . . God . . . my God . . . my — *Ain't* no God! Beth, at the letter the cops'd left her with. From (it can't be real) her. Grace. (My dead girl. Speaking to me. To Mummy. *To her mother!*) Beth screaming inside. Weeping inside. Weeping and screaming and not fully comprehending.

Over and over she read the scrawled last words of her daughter. But still the message not reaching home. So reading it again. Again (Got to get it right.) But each time the message so overwhelming Beth could not think straight. As if being dead — by her own hand — is not enough . . . now this?

And a day passing with a mother her mind hardly knowing where she was, who she was . . . just this message going over and over in her mind: . . . *Mum, I was raped. I feel so, I don't know, dirty or something. As if I did something to deserve it. I feel so bad, Mum, I just want to die* — Beth unable to get past that part without shoving the letter away or other violent recoil . . . *Mum, I think it was Dad* — AEEE!! the scream going up in her mind. *Dad* — Dad? *Dad.* Jake? *Dad.* My *husband?* My kid's own *father?* Hate building.

I'll *killim.* I'LL KILLIM! (calm down, Beth.) Telling herself, you gotta keep your anger under control. Wanting a drink — No, I won't drink again. Lighting yet another cigarette. Mind arguing with itself: Why shouldn't I have a drink? Not as if I ain't got good cause. Deciding, several times that day, Right, I'm going next door gonna borrow some relief from this damn nightmare. Yet each time overcoming the desire. So eventually the voice in her head trying to persuade her to have a drink faded away.

Waiting up there, in her bedroom — *my* bedroom — all evening; had sent the younger ones to her sister for the night. Just her and Abe left, and not that he was actually physically at home; kid

154

spent most of his life out on those miserable streets, wouldn't surprise a mother if another of her kids'd up and joined the Brown Fists. And thoughts of her family picturing in her mind like some ruin, some terrible accident that'd befallen half her brood with em lying all over the road. Dead and dying. Knocked over by life. By being Maori. A loser. A member of a race on its way out. Kaput. My own children. And all that *hope* a woman'd once had forem. Though it did occur to her that never had she anything specific laid out in her mind as to how to secure this future for her kids. It was just hope, with no structure, no game plan to apply to it. No structure, woman. You got no structure cos your race ain't got no structure. We just wake up each day and take what comes. Which, when you think about it, ain't a hell of a lot. And why should it be? Life don't come marching into your kitchen saying, Here take me I'm free and there's plenty of me. Does it? You got to . . . you got to . . . Well, work for it, Beth supposed in her unenlightened state and general misery. Oh, but don't forget the anger.

Hours of it — thinking. Just thinking. And waiting. For him. The black bastard. The *rapist*. Of *his own daughter!* To come home. And praying — for once in her life — that he'd come home with a bunch of his precious boozing mates in tow. Lots ofem. So angry she almost relished the thought.

A whole bunch ofem. (Oh *good*.) Beth all purpose. All fixed determination. Yet scared out of her mind: (Maybe he didn't do it. Grace said she *thinks* it was him — Nope.) Unable to believe otherwise now. *I'll killim*. Telling herself, Think of the letter, think of the letter, to give herself the courage.

Lettin em settle in. Coming down the stairs. Stepping into the kitchen. *Just think of the letter*. Hey! It's Beth. Come an have a beer withus, Beth, honey. Sonny Boy Jacobs greeting Beth. She hadn't seen him in ages. Smilin that trademark smile at Beth, Come an give Sonny Boy a kiss. Laughing. And fuck Jake Heke, *I* ain't scared of Jake. Looking at Jake with a confident grin. Beth regretting the timing of Sonny Boy's long absence being marred by this. She brushed aside Sonny's outstretched arm. Sorry, Sonny, but I got something to say to my *husband* here. Spat the word out. Never wanted it to leave her lips again. Ever.

Beth drew in a breath. Went to full height. She caught Jake just about to snarl something at her after his first reaction of confusion. She stabbed a trembling finger at Jake: You, mista. Shaking all over. With rage. (And fear. What if I got it wrong?) *Think of the letter.* Accusing finger at full arms length. You — You! Clutching the letter in her other hand. Lifting it aloft. *You — raped — our — dead — daughter!*

Table went up. And everything with it. Bottles, glasses, ashtrays, lighted cigarettes, packets of them. Everything. And Jake roaring like an enraged bull. And Beth standing there, standing her ground. Ready for the worst. And the worst coming for her.

In slow, mad motion he was coming for her. Except he didn't make it: Sonny Boy Jacobs stepped across Beth's vision of her husband, Holdit. Jake trying to sweep Sonny Boy aside — Man, I said holdit! Sonny Boy slammed Jake against the wall. And the others were picking themselves off the floor, dusting themselves down, picking up toppled chairs, a smoke still burning. And Jake yelling that he was gonna KILL Beth.

Beth staying her ground. (*Think of the letter.*) Jaw jutting. And Jake threatening Sonny, Sonny, you beddda let go a me or — Oooof! as Sonny drove a punch into Jake's belly, asked him, Or what, man? Then Sonny turning to Beth, Show me that letter. Narrowing eyes at her, And you bedda be right, woman. Or you the one gonna cop it. And Beth managing to get out: My Grace . . . she left a note . . . cops didn't want to show me . . . not till she was — She said — she said. She said *he* — throwing the accusing finger at Jake slumped and groaning in Sonny Boy's grasp — *raped her.*

Jake. Walking the streets. The Pine Block streets. Hurting. My pride, man. Of Sonny Boy hitting him. That other matter not yet sunken in. Accepted. It couldn't be, because a man'd not done it. Just Sonny Boy Jacobs then, a picture of him, the feel — the force — of his gut punch. The strength of the man. The *easy* way he handled Jake. But this cannot be.

Walking. Walking and hurting and that other matter drifting round and round in his mind of not being true, it can't be true. I'm not like that. But then again . . . you know how drunk a man gets, he don't remember nuthin half the fuckin time. But surely he wouldn't do *that*? Man don't even have *thoughts* like that, of, you know: havin sex with kids. Let alone his own daughter. But

156

then again . . . thinking of the dreams, how violent they were, how — a man don't have the words — but he knows his dreams are strange.

Sonny Boy! Pop! just like that: poppin up in his mind, even his troubled mind, as this . . . this thing, this idea, this notion, this *force* more powerful than his. Than my force. Than my power. Clenching his big fists, thrusting them up in the early morning cold air with the streetlight giving him a taller shadow, and those mits huger in their black image on the footpath, Than *this!* Feeling his old power surging through him. *Come to me now*, Sonny Boy. Wanting the man. *Wanting* him. And this hot feeling rushing down his face, of shame. The shame of a beaten fighter. Beaten at his own game. And Beth and her accusation, the cause of it, barely a background murmur so strong was Jake's shame at being handled so effortlessly by Sonny Boy Jacobs. And that hurt coming on real strong. Enough to kill a man on. To kill him: Sonny fuckin Boy. Walking.

Car going past. Nother one coming up, slowing. Jake eying it: Lettim stop. Lettim try me on. Let a whole fuckin carload ofem try me. Ready for anything, anyone. (Even him? Sonny Boy?) Car crawling along, kerb hugging. Browns. They're Brown Fists. But Jake not worried. Even if they gotta gun I ain't backin down. Fuckem.

A hand comin out the passenger side, the front. With a woollen glove with the fingers cut off how they do.

Fuckem.

Hand givin Jake the fingers and him immediately thrusting the same in reply.

Fuckem.

It then occurring to Jake that his own son might be one ofem in that car now stopped, its engine idling. Who's that meant ta scare? Jake thinking in contempt of the engine revving, dying, revving up again. Stopping himself. Staring at them. Not that he could see their faces in the light, how it was falling from the power poles. And no moon, not even a lousy star to help see em with. But it don't matter.

Fuckem.

Standin there. Feeling warrior. (I'm a warrior, man.) But a voice same as Sonny Boy's tellin Jake, Ya suck, man. (And ya fucked ya own kid. And that's why she killed herself.) That's what the voice of Sonny Boy Jacobs was saying . . . starting to come back to a man now. The blood draining from him. Man, what's

157

happening? That Brown Fist car just sat there revving in the poor streetlight, that half-mittened hand hanging out the side. And a man's thoughts returning to him like Grace herself calling. Callin from the fuckin grave.

Swallowing. Courage fleeing. Just up and fuckin off on a man. Just this shell of him standing there, being stubborn, stupid, waiting forem to move first. Inside the man it was like a . . . ? like a kid or sumpthin . . . ? Like a kid was cryin. And that car revving and unrevvin, and a man's tall shadow there on the footpath. And his thoughts. And Sonny Boy's greater strength. And greater confidence. And the streetlight this funny yellow in the outers of a man's eyes. And beyond that this dark. This terrible dark.

Eyes watering — with fear, not tears. The carload a Browns still there. Revving. Easin off. Revvin. Voices in Jake's head goin: *Ya did it!* No, I didn't! *Ya did!* No, honest, I *didn't*, man! Like an adult being answered by a child. Car engine revving. Voices arguing back and forth in his mind and the child losing the argument. Or having its denial disbelieved. Like bein accused all ya life of bein a slave and hardly able ta understand what a slave was, and when ya did it hurt ya to the bone. Way deep inside it hurt. That adult voice in his head, it was like that: hurtin. To the core of him.

Walking off. Fuckem. But the fuckem not like the fuckem of old. Nothing like it. Just a hollow echo. And another in a man's head, his ears, of a voice laughin at him as he walked away: Ya suck, Jake Heke! Ya suck! Laughin. Laughin at a man. At the best fuckin rumbler in the whole of Two Lakes — it wasn't for Sonny Boy comin back ta town. Laughin at me. Tellin me I suck. Tellin me I — No way, man. *I didn't*. I-did-not-touch-her.

Then o — ooooo — a hurt comin on like no hurt ever before. Not in his whole life. Not even in his dreams, his mad bad dreams.

Walkin. The streets. Of not Pine Block but this . . . ? this place, eh . . . this place in a man's mind his bad dreams'd often touched on, hinted at, of terrible, terrible hurt. (Like my mummy and daddy and all my uncles and aunties and cousins and friends — oh, everyone — from childhood. Don't only not like me but hate me. Me. Just a lil kid. And they *hate* me.)

Not understanding it. Any of it. Not Sonny Boy being a better physical man and not that kid's accusation from the grave. None of it. Only hurt. I only know I hurt. Walking . . . in this, uh, this place . . .

158

14
Hark! The People Cometh

Every day; evenings, afternoons when the kids were coming home
from school, at nights when they were out on the streets, Beth
Heke out there with them. With a message: I'm here to help you.
Any of you. You only have to feel you got a problem and I'll listen.
27 Rimu Street's where I'm at. Driven. By what, she wasn't sure.
Grace, yes. But Grace wasn't the all of it. No. A woman'd just
woke up one morning and thought: Streets. I'll go out onto the
streets where all this misery's at and do what I can.

She told them, You're hungry, I'll feed ya. Just call. Though
it took some time before kids started to drift in; hanging around
outside her house at first. Then one kid gettin up the courage to
knock on her door to tell Beth he wouldn't mind, you know, sumpthin to eat.

Soon it was a regular every-night arrival ofem. So money was
the next problem. So she ran food raffles. Had her regular kids
who came to her for food sellin the tickets door to door in the
neighbourhood. Resistance at first but they came round. As Beth
knew they would. Eventually. So a big pot on the simmer all day.
And half the night. Stews, pork bones and spuds and watercress
from the creek on the Trambert property that her own children
picked for the communal pot.

A woman seeing little changes in her adopted charges, like
them responding to her barking at them to use their manners, and
if they didn't have them to use she taught them. A willingness to
help; more and more these half-homeless kids offering to help Beth
at whatever she wanted. You just tell us, Mrs H, they called her.
Mrs H. Pity about the H part being missing. Or kicked out more
like it. Beth hadn't set eyes on the man. (Lettim rot in hell.)
Though there were times when she found herself wondering after
Jake, at how he was doing, where he might be living. And what
was going on in his (dirty) mind now that the whole world knew
what he'd done. (But I can't forgive him. I think of him, but I

can't and I won't forgive.) Besides, too much to do. Too many neglected kids out there.

Then the approach from her home village, a representative of the village, with an offer of financial help, and manual labour if she required. She took both. An idea turned to a project. Even got a mention in the local paper. Oh wow. A woman had to laugh at seeing her own name and an article about her and her village committee.

Self-help, that was the catchcry Beth'd taken from reading somewhere, maybe it was the morning paper she'd taken to getting every day because it was a more serious publication, not so localised, trivial. So a woman felt she was learning a little while she was at it. So it was books: we don't only need to feed these kids but educate them as well. But how? The library.

They gave her a pile of Teach Yourself books; on a range of activities, from carpentry to making things from scraps of cloth material. She converted her sitting room to a rough sort of classroom. Spent the first month teaching to a class of one. But they came around. As she hoped they would. And the Wainui committee kept coming up with money to buy a range of tools, hardware to put the teachings into practice.

Self-help!

She went to sleep at nights with that catchcry exclaiming itself in her increasingly happier mind. Her heart. Like this self-help idea was so beautifully all-embracing it was a wonder they, the Maori people in general, hadn't cottoned onto it before. Why, it helped the helpers, it helped the owners of the businesses they purchased from, it helped most of all the lost, unwanted, ill-directed kids. It was self-fulfilling. Oh but it wasn't all beer and skittles:

Mrs H! Mrs H! Come quick! Racing up the street in the dead of night after this kid. Leading her to a house, just another Pine Block state house, but this one in an indescribable state of filth. And this kid . . . this teenage boy, lying on the floor . . . in his own vomit. A plastic bag beside him. Strong smell of solvent fumes. And all these other waif-looking kids standing around the prone boy going, Oh far out, man . . . This is freakin me out . . . I think he's dead . . . No he ain't, he's just *way*sted! laughin about it. Till Beth slapped one kid's face, told him to get the hell outta my sight. And the rest of you, get.

Going down to the boy, and knowing, instinctively, that he wasn't going to make it. Not through this cold winter night nor

160

any other. But telling someone to go phone an ambulance at any rate. Then picking the kid's spew-stinking head up and cradling him in her lap: There, there, honey. Rocking him like the baby he really was; stroking that vomit- and sweat- and filth-matted hair, and staring at that face skin so smooth yet so sallow, as if he'd spent his whole life indoors, or moved around only in the dark he and his ilk had taken refuge in.

Rocking him. And thinking of a phrase, a biblical phrase of all the suffering children. And what was it He said . . . ? Ah yes, it was: Come unto me. Come unto me . . . come unto me . . . all ye suffering children . . . Thinking of Jesus, and Him saying that all them couple of thousand years ago; Beth wondering what colour the suffering kids were in those days. Because they were surely brown of skin and Maori of feature now. (But we used to be a *warrior* race.)

She thought of Grace's three-day funeral, her elders, the old women, the paramount chief, Te Tupaea. And wondered what'd gone wrong.

And when the kid sighed his last pathetic breath of not utterance but simply expiry, Beth did not yet weep. It wasn't till she heard the distant wail of the ambulance siren, how forlorn was its sound on a cold Pine Block evening. And promising herself, and promising the dead kid: Gonna do my best to give you kids your rightful warrior inheritance. Pride in yourself, your poor selves. Not attacking, violent pride but *heart* pride. Gonna go to my people, my leaders, ask them the way.

. . . every Saturday, man, don't madda if it's raining even fuckin *snowin*, man, ya gotta do it. I mean, he's the *chief*. The CHIEF of all our tribe. And anyrate, he's doin it for our sake. To givus, you know, *pride* in ourselves. No questions asked though, man. Just turn up at Number 27 Rimu at nine *on the dot*. Rain or snow or what, *be there*. Be there and listen. And take it in. And when he says ya do sumpthin like this — like he might be teachin ya a haka — you do it, man. Or else. Or else what, man? Or else, that's all. Ya mean, thas all? Just turn up, bro, and you'll know what I mean.

This chief fulla, man, he's . . . he's . . . I dunno . . . sumpthin about him, eh. Sorta like a god or sumpthin — I know who like: Buck. Buck who? Buck Shelford, bru-tha, who else is Buck? *Cap*-tain of the mighty All Blacks, man. Rugby player supreme of all

161

the world. Well, that's who this chief is like. Buck. Our mighty warrior Maori, Buck damn Shelford, man. Man . . .

Oh, and ya want, you know — I mean, ya feelin like down, on a bummer, got no one ta turn to, call on Mrs H, man. She's *choice*. Wha', she gives ya . . . ? Yep, say it: Hugs? Yeh, hugs. And . . . ? Yep, you c'n cry — bawl ya eyes out ya want. She'll let ya. And she doesn't tell ya you're a wimp? No way, Hosay. So what does she say when ya, you know, like hanging out for a bit of — can't say it, man. Cuddlin? Yeow, cuddlin. Well, she takes you in her arms — and she smells *nice*, man. Clean. And perfume and that — and ya havin a good howl and she goes patpatpat on ya head, eh, and then she says: There, there, now, honey. Have yourself a damn good cry. It's alright. Mrs H is always here.

Is that right? Straight up, man. Sounds choice. She *is* choice. What number'd you say it was?

15
The Will of the People

Waking up, half the time not knowing whose place he was at, having to think; to separate yesterday, last night, from last week, last fuckin month. Of sleeping at different fullas' houses. And head always running strong with them dreams. Them terrible fuckin dreams — *always* violent. Always mad crazy worlds and mad crazy people in em. And me, Jake Heke, one of the craziest. Yet Jake unable to figure it: I don't feel that bad. Not like I am in my dreams. Me and all that blood and guts and stuff and people runnin around with arms half torn off and pulverised faces (usually done by me) and cocks and twats on one person, one minute a man, next a woman, and sometimes both, and me tryin ta grab at em both at the same time and stuff em in my mouth — but I don't *think* like that in the *daytime*?

Slaughtering people, whole armies ofem sometimes, people dying, him killing em, maiming em, machinegunnin em, carvin em up like they're just hams or sumpthin. Man, I dunno about myself.

But no time for that, have ta get up ta use that shithouse before anyone else gets up. I hate havin a shit in someone else's toilet. (Man, what a fulla wouldn't do, sometimes, to be back in his own home.) On the crapper — *jeez!* at a ginormous fart exploding out ofim. Wigglin around on the seat trying to hold the rest in, because of the embarrassment. But impossible. Nature's nature, and booze don't exactly help it come out like a ordinary shet's sposed ta come. And sitting there blurtin and makin these noises and wondering if this house had pretty girls or maybe the lady of the house was good lookin because, I dunno, having a loud smelly shet is worse when ya worried about a pretty woman or a girl (an *old* enough girl) comin in after ya. Not so bad when ya at a house of fatties or uglies. But the pretties. Lighting up a fag in there — ta cover up the stink. Puffin up big clouds to really hide it. Cept the smell still gettin through. So wanting out. I just want outta

163

here. Stay somewhere else tonight. So slippin out if he could, no kiss my arse, nuthin. Always someone else a man could stay with.

Thinking about her a lot: Grace. What he was sposed to have done to her. No way, man. No fuckin way. And any man or woman at McClutchy's even *looked* like they were thinkin that and Jake'd drop em. Even him, Sonny Boy smartarse Jacobs, who's not talkin to a man no more even though his brother, Dooly, is — or was — like a man's own brother. Fuckem both. Even him, Dool, as well. I c'n tell what he's thinkin, that I'm some kinda pervert or sumpthin — *I ain't*. Yet inside never really certain.

Funny thing but a man gettin all the sympathy from people at the pub because of Grace and yet another side sayin he did a terrible thing to her. But the ones who didn't know, they'd come up to man with a beer bought forim and tellim sorry ta hear about your girl, Jake. People ya wouldn't expect to, either. Made a man think that, you know, the kid was somehow *meant* to die: so he could find out who was his real friends and who weren't. Oh, but then there were the ones'd stopped talkin to im but too fuckin scared ta come right out with it, what Sonny Boy Jacobs must've toldem, bigmouthin off to em like he always does. (I'll gettim one a these days. See how *he* goes when he's half pissed and not expectin his own mate to givim one in the guts. Wouldn't a minded one on the jaw, a man mighta been able to come back from a shot like that. Off the ropes like. But in the guts. Takes the stuffin right outta any man, don't care who he is.) But when Jake thought hard about it, he hadn't had that many free beers bought for him of late. Mind you, he didn't expect it. Mean ta say, the kid can't be dead every day. Well she can and she is, but ya can't expect people to still think of her like that and so feel sorry for ya, her old man. How sad ya must be. Deep down inside. But not showin it. Not if ya got a rep. Ya can't.

The unemployment cunts cut his dole money to the same as a single fulla. The cunts. The fuck they think they are stickin their noses in a man's private business? What, they ring Beth up — oops, I forgot, we got no phone — writer a ledda ask her if she's still wither husband? Cunts. How do they expect a man ta live on only a hundred and three bucks a week when a jug alone costs nearly four? What if he had ta rent a place as well? Man'd fuckin starve ta death before those cunts'd lift a finger to helpim. And it's alright for them, they got a job. A *guvmint* job. What about the rest of us dumb Maoris out here don't have work, got no skills, and scared a lookin for a job in case they find one that hardly pays

164

fuckall may as well be on the dole? Fuckem. Any wonder a man has ta drop hints at McClutchy's that he'd be partial to a freebie if it's going. These guvmint cunts take away ya dignity, they do. Fuckem. Man even had to go into the office in town every week Thursday to collect his dole cheque becaue he didn't have no address to givem to send it to. And the way they look at you when you're gettin your cheque, y'd think it was their own fuckin bread they were givin away. Fuckem.

Debts. Man was starting to build up a few debts. Ten here, twenty there. Wasn't so bad when it was just after Grace'd passed away, a man could touch someone up and they forgot it. And so they should. A man'd been good to em over the years; you know, puttin the hard word on some cunt hasslin em, punchin someone over on their behalf. So they should give to a man and forget about it now and then. Plus he'd just lost a daughter in a very bad way. The way she died that is. But they were startin ta hit a man up: Hey Jake, ya got that twenty? And Jake trying to give it the ole Maori pass-off, you know, gigglin about it and saying, Yeow, bro, yeow. Next week, next week. In that way everyone knows means ya not gonna pay back. And McClutchy people, they should know that. They know the rules. Fuckem.

Doin most of his eating at wherever he landed a bed for the night. Taking a shower when he felt confident enough to. Eating at the takeaways — Chinese. I love the Chink grub, man. Specially the spare ribs — when he'd missed out on a freebie or just felt like Chinese. The Chink fulla there'd taken to calling a fulla by his name. Missa Jake. Even feeling Jake's muscles, grabbing him by the arm: Oo, Missa Jake, you velly stong man. Talkin how they do these fuckin Chinks; all the damn time workin, slavin their guts out over them woks. And Jake could tell they were envying him being on the other side, the cussima side as they call it. Him laughin about it, them saying, Oh muss be nice be on your side of counter, huh, Missa Jake? Makin a man feel important, and like he had one over em. Fuckem too. The Chinks. They wanna spend their fuckin lives slavin then that's their lookout.

Though there were times when Jake wouldn't've minded a job — not a full-time one, but so he could afford those little extras in life (even buy her, Beth, a little sumpthin to make up — no, what's ta make up? I didn't do nuthin to Grace. I *know* I didn't.) But he missed Beth sometimes. Maybe more'n sometimes. As the days went by.

Then one day struck by an idea. A brilliant idea. Why didn't

I think of it before? Get a job as a bouncer. Man, I'd make the best (the second-best) bouncer in Two Lakes. Long as someone like Buck Shelford himself didn't walk in and wanna cause trouble, hehehe. Boss, McClutchy himself, said sure, who better. Hired Jake on the spot. Gave him a nice white shirt and a cute black bowtie ta go withit. Best a man'd been dressed since his wedding. And ta think he paid ya thirty bucks a *night* ta bust heads ya would've busted for nuthin. But ya didn't tell him that, McClutchy, clever though he thought he was. As for the no-drinking rules the boss mentioned to Jake, Jake thought it didn't really apply to him. Not me, I'm Jake the Muss, the tougharse around here (wasn't for Sonny Boy Jacobs being around all the damn time).

Friday. It was a Friday, bound to be trouble, always was on a Friday. Jake standin at the bar drinking, fists achin for action. And action takin its damn time in comin. Man'd had four or five jugs downim — and paid for them himself — before a fight broke out. Lovely, lovely. Jake the first bouncer there, and kapow! boom-boom! smash! and three of the cunts down. Ya want some more? Okay, I'll give ya more: into this one prick who dared to want it with Jake the Muss. Man had to really deal to the fulla.

Back at the bar. Gimme a beer, Toby. The fulla he'd beat up being carried out to a summoned ambulance by friends. That'll be — I ain't payin for this one, Tobe. But Toby havin none of it: Can't do that, Jake. Boss's gotta authorise it. Come on, man. I just dealt to *three* of em. It's his pub I just looked after. Then next thing Jake knew was McClutchy's voice himself in his ear tellin im: You're fired, Jake. Wha'? You heard. But Boss? Jake, you don't go beating up customers — But they were fighting, Boss. Your job is to stop them, not join em. And don't let this spoil our relationship, Jake. Walked off.

Left a man wondering what'd hit him, and what relationship did the Boss mean? And that hurt comin on . . . except this time without the surge of power. Of violence come rushing up to the rescue of this hurt person inside of him. Instead, Jake just felt weak. Like his legs'd turned rubbery.

The days became a battle to survive; just to last out the drinking day and then finish with a bed and maybe a free feed for the night. A man was runnin out of places to bed down; people were just givinim the cold shoulder, or they made excuses like having family stayin withem when a man knew they didn't. Or they blamed it on wives, you know: Man, it's my missus, eh, she don't like people staying the night. She can't sleep. Shit like that. And people he thought were his friends — had always been his friends — were more and more givin a man either a gruff greeting when they ran into him or they didn't say a word, not kiss my arse nuthin. Well *fuck them too*. Cept that didn't guarantee a man a roof over his head. And this was turning out a cold winter. And never ending.

Man got cunning in the pub, when it was busy enough to: moving about in the crowd, swiping a jug, a bottle from a table; and even when he was seen, it was hardly anyone who dared say sumpthin. Not me, man, I'm Jake Heke. These people *respect* me.

Spare ribs. Jake'd get a hunger for Chinese spare ribs. Had to havem. But the price: five bucks a plastic pottle container ofem and don't forget the twenty cents because the fuckin Slits don't; even when a man'd tried to hold out their lousy twenty cents, make out he hadn't noticed it read five dollars twenty on the menu board, and Slit'd askim, You have twenny cent, Missa Jake? Ah, ya ain't worried bouta a lousy twenny cents are ya? Mean to say, it ain't gonna bust ya is it? Ah, Missa Jake, price on board say five dollah twenny. Price not go down. When it does, we change up on board. Fuckem. A man didn't have to havem so badly he'd a toldem ta stickit. Stickit right up their slit arses, which I bet are, you know, like their eyes: the hole goes sideways. Sideways! Hahaha!

One night Jake didn't get his usual eleven ribs — *fuckem!* Back into the shop he marched, Oi! Ya only gave me nine. Whassa story? I always get eleven. Bossman Slit not battin an eyelid, askin Jake: But they bigger, yes? Threw Jake. He hadn't thought. He hauled out a rib, held it up for inspection. Looked the fuckin same to him. Glaring at the Slit, wantin to punchim over and not only because of the cheating but the fact that he wasn't showin no fear on his Chink face. And it wasn't that either, it was the fact that they had a nice warm room ta cook in, and they had a choice of all that lovely grub and plus it was *free*. Sumpthin else about em too grated Jake, except he didn't know, had no idea what it was or might be. Mista Bossman Slit himself took out a rib from Jake's container, held it up right in front of a man's nose. It look velly big to me, Missa Jake. Jake looked at it . . . More meat on bone, you see? The Slit smilin. Jake shakin his head, Nah, not that much more. Not two ribs less more. Here. You try. You bite, Missa Jake.

167

So Jake took a bite. (Fuckin nice). Well, maybe it was meatier than the last lot. But fuckim anyway: The container ain't as full as last time neither. Jake tapping the plastic pottle. Ah, less gravy, is all. You wan more gravy, Missa Jake? No charge. Jake going, Alright. I give you nice piece a bread you dip, hah? The Slit laughin in that funny way of theirs. But free gravy *and* free bread? And when the Slit came back he had not one but two slices of bread, and it was buttered, even if it was a bit skinny on the butter, and it came on one a them paper towel things, makin a man feel, you know, posh or sumpthin, like he was at a restaurant even though he'd never set foot inside one in his whole life.

Mondays, Tuesdays and even some fuckin Wednesdays, man, it'd got so a man wasn't sure of a bed. Had ta sleep out under the stars. First time it occurred to Jake that he was homeless was one Monday night when the bar was near empty and so no one to touch up for a bed for the night, no party to go to where he might just stay on after it was over, flake out on the couch or sumpthin. Had a man walkin the main street and wondering what the fuck he was gonna do with himself for the night. But laughin about it because, well, it was a fine night, a bit cold but nuthin to a tough-arse; and he enjoyed walking down Taniwha Street playin the window shopper when ordinarily mosta the shops sorta scared a man. During the day when they had people inem. Made him feel, you know, inferior. So.

So eleven at night and here was a man strollin down the main street whistling and enjoying lookin in all the windows. And criss-crossing the street so he could get to see his reflection — but makin out he had business on that side when he did cross, lookin at his watch, the digital he'd stolen from a sleeping drunk in the McClutchy toilets, lappin up that image of tall, beautifully — *budeeful* — proportioned man a muscle. Even with his clothes on you could still see a man was well made underneath. Fuckem. Sayin fuckem, to himself. At them. The fuckin world. Sonny Boy Jacobs. The Brown Fists. Her, Beth. For sayin what she did in front of everyone even though it wasn't what she'd said herself, he knew that, it was what Grace musta wrote in a, you know, last letter, suicide note. But it wasn't true. It *wasn't*.

Down at the lake end of town and Jake could smell the aroma from the first Chinese takeaway where he always went and never the other joint, dunno why, just that a man took a dislike to that other joint, and these aromas comin to a man makinim starvin but no dough, man. Felt like marchin in the place anyway and haulin

the little Slit jerk over the counter and robbinim. But Jake was no
robber. And besides, the little jerk might know kung fu or sumpthin. Turn the tables on a man. Chop-chop a Maori boy's neck off,
hahaha! his laughter echoing down that deserted street, and not
long after being followed by the town clock chiming . . . ? Jake
stopping to count the dongs: twelve ofem. Midnight. My, how
time flies when ya havin a good time.

Found himself in Samuel Marsden Park, named after some
white colonial fulla from the old days when the Pakeha first
arrived and changed the Maoris' way of life forever. Man, did
they what. Mind you, a man, Jake Heke *and* his entire family,
woulda been a slave in them days. Magine that, bein a slave,
havin ta have some cunt givin ya orders, havin ta do all the shit
jobs. And being *born* to it? Fuck that. Man's lucky he's around
now and not then, was how Jake Heke saw his first night in the
park.

Now, he was used to it. Didn't like it, but used to it. Accepted
the fact that his life wasn't, you know, right any longer. That
things'd changed. And that maybe even he'd changed. But a man
was still a tougharse, make no fuckin bones bout that.

Fridays and Saturdays a man could usually find a bed somewhere, get a decent feed into him, get cleaned up. Clean clothes
from the plastic rubbish bag of clothes he had stashed now at
the park and which he washed in the toilet bowl of the public
Lavatories, which it said above the door, not Toilet as a man
expected it to read, without soap or maybe there'd be a bit in the
handbasin if a man was lucky. But the rest of the week, man
. . . sittin shivering ta death under a drippin tree or pouring with
rain and the fuckin wind howlin all ovah ya; too cold and wet ta
sleep have ta walk to get warm. Walkin all fuckin night. Like a
tramp. A real tramp ya see on the TV in them olden-day movies.
Man, what'd happened to a fulla? And in such a short time? And
ya mind, man, thinkin weird things, sorta like dreams: distorted,
everything fucked up, yet a man is awake so thinking you were
going, you know, mad. But maybe it's just the cold and the wet?
Or maybe a man's missin his wife (her warm body, ahhh . . . *why*
didn't a man appreciate what he had when it was there on tap
forim?) Oh, and his kids too. Wonder how Boogie's gettin on? And
thinking of the others: Nig in the Brown Fists how was he doing,
the kid can fight, just like his old man, but I wouldn't a thought
he had that meanness, a man's gotta have a mean streak he wants
ta run with them cunts. Oh well, he'll find out. And Poll? And her

little doll, what's its fuckin name now? A man can't remember. Or maybe he never knew the name ta start with. You know how a man gets: he forgets he's a father to all these kids. It's the drinking, see, his whole fuckin life moves around the drinking. But that don't mean a man don't think of his kids now and then. And Huata? How's my baby boy doing? Ahh. A man gettin all sentimental over his youngest, the baby of the family. Enough ta make a man weep — Well, not actually weep. I don't weep for nuthin or no one. But tears in his eyes. And Abe? Now *that's* a kid with a mean streak. Hahaha. Cunning as a shithouse rat. Cept he can't fight. Or not well enough to takeim to the top. Like his old man.

And Grace.

All the time wondering: Did I touch her? But immediately the denial: *I can't have.* Because a man'd know, wouldn't he? In his heart of hearts he'd know, surely ta fuckin God? Thinkin of going to her grave, but what the hell, what'd a man say to a grave? He might even get angry ater for writing that suicide note. I mean, she could've just left it out that someone'd done bad things to her, or she coulda left *me* out. I mean how'd she *know*? Know for sure that it was a man, this man, that'd stuck his — No way, man. That ain't Jake Heke. But haunting him. Always haunting him.

And now even the cops knew a man was sleeping rough: Evnin, Jake. Not so nice tonight, eh? cop on the night beat'd greet a man. Like I'm an old friend — no, not that. More like an old tramp. Or a wino. Not that ya see many winos in Two Lakes, ya don't. Small town, see, they don't end up on the streets (in the gutters) like on TV. But no shortage of streetkids, Jake was more and more noticing. And some ofem with strangely familiar faces like he knew em but that being impossible, Jake figuring it might be that he knew their fathers, had seen their mothers around, you know, at McClutchy's, a party, just around in Pine Block general.

But tryin ta say hello to em ya may as well be talkin to a fuckin brick wall: they'd just look at a man and move off. Remind a man of stray dogs. And feeling sorta sympathetic withem, or in tune withem. If only they'd give a man a chance, just stop for once and have a chat. I ain't gonna bite em. A man feelin hurt. But no anger with it. Just hurt and lonely, and wanting company. Any company.

So one day at McClutchy's strollin over to the table where the alkies drank, four ofem, every day, six days and nights a week and

Sundays boozing at their shared flat just up the street a bit. Smilin atem, How's it, boys? Greetin em in turn and order of known seniority: Patch (the boss). Red. Hey Red. Hey Jake. Smilin at a man, makin him feel warm inside. And hello to Jock, and how ya goin, Wally? Then waitin. For what they might say to a man. A sign or sumpthin, a hint.

Patch eyein a man all ovah, that in the old days woulda had Patch flat on his arse with a broken jaw lookin at a man like that. But Jake as nervous as hell. At Patch eyin him all ovah. And eyeballin Jake ta finish. Then finally: Whatcha havin, Jake? And Jake keeping his gladness under control, not wantin to scare em off. Oh, whatever you fullas're drinkin.

Sherry. (Jesus Chrise.) With beer chasers, they called it. A beer man all his life and havin ta drink fuckin sherry. And at one o'clock in the afternoon. Jake swallowing the stuff like it was poison. But thinking it was better — oh far better — to be in than not. Reminding himself to stay cool, not make out how desperate he was. That he needed em.

So where ya been stayin these days, Jake? Patch asking a man. Oh, around. You know. Shrugging. Pretending to be casual about it. Seein em lookin at each other again. We heard ya been doin it a bit hard, Jake. Sleeping in the park we heard. Only sometimes, Patch. Lookin at Jake again. All fuckin ovah. Makin a man feel stink. We share a house, Jake, as ya know. Yeah, know that. Heart hammering. We share everything: the rent, the food, the power. Lookin at im. And booze. We share our booze, Jake. Oh sure. Why not, eh? Giving a chuckle that he hoped they didn't hear the nervousness in. Each of us picks up his sickness benefit each week and it goes in the centre, Jake. The Pool, we call it. And no one draws more than the other, Jake. No one. Eying im. Gotta have rules, eh Patch? And the old alcoholic smilin at Jake, goin Yeah, Jake. Ya gotta have rules. And Jake nodding; feeling like it was a power comin off Patch. As if Patch was in charge of him. And as if that was how it was meant to be. And Patch stickin his old whiteman freckled hand out: Put it here, Jake. And Jake puttin it there. And ya need a place ta stay, Jake, you just let us know. And Jake saying: I might just take ya up on that, Patch. And smilin at the man. Oh, and the other three. Like they'd been waiting for him all these years, and he for them. It just seemed to fit. And he raised his sherry glass: Cheers, lads. Cheers.

171

16
Deep Tattoo

And he was talking in English, tellin em all gathered at his feet, his constantly moving feet, that their inheritance was their past and without the past they were nothing and, why, indeed, they *had* been nothing till he and his tribal elders and helpers and committee members came along at the request of this woman here, Beth, who used to be a Ransfield when she belonged to us. Hadn't been for not so much us but what we bring, the knowledge — the *knowledge* — of your great history, your illustrious ancestors, then you lot, boy, I have to tell you fullas and you girls and women (and there woulda been a hundred, oh, over a hundred ofem gathered there on the front adjoining lawns of Numbers 27 and 27B Rimu Street) you lot were gonna kill yourselves. Tapping his heart area, the paramount chief, Te Tupaea, and then his forehead. Dead in your heart, so dead in your minds. So.

He breathed out a long sigh and the people they shifted position and tried to make out it wasn't freezing but it was hard, boy was it hard; just as he, this great chief come amongst them, was hard. And some lit cigarettes and the smoke got instantly snatched by the chill wind but still no one got up and moved off to warmer parts, not even the kids, the unwanteds whose needs'd got one woman starting all this; they just sat there. And listened as history flowed down on them from above.

He told them of great acts of chivalry during the warring with the first white men: of warriors — that's *Maori* warriors — slipping out into the battlefield at night to tend to the wounded enemy, giving the enemy food, drink, even touches of comfort. And the gathering going, Wow, far out, but why? And the chief's eyes with that fighting fire in them saying: So the enemy might have more strength to continue the battle in the morning. And the crowd went, Ooooh! Smiling all over. Thinking: But we never knew that.

172

No one taught us this at school. They taught us *their* history: English history. They forced us to learn, off by heart, dates and names of great Englishmen and battles fought in a country none of us have ever been to nor are likely to go. And they gave us no marks in our exams when we couldn't remember these dates and funny names and strange-sounding places, and they never understood that to remember things of knowledge ya have to have fire in your belly for it, like the great chief there, or just ordinary passion of wanting to remember it because it, well, it's about yourself, historical knowledge most easily remembered.

And the chief putting into words their vague thoughts, giving their minds a shape they could visualise: We fought em at every turn. We *never* gave up. They came to this land with their queen and kings, and we, the Maori, set up our *own* king in defiance of them. YOU HEAR THIS? And the crowd roared, YESSSSS!!

And when they knew we would never give up they signed a treaty with us. The Treaty of Waitangi. You all heard of that? YESSSS!! You all know what it was? Individuals answering they thought it was an agreement between two peoples to share the land, its resources. *As equals!* their fiery chief exclaiming.

A contract! IT WAS A CONTRACT. Then silence.

And just the coughs and sighs and rustle of movement.

Te Tupaea just stood there, legs astride, fists on suited sides. A contract . . . Whispering it, so the ones at the back had to ask what'd he say, and then their whispering dying down. And Te Tupaea again whispering: Which — they — broke.

Suddenly he was bursting into a roaring cry signifying the start of a haka. And so a line-up of older males behind him stood. Like a row of fierce-faced guards. And they danced. The dance of war. The expression of anguish. A dozen, no more, thundering voices led by their chief. A dozen chest-slapping, thigh-slapping, elbow-slapping, arm-out-thrusting, arm-dancing, feet-stomping warriors from yore. And this man in a suit and a carved walking stick dancing back and forth across their front, twirling his tokotoko this way and that. Gold fob watch flying. Spit flying. And joined by four women, who launched themselves into it with even greater ferocity than the men.

And the people sitting there with chills running up and down them and not from the cold either. And this incredible beat of war setting off things in their heads: of understanding themselves, some locked away part of themselves suddenly opened up, sprung by him and them up there, shuddering this very ground we sit upon. And their movements all as one. The near-shrieking and roaring wording in exact time.

And in every line of mad, rhythmic shout, this familiarity just impossible to know where it was coming from or why. Just this sense of: This is me. At them, the sight of your warrior past stood in animated defiance of all that this struggle of a life can throw up. Sorta like a, you know, a culturalised way of saying: Fuck you! I am me! I stand here, I fall here. Sumpthin like that.

Hardly a one in the crowd knowing what'd struck him and her. Only that sumpthin good'd happened.

It ended. Chief gave a sharp look when some ofem started to applaud. But their beating hearts were applause enough. Te Tupaea gave one of his sighs, then a single word: Moko.

Looked at em. Tapped his face, then his pinstriped rump, with a chuckle. Tats, that's what they call it nowadays, eh? He told them of how the warriors of old used to have full-facial tattoos and on the nono — patting his rump with a smile — down to their knees, to signify their warriorhood. Silence. Looking over them. You got that? *Warriorhood*. And it was — pausing, with the skills of an accomplished orator — It was *chiselled* in.

Pausing again. Eyes going over them. And telling them in a half-whisper how not one cry was to be uttered during this long and painful process. Not one cry.

And the warrior — *your* warrior ancestor — his whole face became puffed up . . . so he would have to be fed through a funnel . . . and this process, people, this *manly* painful chiselling went on for months . . . But never did it occur to the warrior to show in sound or sight his terrible pain . . .

Lookin at them in that kingly way again in the pause, this time long, and having the people wondering what was coming next . . . It was a finger. Pointing. Then slow swinging over all of them. Accusing them. Or maybe just embracing, they'd know in a moment.

Pain, he said. Your ancestors endured the pain of moko . . . pain, my people. Like you are suffering in here, your hearts. But —

The look was of contempt. No bones about it. But why? Yet *you*, most of you gathered here — stabbing the finger this time — You have been enduring your pain like — like — Seeming to be struggling for a word and not like him, they knew that much of him. Like slaves! it hissed out of him.

And the crowd let out a collective sigh of surprise, even mild

174

outrage. Waited for the man to explain himself. Many shifting position, as if ready to up and go should the explanation not suffice.

Beer! he spat the word out. You endure your pain only by the false courage of *beer*. The word bad on his lips. His eyes darting all over them now. Beer.

And this . . . *beer*, it has you beat up your wives, your children, turn against each other. Yet you dare to call yourselves *Maori*? Pah! He made a downward stroke with right arm. Not Maori. *Not Maori*, he thrust his jaw skyward. Dismissively. A don't wanna know you gesture.

Then an arm came lizarding out in front of him, in an arcing sweep of pinstripe and bladed hand. The eyes absolutely fixed on the movement of the hand. And his stance, everything about him fitting. Something in the pose, the people recognising without really knowing that it was classic poise. Trained classical poise. Then came a chant . . . begun by a sobbing, of emotion choking on a word. But then it flowed. And the twelve men and four women stood once more . . .

Up the street, around the corner and up a bit, a fulla getting tattooed. Electric job. Tattooist in town he came out to the Brown Fist's HQ they only had to call and he'd be there. Charged em for it mind you. The electric needle with its ink injection going *bzzzzzz* along the pre-drawn lines on the fulla's face. Only a young guy too. Handsome young fulla, can't be more'n eighteen, nineteen. And going for the full facial too. And laying there on this (filthy) couch, jaw clamped shut, eyes squeezed closed but opening now and again so the tattooist knew the kid was feeling it alright, but making a damn good showing of manhood he was. Except for the tears of sheer pain.

Design a replica of olden-day moko, which the tattooist'd copied out of a book from a photograph of a real tattooed Maori head. Now, he knew the design and its stock of variations so well he could do it by heart. Was the big thing to do these days amongst these gang members. And a man tried to do a very professional job because even if it wasn't exactly his cuppa tea, the design, the original he'd taken from, was no less than exquisite. A man'd heard that the real thing back in the old days was chiselled in. Man, these Maoris are devils for punishment. I think it must be still in their blood. They like tough things, deeds, acts.

175

And this gang sheila standin there lookin over the tat operation, making a man nervous, specially a white man in a Brown Fist house. This sheila not responding to his attempts to converse. Just grunting. And giving him funny looks. And the young guy — Nig he said his name was — asking every so often, It look alright, Tania? She grunting, Yep. Choice. And the kid's face transforming before a man and his apparent girlfriend's eyes. (Poor bloody mixed-up kid. What they do to show their toughness.)

The gathering gaining more and more as people strolled from up the street, down the street, from all over Pine Block as telephones passed the word around. And this flashly dressed Maori fulla addressing the growing crowd, and the venue the Heke place of all the places. And boy was he laying it on the line toem: tellin em to jack their ideas up. Ta stop being lazy. (Who's he callin lazy?) Ta stop feeling sorry for emselves. Ta stop blamin the Pakeha for their woes even if it *was* the Pakeha much to blame.

So what? he asked them in this booming voice that didn't need no microphone. Do I accuse the storm that destroys my crops? (Well, come ta think of it that way . . .) No! No, I don't accuse the storm. I *clean up*. THEN I PLANT AGAIN!

On and on he went in this vein. Sometimes breaking off into this haunting, chanting waiata; and the others with him joining him. Or they let loose with these amazing *haka* that sent shivers and chills through ya, don't care who ya are, it just gets to you. And the wind so cold and yet, funny thing, ya only had to be there for a little while and you hardly felt the cold. Just this, I dunno, pride I guess you'd call it, that you'd never felt before, at being . . . well, I guess, a Maori. Make that Maori warrior. Oh, and Maori warrioress. After all, we ain't nuthin without our women.

And the woman, Beth — disowned of her married name. Just Beth — sat there with this glowing look on her face. And people that knew her sayin they'd never seen her looking so well, and when you consider, you know, what the poor bitch's gone through, it makes you really wonder about this weekly Saturday get-together that she got organised. Like she's sorta come amongst ya . . . I dunno, hard to find words when you're a Pine Blocker. As if she's gone through all this pain so you, the rest of you rotten ne'er-do-wells, might sorta gain from it. From this.

From a newly inspired Beth, along with this chief fulla inspiring ya with his speeching and his words of history like he's

showin ya the light but without the Jesus saves ya crap. And as if
Beth Heke is some kinda saint but without a god hovering there
behind her: you feel if she can do it, more or less alone, then
dammit, maybe you, a previously hopeless Pine Block case, can
too.

17
Love Is Where You Find It

Hey kid? Hey, k — Aw, c'mon, I ain't gonna hurt ya. Jake shaking his head at the kid backing away out of the light of short-heighted lamps that lit the meandering path through the park. He blew into the air, Smell me, kid. Jake hasn't even had a beer. Chuckled. Too fuckin broke, that's why. But tomorrow, boy . . . He used it as a tantaliser. It's dole day tomorrow, boy. I might be buying.

But the kid stayed where he was, in the shadow of a big spread of tree untouched by the lamplight, just visible as a shape. It's Christmas next week, know that? What ya doing for Christmas day? No answer, not even a breeze rustling through the leaves. Just a few crickets going, and a lonely man and a wary boy. What, your mates leave ya? I thought you streetkids stuck together? They left ya cos ya can't fight, right? No answer. You useless at stealing things? No response. But Jake knew the kid had been deserted by his fellow streetkids, he'd seen the face when it was a member of a group ofem who'd always kept their distance from his overtures to come talk with him. But now there was a stray sheep.

Ya like the Chinese food, boy? Maybe. Jake's heart leapt at the first response in maybe an hour of trying with the kid. Spare ribs, mmm? Jake smacked his lips. Cept I don't like the Chinks that sell em. Nor me. Another response. (At last!) Want me to buy you some spare ribs Christmas day? Yep, but he'll be shut. No way, boy; these greedy fuckin Chinks they don't close on Christmas day. Bet ya a buck they're open on Christmas. I ain't got a buck to bet. Well, fifty cents, twenty cents, who cares, just make a bet. Ten cents? Ten cents, fine. But still the boy stood in the shadows.

Know what? I got kicked out myself. From where — home? Home and then the winos kicked me out. The winos? Them who come and sit in the park here and talk shit? You mean that lot? Yeah, that lot! How come? They didn't like me. Why not? Cos I'm no alkie, that's why. Cos a man didn't wake up and have a drink

178

of sherry withem first thing in the morning. That's why. How come? How come what? You didn't want a drink of sherry in the morning?

Jake had to think a moment . . . Cos that's what alkies do, boy, and I ain't no fuckin alkie. We thought you were. Who, the streetkids? Yeah. You tellem ta say that to my face an — *I* didn't think it. But they did. Yeah, sure, kid. Sure. Honest, I didn't. So what else you fullas been saying about me? That you're tough. Made Jake smile. That right? Tough as. Tough as, eh? Toughest in Two Lakes, that's what they said. Are you? I — used to be, boy. What happened? I — Again Jake hesitated: he didn't want to lie but nor did he want to face the truth. I got older. Can't you fight now? I can fight alright. You wanna go? No way, mista. Only joking.

How long you been following me? Bout a week. A *week?* So you know where I live? Yeah, sure: you live in the bamboos. You got a neat little hut there. With blankets. And a mattress. And you got plastic underneath to keep it dry. The kid stepped partway out of the shadows. But, man, you're *old* for a streetkid. I ain't a street- kid, I'm a — Jake didn't finish it. Couldn't. What's the name, kid? Cody. Thassa a neat name. Thanks. I'm Jake. I know. How do you know that? Everyone knows. Everyone? The streetkids. Oh. You fullas been spying on me? We spy on everyone comes here. Had Jake thinking about what he might've been up to, mastur- bating, talking to himself, the usual. Him asking suspiciously, What sorta things you seen? Your hut. You drunk. You asleep on the ground. You grinding your teeth. Man, but do you grind your teeth. Kids say you sound like a horse. A horse? Yeah, a horse. Sorry, mista, but that's what they say. Fuckem. They don't mean any harm. I'll givem harm they call me a fuckin horse. No, only you *sound* like one. What else you seen? Not much. How much? Oh, you know, you being drunk and saying things to yourself . . . And? And nothing else.

Jake shrugged, oh well, if he'd been observed in his most private moments so be it. Least he was talking to someone. How old're you, uh . . . ? Jake'd forgotten the name. Cody. Cody. I'm fifteen. I got a boy fifteen. I know. And you got one in the Brown Fists. How do you know all this, man? Jake getting annoyed. Everyone knows it. And the one in the Brown Fists he can rumble. That right? Jake feeling proud. Who told you that? We seen him. He wasted two dudes on his own in a rumble outside the Palace. Jake grinning all over, Did he just? Thinking: Thas my boy Nig.

But he — You spend your life spying on people, kid? Nuthin else to do. Saves thinking about grub. You hungry? Always hungry, Mista Jake. (That's what the Chink calls me: Mista Jake.) So what they kick you out for? I — No further words. You cry too much, I bet. How'd you know that, man? I know these things. I can't help it. That's alright. Jake ain't saying it's wrong. Aren't ya? the kid sounding suspicious. Nah, not me, kid. Everyone has a cry. You musta seen ole Jake here having a cry once or twice, eh? Jake half fishing but no less in earnest. Yeah, we seen you crying. But I'm still a tougharse, eh? You sure are! How do you know I am? Cause *everyone's* heard of you, Mista Jake. (Is that right? Well, how about that. People who *know* who Jake Heke is.) But why'd you let the alkies kick you out if you're tough as? It's their place. I was just a boarder.

Poor you.

That got to Jake. He could've taken the boy in his arms and wept.

What, they actually kick you when they booted you out? No way, boy. Anyone laid a hand on Jake Heke and he's dead meat. Man, I thought so, the kid's voice came excitedly from the half-in-shadow.

Where you kids sleep? All over; in old houses no one lives in, on sheds on the sites, under bridges, in people's backyards long as they don't have a dog. Anywhere. Why don't you build a hut like I did? Don't know how. It's easy. For you, maybe. For everyone. Warmer than sleeping out, boy. Ah, ya get used to it. Not me, kid, I never got used it; why I made myself a hut. But why'd you come here in the first place? My missus told me to get the hell out of it. Whyn't you waste her then? Couldn't. Why not? Did it too many times before. And my daughter, Grace, she'd just died; killed herself. Yeah, we heard. You heard everything about me? We heard a lot.

So's that why you didn't waste your missus for kicking you out, only because of the girl — uh, your daughter — killing herself? That's right. Otherwise, what, you'd've smashed her face in? Jake not knowing how he should answer that one, didn't have an answer anyway. Nah, I got sick of hitting her. No good for the kids, either, Jake just said on instinct. And Cody stepped fully from the shadows.

They walked. Up and slowly down the winding concrete pathway lit every thirty of Jake Heke's paces and, Jake'd read somewhere, a hundred and twenty acres of park. They talked. Trust grew as the hours went by and a chill came over the park, and so too did the moon disappear beyond a sky of cloud. So where you sleeping tonight? Oh, around. You can sleep in my hut you want — Suddenly the boy broke away in a sprint, stood off at a distance warning Jake: You touch me and I'll get the cops. Jake confused at first: Huh . . . ?

Oh, you think I'll . . . Chuckling. Kid, I'll sleep outside you want. Yeah, and then what when I'm asleep? Someone done things to you, kid? None a your fuckin business. So Jake shrugged. Oh well, you know where I'll be. Turned and walked off; kind of knowing the boy would follow. Smiling to himself, feeling fatherly.

Later, they lay side by side under the warmth of several blankets and listened to the distant chime of the town clock striking one o'clock. And the boy yawned, which had Jake do the same.

They could see just a glimpse of the stars, a tiny pocket from a cloudbreak. See them stars up there, boy? Your ancestors they used em to navigate when they came here on their canoes. Navigate? the boy asked at the same time he slipped his head over Jake's outstretched arm. What's navigate mean? It means to guide. The stars guided them. But don't ask a man how, I'm juss dumb Jake Heke who don't know much about this crazy damn life. Grinning. Yeah, and I'm just dumb Cody McClean who don't know nuthin about nuthin.

Cody snuggled into Jake. Your ole man used to cuddle ya, boy? Jake trying to sound gruff so the kid wouldn't think he was a softie. No way, Hosay. He just beat me — and my brothers and sisters — and my old lady too, she got it worse. Had Jake wincing with guilt. Well, maybe he was angry at sumpthin, your old man, ya think?

Angry? Mista, how angry are ya ta smash ya wife to pieces for just, you know, bein there? Nope, can't tell me it was angry. Well, it musta been sumpthin, boy, or why'd he juss wanna smash you and ya mother? I dunno. Silence. Not even a breeze in their little world.

Mista Jake? Don't call me Mista, I ain't a Mista. I'm juss Jake. Jake, I bet you cuddled your kids, did ya? (Nope. I didn't. Man never thought to. Dunno why. Just never thought to.) Jake sighing, drawing the boy closer to him, sayin nothing.

The boy's sigh of contentment making a man feel warm inside. And the smells of their unwashed bodies barely registering.

181

Gonna get us spare ribs tamorrow, boy. Thanks, Jake. And a coke. Ya like coke? Yeow. What about Christmas, Jake? You and, uh, me, we gonna be together then? Well, I don't *think* I got nuthin else planned for that day, boy. Tousling the boy's hair. What if I don't like these rib things, c'n I have sumpthin else? Whatever ya want, kid. Whatever ya want. Long as I got enough left to get drunk on.

Talking on and the town clock donging two. The boy yawning, Think I'll go ta sleep now. Yep, me too. Goodnight, boy. But nothing comin back in reply. Kid . . . ? What? I said g'night. But still nothing, and Jake thinking his usual: Fuckim, then. Then Cody askin: Uh, Jake? Ya won't, y'know, like, do nuthin to me when I'm sleepin, will ya? Fear in his voice. Alarming Jake. Kid I — Having ta suck in a breath or a man'd've near sobbed. Won't touch ya, Cody. Ya promise? Kid, I promise ya. (I *promise* ya. I'm *not* like that.)

Sleep finding Jake some time after the boy'd gone to sleep. And dreaming, as always, except waking up during what was left of the night and being amazed each time that his dreams were alright. Not mad violent. For once. Violent, sure. Life is violent. But nuthin mad, and not ripping people's eyes out and tearing their arms off and pulverising their faces till they were flat in his hand. Just ordinary ole fights. And winning em too.

The youth with the tat-swollen face had a dream. It was as clear as the reality of sleeping in the sheetless bed with its stinking blankets; as clear as the floor covered aroundim in fellow Browns sleeping drunk, stoned, pilled, bombed outta their brains and snoring, whistling, wheezing, moaning, thrashing, crying out and even a scream coming from their fucked-up heads. Clearer even than that; for this dream had kinda like this wisdom he didn't know. Like he was being told sumpthin but he couldn't get the message.

He dreamt he came upon several men with facial tats of exquisite design. They were beating someone. Over and over with steady, rhythmic punches going thud . . . thud . . . thud into the man's face. Nig askin em: Are you my Maori ancestors? Because they looked so much like him, mirrors of himself. They paused from the beating to give a kid hostile looks, and one answered, No. We are not of your cowardly blood, for we know you are knowing fear. We are warriors.

182

Nig gestured frantically toward his face, his new tattoos just like theirs and freshly swollen from doing. But when he looked into the eyes of them all at once, he saw that terrible glaze of reason gone. Quite gone. And their tattooed faces were deeply etched, whilst his manhood markings were but lightly marked. Then they had blue and white bandanas around suddenly wildly frizzy locks. And they kept punching this face till he rattled. Yes, rattled. Nig could hear it as clear as anything the broken shattered bones like bones in a jar, or a gourd made of skin.

He asked them: But why are you doing this to him? And one replied: Because he is no longer one of us. And Nig said: Isn't there a way he can make up? And the warrior said, No. He no longer thinks as we do. And for this he dies. And Nig said: For that you kill a man? You beat him till his shattered bones rattle inside him? Because he does not *think* like you? And they looked at him and laughed.

He woke and wasn't sure where he was, who he was; thinking, thinking hard on that dream; and those bods all around him, on the floor, in the opposite bed; light starting to come in through the curtainless windows; so he could make out the features, by and by, of the sprawled-out bros, pick the tat marks, the stars, the full facial of The Beast, the scowls most ofem wore, even in sleep. And he could still hear that awful rattling in his mind. And looking at his fellow gang bruthas and one sista over there curled up in the corner like a lil babe, and they coulda been the same gang/warriors as in the dream.

So the sweat broke, because the fear was his own. And so was the face of the bone-rattling victim.

18
And Still They Cometh

Now Beth had got Mavis Tatana. Had Mavis place her great
frame and singing voice amongst the people. Five nights a week
down at the local community hall, which the people'd hardly ever
used but had now painted and given new life to, the giant woman
(with her unrequited singing talent and years of accumulated
fat from years of wanting but unable to have because she was
afflicted with the old Maori shyness) had the people in voice,
unified voice, learning funeral hymns because, well, a woman
figured they were a good starting medium in good old minor keys
with a sense of worth to them that the people, these ordinary Pine
Block people, could fix their simple outlook to.

And you could go past the hall and see gatherings outside, even
on bad weather days, of kids and adults and even the odd Brown
Fist (pretending it was just by accident and that the sounds he was
hearing sucked) see them stood there listening; and with looks on
their faces that closer inspection revealed as almost joy — it was
joy — and that quiet smile of pride in themselves, since it was
someone they were related to, close to, inside there doing his and
her bit to that wonderful sad singing. Brought ya out in blimmin
goosepimples them hymns. And as for that Mavis, could she sing.

Yet every day word was out that another Mavis'd been found
amongst this Pine Block rabble, ya juss wouldn't believe it. Even
three months ago. Ta think that this was Pine Block. And ta think
it was one woman started it. And ta think it was the wife of Jake
Heke. Ya wouldn't read about it. Not when ya, you know, added
up what that poor woman'd gone through. And now this.

Word going round all over Pine Block that something good
was happening; you know, change. That change was happening
to some of the people living there. And every Saturday, nine in the
morning sharp, y'c'd see the crowd gathered at Number 27 Rimu,
to listen to this high chief fulla, Te Tupaea, tellin the people of
their history. Our *proud* history. Oh but that wasn't all he was

184

about neither: he told the people off, shouted and speeched atem to change their ways before the ways changed them; you know, in that funny poetic way he speaks. Nor was Chief into blamin people, the Pakeha, the system, the anything for the obvious Maori problems; you know, our drop in standards just in general. He didn't care bout no damn white people ta blame, no damn systems meant to be stacked against a people, he just toldem: Work! We work our way out. Same way as we lazed ourselves into this mess.

Every Saturday, man, y'c'd hear this dude. And could he dress. Different suit every week on a six-week cycle, the observant noticed. Pinstripes. He favoured dark pinstripes. And different ties. Stripy ones, ones with club emblems, like rugby clubs. And he'd turn up with someone well known, a local Maori fulla who'd become an All Black, a Maori lawyer, a Maori doctor, a Maori surgeon; and he'd prance these fullas out before the crowd there on Beth's front lawn as well as her neighbours', tellin the crowd, *This* is what you can achieve.

And you sitting there, eh, and looking at these Maori fullas and the odd woman, and thinking, Yeah, maybe I can, you know, better myself. If those Maoris can do it, so can I. Oh not that Pine Block was running full with people all of a sudden wanting to educate emselves, play rugby for their country, things like that. Just this slow change comin ovah the place. And this sense that it wasn't here today gone tamorrow. No. It gave you a feeling of permanence.

And each Saturday you turned up or even went past, it seemed more and more faces you knew were up there when this paramount chief fulla was leadin em in their many hakas of the day. And ya'd think, Man, if Smoky can do it then why can't I? But you know how a fulla is, he gets into these slack habits, can't get off his arse, so another few Saturdays'd go by and there'd be several more faces you knew up there doin that neat cultural stuff. Their faces glowin with first a mixture of embarrassment and pride, then it was just pride. You could see it, plain as day.

Then one day the chief didn't show up, and y'c'd see on the people's faces they were thrown by this. Lost. Mumbling and whispering and feet shuffling and head scratchin amongst emselves when who else but Beth stands up, asks, What, we playin follow the leader or sumpthin?

The crowd lookin ater but no one movin or sayin nuthin. Then she started singing this real old chanty thing that the chief musta

185

taught her because no one ever knew Beth singing that sorta thing before. Then she was joined by one of the Moke brothers from Alligator Street, wildest buncha black Maoris you ever saw, those Mokes. And it seemed to be the signal for everyone to join in, even though most ofem didn't know the chant. It was just the, you know, the sticking togetherness, eh.

And all this time the chief was across the street in a friend's car laying low.

Another day and a fulla had ta join, or he was gonna miss the fuckin bus, man. He was. Like half of Pine Block was behind this thing now. This . . . this force.

The other half, the ones didn't wanna give up their all-day every-day boozing, well they went on as always, and their kids still ran wild at all hours, and y'c'd hear their parties raging half the fuckin night and fights break out and yellin and that old usual shit stuff ya'd think they'd get sick of it. But who cared about them? The chief didn't. He said they got their chance. They don't wanna change then we can't force em.

But the rest of you, ya got, I dunno, sorta in contempt of them, eh, these diehard arseholes just hellbent on emselves their own selfish pleasure, a guvmint payin em to carry on that way. Feedin their rotten habits, as Beth used to say in her speeches. So ya stopped talkin to em, it just happened that way: like ya couldn't like identify withem no more because, well, they weren't like you anymore, were they? Or you weren't like them.

And all the time this feeling, eh, that sumpthin important had happened. And that maybe it'd last. And not so much hoping it would but, you know, determined it would.

Carload of Black Hawk prospects pulled up outside the court-house, parked their mean machine on the yellow line (fuckem) spotted a trio of Brown Fists — What the fuck! This is our day, Wensday. Instantly wild. Even though it was obvious a court official must have ballsed up on scheduling the two gangs apart. This is *our* fuckin day.

Browns! yelled the lead Black Hawk and he leapt from the car, raced for the trio, and his mates spilled out at similar mad haste. YA CUNTS! the front one yelling. *This's OUR day!*

Nig Heke was the first of the Browns to see what was happening. And first thing he thought was: Set-up. Jimmy's set us up. Then it was too late for anything, ya just have ta fight. And the

186

last thing he remembered thinking was, I'm a Heke, before he met
the charge with a blasting right that caught the Hawk full in the
mush. And the fuckin Hawk went down. And all hell broke loose.
And such a nice spring Wednesday morning it was too.

Back at the HQ and Jimmy Bad Horse thundering at the trio,
YA WHAT!? at them reporting what'd happened, that they did
their best but too many of the cunts, man. Too many. And the
Hawk cunts were tooled up too: iron bars, blades, the fuckin
works.

Nig Heke with a stab wound deep in his right thigh and
numerous other marks of a beating; his two mates the same. But
feeling proud, despite their eventual loss — till they got back to
Leader that is.

Didn't understand his reaction — he was *mad* atem. And it
was Nig Heke he laid most of the blame on: I sent you as a fuckin
escort for Mat and Chappie here. I told ya ta look afterem. And
when Nig said, But it was a Wens — Jimmy cut him off — Fuck
you! Slapped Nig's face. Shook his big bearded and shaded face at
Nig. Man, have you got some making up ta do.

Nig more confused and hurt than he'd ever been in his short
seventeen years of life. And catching the eye of the newly patched
Warren, who seemed to be taunting him, mocking him for not
having earned his patch when they'd gained their first probationary
entry the same time.

Nig went over to Tania, asked if she could look at his wound,
the knife wound. But she looked up at him from where she sat on
the (filthy) floor drinking beer straight from the bottle and told
him, Ya suck, muthafucka. And guzzled for what seemed an
eternity.

That night Tania announced: I'm on the block tonight, boys.
Slurring, with a sway on, and giving Nig Heke this terrible look
as if he was ta blame her putting herself on the block for all the
fullas to fucker.

Then she tripped and stumbled over to the table where they
sometimes ate from but mostly perched on and rested their beer
bottles on, and anytime there was a sheila for blocking it was
usually there they did because it was easier just ta flop yaself out,
walk up toer and giver one.

And they watched, beady-eyed, as Tania struggled out of her
tight jeans, her gang denim jacket, no underpants ta take off, who

187

wears undies, man, they suck. Then she sat up on the edge of the table, eyes downcast, nice tits goin up an down in what the fullas assumed was excited breathing but Nig Heke knew different.

Then he could but watch as Tania lay down on her back but wither legs not spread — he knew she wouldn't, that the first one'd have ta do it — and all the bruthas grinning and chuckling and lookin horny and suckin on their piss and their fags.

Then The Beast, sergeant-at-arms, went, Oh well. Sauntered over to the table.

Chief was giving his usual oral history lesson as men and youths of both sexes hammered and sawed on the latest community project, a changing room and shower block on the donated Trambert land for the newly ploughed and sown rugby field. Telling them of how their warrior ancestors were taught chants to gain strength from before battle, giving them the English translation:

> Give me my belt,
> Give me my loin cloth,
> That they may be put on,
> That they may be fastened,
> That wrath and I may join together,
> Rage and I.
> The loin cloth is for anger,
> The loin cloth is for destroying war parties.

And the men smiled and nodded their appreciation of this imparted knowledge of their past (and thus, so sayeth *always* the Chief, their future.) And they hammered and laboured and their chief sang this ancient war chant in the language of its origin. And even out there, in the wide open of the land and the vast expanse of blue sky up there, it seemed to be coming (messaging) down from yonder hilltops.

Bad Horse walking amongst his warriors like some great chief; in full gang regalia, big round patch on his broad back, urging them, yelling at them, firing them up to a state of war. And his unshaded eyes seemed to be mostly directed at the pros, Nig Heke. And his words too.

A jacket with the Brown Fist emblem dangled from Jimmy

188

Bad Horse's brown-mitted hand. He kept shoving it up in front of Nig, asking him: *What's this?* And Nig answering, My patch, brutha. And Jimmy'd go, *Riiiight!* and his teeth'd flash broken white and yellow stubs amongst mo and beard. And, man, all the mad bruthas and sistas standin around and juss dying ta go ta war.

Nig Heke there with his face tats lookin good, real Maori warrior stuff, man, and soon as the scabs healed it'd look mean as. Nig frowning in pain from the stab wound, the one in his leg. And the fullas earlier laughin and sayin the Black Hawk shoulda washed his knife. The thing infected, probably. But ah, you'll be right, Nig. Whassa lil cut, man? Get one a the sistas ta piss on it, man, that'll heal it. Hahaha!

Jimmy really working up to a pitch now: screamin at them. At them, the chosen frontline trio, the three who'd fucked up at the courthouse, allowed emselves to get dealt to by a buncha Black Hawk cunts. Screamin at them that this was their chance: *Hatred! Ya got that?* And the three pros's goin, YEOW!!! Man, enuff ta make ya deaf.

YA GO OUT THERE WITH YA FUCKIN HEART, YA MIND, *YA SOUL* — Jimmy taking a breath — *On fire with hatred!* And the pros's went: HATRED!!!! HATRED!!!!! HATRED!!!! AEE-ARHHHHHHHHHH!! The fuckin veins, man, stickin out on their necks and faces like they were gonna explode. I tell ya.

And the sounds, man, of carload after carload ofem rumblin outta Pine Block. Made ya shiver in awe. All these mean machines, man, these grunt machines, headed into town loaded to the eyeballs with Browns achin ta do murder. Achin for it. (And a boy's heart aching. Oh just aching.)

And Beth watching from her bedroom window of her new house the pass-by of the Brown convoy. And she knew. She just knew. And so her heart ached too.

19

So Life, It Is for Those Who Fight

Gathered at Two Lakes cemetery, musta been mosta Pine Block there. And the cops. But they were parked up at the entrance, and formed in a line to prevent trouble from comin in. Black Hawk trouble. And Brown Fists goin off their grievin faces. With two of their number ready to be given unto the ground, the spaces created for them there.

Two separate groups; the main body of mourners waiting for the Browns to do their last farewells, then it'd be their turn. The people from whose loins and past troubled ways did spring this monster calling itself Gang. And the mother of one of the dead gangsters in a mind of absolute clearness; and even her grief tempered with this sense of clarity and even well-being.

The gang members finally sauntering and swaggering past the main lot of mourners, giving them all the bad shaded eye but there being plenty of unshaded eye in return, and the main with the numbers. And you better believe, the righteousness on their side.

Specially him, the man in the black pinstripe suit standing fiercely proud and erect with his carved tokotoko held across his chest like a weapon, and staring at the file-past of filthily dressed young men and their handful of women with contempt and yet pity, even if it was almost a sneering pity. And especially her, the fine-looking woman in black who had the huge woman beside her, it wasn't for the scars and linings of life leaving its mark on her, looking not at any of the headbanded wild things filing past but up there, at yonder hills with a cloud formation shaped like nothing much though it could've been a boat, a water vessel of some sort, at a push, you were looking for that sorta thing which she wasn't. It was simply where her eyes inclined, and so she should not have to look at those who had murdered, by association, her eldest son. (My Nig.)

Nor giving away her surprise when the last of the Browns stopped at Beth Heke and just stood there . . . then her uniformed arms went out in a hapless manner, and you could see her grief even though her eyes had them hug-around shades. And her mouth was trembling and she was trying to say something, but it wouldn't come. So she, uh, well . . . she stepped up to Mrs Heke and put her arms around her. It was a very moving sight.

But not so moving as seemingly most of Pine Block, people you would never have picked as, singing the sad refrains of a hymn in Maori being led by that huge woman Mavis, and the mother of one of the dead Browns standing beside Mavis singing too.

And so *proud* she looked.

Oh but don't forget The People. Their new-found pride. Made ya wanna bawl ya eyes out. With happiness. Yep, even at a graveside.

Chief Te Tupaea gesturing to Beth: Step over beside me. Pointing to Mavis as well, You too. Oh, and this Pakeha family, eh, dressed spick and span (I mean, they *know* how to dress, don't they? Though not as smart as our chief.) right up at the graveside there, and Beth excusing herself from them, and they giving just a little nod they know how to, you know, comport themselves.

The birds tweeting from line of pines along the boundary, the lake-end boundary, and bees and flies buzzing away, and the odd car and truck going past as reminders of not only life carrying on but the time too, eh. The century. The year: 1990, brother. Got ta move with the times or it leaves ya behind. But not yet, not yet, brothers and sisters and all of you wherever you are. For there is one more thing to do.

And Chief began it:

> *O my son,*
> *Now you are gone, alone.*
> *Love has no power to restore the heart,*
> *So slow to live, swift to die . . .*

. . . man, and it was maybe four hundred voices adding to those of first Chief Te Tupaea and Beth Heke and Mavis Tatana, but you would not believe such force could be generated from mere voices, four hundred though they were.

> *. . . Your blood soaks into the wood*
> *But you have flown —*
> *You will greet your ancestors,*
> *The great await thee . . .*

191

(As the great do farewell thee . . .)

And this fulla with this equally bedraggled boy, over in the pines, concealed, peeping out like thieves, or shamed children of slaves.

And tears trickling from him — Him. He who they used to say was toughest in all Two Lakes. Bad. Mean as. Jake Heke. Now just child weeping for another child.

And the chief leading the gathering:

> . . . *O my great fish, rise from the depths.*
> *No! That cannot be,*
> *Death has swallowed thee*

(Ah but so does life stem from thee.)

So go now, boy warrior . . . your mother shall see thee (as shall your daddy, boychild. And we'll showem, eh boy? In the next life we'll showem . . .)

The last refrains of sweetsad hymn more mighty than the departing rumble and roar of Browns. And a sky stayed blue. And that cloud formation had changed shape — Oh, but only if you're looking for that sorta thing.

The Last Good Time by Richard Bausch	0–679–75556–X
A Man for All Seasons by Robert Bolt	0–679–72822–8
The Sheltering Sky by Paul Bowles	0–679–72979–8
Mildred Pierce by James M. Cain	0–679–72321–8
The Postman Always Rings Twice by James M. Cain	0–679–72325–0
Breakfast at Tiffany's and *Three Stories* by Truman Capote	0–679–74565–3
In Cold Blood by Truman Capote	0–679–74558–0
Short Cuts by Raymond Carver	0–679–74864–4
O Pioneers! by Willa Cather	0–679–74362–6
The Big Sleep by Raymond Chandler	0–394–75828–5
Farewell, My Lovely by Raymond Chandler	0–394–75827–7
The Lady in the Lake by Raymond Chandler	0–394–75825–0
A Tale of Two Cities by Charles Dickens	0–679–72965–8
Babette's Feast by Isak Dinesen	0–394–75929–X
Out of Africa & *Shadows on the Grass* by Isak Dinesen	0–679–72475–3
The Book of Daniel by E. L. Doctorow	0–679–73657–3
Ragtime by E. L. Doctorow	0–679–73626–3
The Commitments by Roddy Doyle	0–679–72174–6
Madame Bovary by Gustave Flaubert	0–679–73636–0
September September (the basis for *Memphis*) by Shelby Foote	0–679–73543–7
Howards End by E. M. Forster	0–679–72255–6
A Room With a View by E. M. Forster	0–679–72476–1
Where Angels Fear to Tread by E. M. Forster	0–679–73634–4
A Gathering of Old Men by Ernest J. Gaines	0–679–73890–8
Wild at Heart by Barry Gifford	0–679–73439–2
Shoot the Piano Player by David Goodis	0–679–73254–3
The Tin Drum by Günter Grass	0–679–72575–X
Claudius the God by Robert Graves	0–679–72573–3
I, Claudius by Robert Graves	0–679–72477–X
Monster in a Box by Spalding Gray	0–679–73739–1
Six Degrees of Separation by John Guare	0–679–73481–3
The Maltese Falcon by Dashiell Hammett	0–679–72264–5
The Thin Man by Dashiell Hammett	0–679–72263–7
A Raisin in the Sun by Lorraine Hansberry	0–679–75533–0

A Rage in Harlem by Chester Himes   0–679–72040–5
The Remains of the Day by Kazuo Ishiguro   0–394–25134–2
Gideon's Trumpet by Anthony Lewis   0–679–72312–9
Common Ground by Anthony Lukas   0–394–74616–3
Death in Venice & Other Stories by Thomas Mann   0–679–72206–8
At Play in the Fields of the Lord
    by Peter Matthiessen   0–679–73741–3
A Year in Provence by Peter Mayle   0–679–73114–8
The Cement Garden by Ian McEwan   0–679–75018–5
The Comfort of Strangers by Ian McEwan   0–679–74984–5
Bright Lights, Big City by Jay McInerney   0–394–72641–3
Moby–Dick by Herman Melville   0–679–72525–3
Lolita by Vladimir Nabokov   0–679–72316–1
Shattered by Richard Neely   0–679–73498–8
Swann's Way by Marcel Proust   0–679–72009–X
Kiss of the Spider Woman by Manuel Puig   0–679–72449–4
Jazz Cleopatra by Phyllis Rose   0–679–73133–4
Cyrano de Bergerac by Edmond Rostand   0–679–73413–9
Iron & Silk by Mark Salzman   0–394–75511–1
Dr. Jekyll and Mr. Hyde
    by Robert Louis Stevenson   0–679–73476–7
Sophie's Choice by William Styron   0–679–73637–9
The Joy Luck Club by Amy Tan   0–679–72768–X
After Dark, My Sweet by Jim Thompson   0–679–73247–0
The Getaway by Jim Thompson   0–679–73250–0
The Grifters by Jim Thompson   0–679–73248–9
The Player by Michael Tolkin   0–679–72254–8
Life on the Mississippi by Mark Twain   0–679–72527–X
The Adventures of Tom Sawyer by Mark Twain   0–679–73501–1
Birdy by William Wharton   0–679–73412–0
The Hot Spot by Charles Williams   0–679–73329–9

SCREENPLAYS

Hannah and Her Sisters by Woody Allen   0–394–74749–6
Three Films by Woody Allen: Broadway
    Danny Rose, Zelig, The Purple Rose of Cairo   0–394–75304–6

Available at your local bookstore, or call toll-free to order:
1-800-793-2665 (credit cards only).